Rules of Engagement

ICE PRINCESS

CAITLYN WILLOWS

Ice Princess
ISBN # 978-1-83943-837-0
©Copyright Caitlyn Willows 2018
Cover Art by Erin Dameron-Hill ©Copyright December 2018
Interior text design by Claire Siemaszkiewicz
Totally Bound Publishing

ICE PRINCESS

Chapter One

Sharp, painful jabs of sunlight forced open Claudia Stuart's eyelids. She squinted against her pillow, trying to focus on her surroundings through bleary eyes. *Why the hell did I leave the drapes open?* She closed them every night, her protection against the world.

"Oh my God."

Her soft mewl of agony felt like a shout. Wincing, she fought against the pounding beat of a headache reverberating throughout her aching body. She tried to center herself by focusing on any one part of her anatomy that wasn't sore. None existed.

A faint, persistent sound filtered through her pain. The foghorns from San Francisco Bay had never seemed this close before. Her senses slowly emerged from the blanketing haze. She wasn't in San Francisco. She was in Las Vegas. And there was an odd noise coming from the far side of the king-size bed.

Stretching out a shaky hand to balance herself against the spinning room, Claudia brushed against something warm, solid and most definitely male. She held her breath and twisted around to see a dark head partially buried in a mass of tangled covers. Horror clenched her gut.

Franklin?

The very idea churned her stomach. Franklin had made his intentions clear. She'd made hers even clearer — *no.* If he'd slipped something in her drink and taken advantage, she'd see him behind bars.

Claudia shook her head. *Not possible.* Franklin was in San Francisco. He had no idea she'd gone to Vegas. He thought she was on vacation, visiting her brother in Twentynine Palms, California.

So, who am I in bed with and why the hell can't I remember how I wound up like this?

She squinted at the waves of dark hair.

Wavy? With growing horror, she realized that the hair was clipped military-style — sides cut tight and the top allowed to grow a little longer, permitting the errant waves.

"Oh my God!"

The loud croak of disbelief aggravated her headache. Claudia didn't care. This was too horrible to believe. *It can't be. It just can't. Of all the men in the world, why this one?* The one who did things to her insides she would deny to her last breath. The one who made her want what she refused to allow again...ever.

She lashed out under the covers with her foot, whacking Zach Taylor squarely in the ass. "Get out! What are you doing in my bed?"

A muffled 'oomph' and a string of curses emerged from the pile of bedding. "What the hell?"

Zach bolted upright, clutching the edge of the sheet to his chest like a maiden bride. It did little to cover his naked body.

Make that gorgeously naked body.

Claudia shut down the fuzzy image of running her fingers over his carved chest. *What is he doing here – in my hotel room, in my bed? More to the point, why is he naked?* And she, too, for that matter. But if the tingle between her legs was any indication, she already knew the answer.

What have I done?

Scowling, Zach pushed himself upright.

Nothing made sense and all her thoughts were a jumble. She dredged up her only defense – the one that had failed her last night – control.

"I said get out."

She reared her foot for another attack against his oh-so-fine ass. With a lithe twist, Zach avoided the kick and pinioned her leg under his arm. Electricity zinged up her thigh, aiming to roost in the warmth at the top.

His quick jerk pulled her off-balance. She flopped back down onto the bed. The sudden movement brought waves of nausea.

Her distress must have been plainly written on her face. He jackknifed over the edge of the bed, scooped up a nearby trashcan and shoved it under her nose. Two used condoms stared back at her. It was all her stomach needed to tip it over the edge. Ignoring the trashcan, she dashed to the bathroom, trying and failing to drag a blanket with her.

She fell to her knees before the toilet with images of those condoms etched in her brain and threw up, naked and puking in a hotel toilet, fighting her hair. Humiliation overwhelmed her. Zach would never let her live down this moment.

Kill me now.

"Here... I got you."

Zach wrapped the blanket around her then pulled back her hair.

Claudia clutched the edges of the soft cover in one hand as another wave overcame her.

"Why are you being so nice to me?" she asked when she recovered.

"I'm thinking I might have a masochistic streak in me," he replied.

After what seemed like hours of wrenching heaves, she levered herself upright, still shaking.

"Do you want to go lie down or stay here for a while?" He combed his finger through her hair—petting her, soothing her, breaking down her defenses.

She shrugged his hand away. "Bed."

He helped her stand. "Rinse and spit first. You'll feel better." He ran a glass of water for her then held it to her mouth. She complied with his suggestion, ignoring their reflections in the wall-sized mirror. Zach cupped her elbow and helped her back to the other room. Once she caught sight of it, Claudia wished she'd remained in the bathroom.

The room was an unholy mess. Clothes—hers *and* his—were strewn from one corner to the other. A pair of panty hose was draped over the lampshade. A bottle of champagne was upside down in the ice bucket. Another rested unopened on the desk. Room service trays were piled with dirty dishes. Money in denominations ranging from twenty to one-hundred-dollar bills lay scattered over the bed and on the floor.

She sank to the edge of the bed and buried her head in her hands. Zach left her, only to return and press a cool, damp washcloth into her hand. She ran the cloth over her face and tried to gather her wits.

"Here." He held out a glass of water and a handful of aspirin. "I think you could use these."

She glanced up. He'd pulled on a pair of white boxers but hadn't bothered with a shirt or shoes. His muscular chest was bare. A sprinkling of hair that narrowed to a distracting line leading down into his waistband grabbed her attention. More hazy images intruded — wandering her tongue down the bunny trail while she divested him of his boxers. At least she'd maintained some measure of power and control last night, but how much had she lost?

Claudia accepted the glass and the pills with shaking hands. She drank, darting surreptitious glances toward her unwanted companion.

Captain Zach Taylor, attorney and United States Marine, epitomized everything she distrusted in a man. Darkly handsome with full, sensuous lips and a flashing dimple, he represented to her the typical carefree philanderer — the kind of man who could break a woman's heart and never think twice about it. She'd already had her heart broken once and that was enough to last a lifetime. Her older brother Phillip had introduced them years ago, and ever since, the antagonism had been mutual.

Yet that was nothing compared to the lust-filled fantasies of him dancing through her head every time she made herself come. Her first glance at the man had sent her heart and stomach somersaulting with glee. All her hard-won control had sifted away. Zach was the one in charge and she'd done everything in her power to keep him from realizing that.

'You need to loosen up, Claudia Stuart, and stop being such a prude.'

Zach's teasing remark had been made in front of a crowd of friends at a Christmas party in Phillip's home — mostly fellow attorneys from the Judge Advocate's Office at Camp Pendleton. The jibe had drawn a big laugh from the Marines. Zach had been one of them, and his personality was in a league of its own.

She recalled that he had wanted her to give him a simple kiss under the mistletoe. Cold rejection had been her answer, delivered publicly to humiliate and discourage further interest. In retaliation, he'd dubbed her Ice Princess. The nickname had stuck — and so had the animosity and that damnable unrelenting want for him.

She'd let him egg her on at that party. There'd been a stupid bet. She'd lost. The price? That blasted mistletoe kiss. But there hadn't been anything simple about it. Claudia would never forget the fire, the raw sensuality that had engulfed her, threatening her carefully erected defenses. She swore the heat from his erection that had been wedged between them had branded her. There were times she could still feel it throbbing against her. She'd done her best to avoid a repeat incident. The only time Zach had ever been in her bed was in her fantasies. Until now…

Claudia put down the glass, forcing a calmness she didn't feel. "It looks like we robbed a bank."

"Hit the jackpot, as I recall."

"I remember something like that, but it's about all." She rubbed at the ache in her head. "God, this is my worst nightmare."

Zach leaned against the dresser and stared at his toes. "I've never had a woman complain before, but in this case, I'd have to agree."

Claudia soaked in the sight of him, standing there unguarded. Her focus wandered to the scar on his left biceps from a bullet wound. Old fear gripped her heart. He'd been injured trying to protect Phillip and Rowan's son the previous year. The news had brought her to her knees. She cared for him more than she'd ever admit, making her more determined than ever to never let him near her heart.

He lifted his gaze to hers, nailing her in place with its dark brown intensity. "We're married."

Claudia's jaw worked, but it seemed an eternity before she could push out the single word. "Impossible."

"But true," he replied.

He shoved away from his perch and walked to the desk. With a flick of his wrist, he dragged out a paper from underneath the champagne bottle. Thrusting it at her, he said, "I found this when I got the aspirin from my ditty bag."

Claudia craned her neck at the paper but refused to touch it. A different wave of nausea engulfed her.

United this day in Holy Matrimony, Zachary Stephen Taylor and Claudia Marie Stuart...

Their signatures were sprawled with untidy abandon at the bottom of the document. Two of the people who had accompanied them to Vegas had signed as witnesses.

"This has to be a joke," she muttered, although the document and the evidence throughout the room left no doubt.

"Oh, how I wish that were so."

A little melodramatic, but it certainly echoed her feelings.

"Listen—" he began.

Claudia held up her hand. "Put on a shirt or something. I don't need you walking around here half naked."

"What's wrong? Too tempting for you?"

There it was, that killer smile guaranteed to make a woman's heart stutter and her lady parts stand up and take notice—Claudia's included. She narrowed her eyes. "Why, you self-serving—"

"You're pretty tempting yourself." He waved a finger at her.

Claudia glanced down. She'd let the blanket fall, exposing her nudity. Nothing was left to the imagination. Embarrassment burned her from head to toe. With as much nonchalance as she could muster, she tugged up the blanket.

Zach half-grinned. "Pity. I was rather enjoying the view."

"Shut up."

His grin widened. "That's a fine way to speak to your new husband."

She rubbed her forehead and tried to control the laughter that was threatening to turn hysterical. "You would be the last person I'd consider marrying."

"But, to put it bluntly, that's what we did. We're husband and wife." He waved the certificate once more then tossed it to the rumpled bed. "Legally married by Reverend Thompson at the Vegas Chapel, wherever the hell that is." Any humor his voice had held was gone.

Claudia tugged the edges of the blanket closer. "I didn't think they were allowed to marry people who were drunk."

"Maybe they didn't realize how far gone we were" — he clutched his hands to his heart—"or maybe our boundless love and devotion for each other was too much to deny and they married us without delay."

"Cut the melodrama," she snapped. "In any event, it's something I plan to rectify at the earliest opportunity. I'm sure I won't hurt your feelings when I tell you I'll be filing for divorce as soon as possible."

"Summary dissolution," he corrected.

Here they were in this lousy predicament and he wanted to debate technicalities. "I need a lawyer."

"You just married one, remember?"

Claudia wanted to screech at him. Instead, she kept her voice level, maintaining her control, speaking in cold, clear tones that even a moron would have no trouble understanding. "I don't care what you call it or how it's done. I want out of this alcohol-induced nightmare. Do you understand me?"

"Loud and clear." The ice in his voice matched her own.

Good. At least there's something we agree on. Although, from the looks of the room, they'd found other mutually agreeable matters during the night.

Zach sighed. "Despite us being drunk, it appears we were careful. There are two condoms in this trash can, two more in the bathroom. I know you think I'm a sex-starved animal, but believe me, I have my limits. Frankly, I'm surprised to find more than two. But on the off chance we weren't and you discover you're — "

"I'm on the pill." Her body, her rules. She trusted no man — and certainly not a flimsy piece of rubber.

"Okay...good."

He sounded disappointed.

Trying to ignore her aching stomach and pounding head, she wrapped her blanket around her rigid body and headed for the bathroom to change. His silence followed her

Shutting the door, she caught a glimpse of herself in the mirror. Her platinum-blonde hair was flying out in all directions and her skin had a tinge best described as pasty in the overhead lighting. Her blue eyes were almost black in her pinched face. They were bloodshot, as well.

A stunning sight. She dropped the blanket and stepped into the shower.

"If you can't remember it then it never happened," she whispered into the biting chill of the spray.

But it *had* happened. If she wanted to deny the evidence around her, that was one thing, but her aching muscles and soreness were quite another.

Was it as wonderful as I'd fantasized? Damn, I wish I remembered.

Claudia laughed at the contradiction. She didn't want him, yet she wanted it to have been a night she'd remember forever? More input for those fantasies.

She warmed up the spray and let the water beat life into her system. Sinking into the bottom of the tub, she hugged her knees to her chest. She tried to focus on the last twenty-four hours and figure out where she'd faltered, where her defenses had been breached.

Her sister-in-law Rowan had talked her into going to a wedding. Phillip had been the best man. Zach had been a groomsman. Immediately following the ceremony, Rowan delivered a son, after successfully hiding the fact she was in labor *during* the ceremony.

Then there had been the wedding reception. Drink had flowed. Claudia had abstained. At some point, the wedding party had decided to take a road trip to Vegas. They'd wanted to borrow Phillip's brand-new minivan. He'd agreed, on one condition—Claudia must drive. She'd been the only sober one. She'd agreed as a favor for her brother.

They'd arrived at midnight with Zach and six other people. All Claudia had wanted to do was find a room and go to sleep. But, as usual, she'd allowed Zach to bait her.

'Just one slot. Play just one. I'll even give you the dollar.'

Anything to shut him up and put much-needed distance between them so the buzz he always gave her would die. She'd fed the dollar in…and had gotten a thousand back. The cocktail waitress had brought one drink after another. She and Zach had gambled and kept winning. Champagne, wine and beer had mixed with lethal intensity.

She dropped her head to her knees. A vague memory of one hell of a kiss with both of them plastered against the slot machine drifted into her foggy senses. A glint of gold and diamonds caught her eye. He'd even bought her a beautiful ring. None of it made any sense.

They didn't get along. Their constant sniping at each other proved that. Hell, she'd fueled it to save her heart. *How in the world could we have gotten married?*

A knocking at the bathroom door startled her from her thoughts. She tensed, afraid he might barge in.

"What do you want?" she shouted.

"I have to pee," he snapped back.

"Can't you wait?"

"You've been in here for half an hour already. I can't wait much longer. If you don't come out, I'm coming in whether you like it or not. I'm giving you another five minutes."

Claudia balled her hands into fists and stood. It was going to be a long drive back to Twentynine Palms.

Chapter Two

Zach shoved the last of the room service trays into the hallway. The smell of leftover food turned his stomach. It was either that or the stench of liquor exuding from his body. In all his life, he could never recall having drank so much. It was a wonder his head wasn't shoved in the toilet next to Claudia's.

He and Claudia Stuart married. A dream come true for him. A nightmare for her.

He'd wanted her from the second he'd first laid eyes on her, had loved her the instant his lips had covered hers under the mistletoe and had known a heartbeat afterward that a union of any kind would never happen. Women like Claudia — beautiful, surreal, sophisticated — did *not* marry men like him. Until now. *Too bad it isn't real.*

He eased back on the bed while he tried to piece together fragments from the night before. Nothing coherent stayed with him.

A pity. After all these years, he had managed to get beneath Claudia's icy armor, only to discover he could barely remember a thing.

What he did remember tantalized him. Her normally indifferent dark blue eyes had lit with wonder the instant the reels had aligned on her slot machine. From that moment on, he'd done everything in his power to keep that spark of humanity on her face—anything to keep her favor.

They'd traveled from one slot machine to another, each time winning more. He glanced around the room at the money scattered about.

Damn, how much did we win?

The cocktail waitress had kept bringing them more drinks until they were beyond rational thought. *Then I kissed her.* He remembered that much—and the fact that he wanted her so badly he couldn't walk without his cock hurting. But that was a common occurrence whenever he was around her.

Her slurred response had been...

Zach squinted. *What did she say?* Then he recalled.

'I can't let you in unless we're married. I promised myself. You've already shattered my control and made me crazy. I won't compromise on this.'

'Then let's get married.'

He stared at the gold ring on his finger. Married to Claudia. It was what he'd always wanted. It was equally obvious that they'd had way too much to drink because she wouldn't have agreed to go out with him, much less marry him, otherwise. Thank God, they'd exercised some caution the previous night and used protection. Not that it mattered, since she was on the pill. A woman as fine and savvy as Claudia would take no chances. Odd how that news made him sad. A baby would ensure they'd always be a big part of each other's lives—and always at odds, if it'd been an accident.

He heard the door open and watched her slink into the room, blanket clutched around her like a suit of armor, hair wrapped in a towel.

"If it's your virtue you're concerned about, don't worry. I won't attack you." He hoisted himself to his feet and glanced down at his boxers. "Besides, I think you broke it."

Claudia blinked then laughed—an honest-to-goodness laugh. The husky sound set his body tingling and woke his cock. Zach ducked into the bathroom before she noticed his erection—not that he had any energy to do anything about it. He felt like shit, too. His head was killing him and his stomach contents threatened to abandon ship. He'd barely been able to hang on when he'd held her hair back while she puked. He doubted she'd award him hero status for his efforts. Once she recovered, she'd be pondering ways to flay his hide and use the skin for new shoes. Reminding her that she'd been an active and willing participant last night wouldn't earn him points, either. No. If he hoped to salvage anything from this, he had to man up and show Claudia his true self, not the man who teased and traded barbs with her.

He relieved himself then wasted little time getting into the shower. A flick of his wrist doused him in cold water. His cock deflated and his balls tried to crawl up his ass to get warm. He turned the heat up and started to bathe. The sooner he was done, the sooner they could leave and retreat to their corners. He hated the idea. He didn't want the old Claudia to reappear. He wanted this version to stay—the Claudia whose laughter swelled his heart, whose bright eyes crowned him king, whose kiss devastated his senses.

She had a body to die for, and up until this point, she had barricaded herself behind walls of ice so thick that a blowtorch couldn't have melted them. He liked this unexpected facet, the genuine humor, the loss of restraint. It made him wonder if the feud between them had been dispelled during the night and now he could discover the real Claudia, let her know how he truly felt. The question was, did he want to set himself up for rejection?

Women like Claudia were all class. Beauty, grace and style shimmered beneath her frosty exterior. Even if she did decide to give him more than the time of day, it would never last. Women like her didn't go for guys like him. She was a heartache waiting to happen.

By the time he walked into the room again, she was ready to leave. Her shoulder-length blonde hair was pulled back in its normal French twist. Not a single strand was left to wander. The peach-colored dress she'd worn the day before was pressed into perfection with no hint it had once been a crumpled mess on the floor.

"I won't be long." He reached for the tuxedo he'd worn at the wedding and found it ironed and neatly draped over the back of the chair. In fact, everything about the room was back in order — the bed made, the money stacked on the dresser, the champagne bottles gone.

"Did the maid come while I was in the shower?"

She walked to the bathroom. "Don't be ridiculous. Do you think I'd actually let another person walk into this mess?"

"Crazy me." He managed a grim smile. "I don't know where my head was." His Ice Princess was back in all her glory.

While he dressed, he watched her tidy the bathroom and had to grudgingly admit she was right. No one deserved to have to clean up something like this.

Score one for my Ice Princess.

"There was a message for us from your friends." Claudia smoothed out the bed coverings where he had sat. "They rented a car and left without us."

"That was dumb."

She straightened and faced him, mouth set in those stern lines he hated. He longed to kiss them away, to pull her hair free and comb his fingers through it. Fear of having her knee plowed into his groin kept him in place.

"Not considering their perspective." She arched one finely shaped eyebrow. "They wanted to give the lovebirds some privacy."

"Fuck." He raked his fingers through his short hair. "I'm guessing we made quite a spectacle of ourselves last night."

"So it appears. I only hope we can get back before they start spreading the good news."

"Want to call from here?"

Claudia closed her eyes and drew in a breath. "What I want is to leave this nightmare as quickly as possible."

Zach tossed his jacket over his shoulder. "My sentiments exactly, Princess."

She gathered the two piles of money and handed him one.

"Keep it," he told her.

"We have twenty thousand between us."

His eyes widened. "It'll be safer in your purse for now."

"I disagree. It's better to split it between us — or would you rather I stuff it in my bra?"

Is she joking or serious? It was always so hard to tell with her. A smile lifted one corner of his mouth. "I doubt there'd be much room in there."

A faint flush crept to her cheeks. Without another word, she stuffed the wad in her purse then jerked open the door. She was at the elevator waiting when he caught up with her.

Claudia tried to not watch him from the corner of her eye as they rode down. It was impossible. His comment had been typical Zach, but he'd spoken nothing more than the truth. Her bosom was out there for the world to see. Heaven knew there was certainly nothing small about it. But no matter what truth his words held, they had also possessed an intimacy with which she was unable to deal. He'd seen her, touched her, likely wrapped his hot mouth over her turgid nipples. The thought, coupled with the knowing comment, sent fire and ice racing through her body.

How much does he remember from last night? Part of her longed to demand the information. The other part prayed she would never learn. It would only make her want more.

The elevator door opened. The incessant ringing of slot machines assaulted her aching head. Greasy smells from the breakfast buffet drifted her way, twisting her stomach into churning revolt.

Zach pressed his hand against the small of her back to guide her forward. The protective gesture made her feel safe. The way he brushed circles on her back with his thumb comforted her. Claudia leaned into his touch, wanting more, wanting to tuck under his arm and curl against him. Odd, when she'd spent five years avoiding him.

She reined in the wayward emotion. That was more evidence of how easily he could wrest control from her hands. There was nothing safe about Zach. He was nothing more than a womanizer and she had become his latest conquest. She should be feeling disgust with herself and with him for putting themselves into such a stupid predicament, not wanting to cuddle up and feel his arms around her.

Checking out was more agony. Pasting on a smile, Claudia dealt with the congratulations of the desk clerk, the bellman, the concierge and the valet. Finally, her brother's minivan was brought to the entryway. Once safe behind the closed door, she sank into the cushiony seat and let the happily-married façade drop.

Zach snapped his seat belt in place. "If we'd been the happy couple, that would have been very nice. We'll have to stop for gas then we can be on our way."

Claudia nodded, found the armrest with her elbow and propped her chin on her palm. Her stomach lurched with the first movement of the vehicle. She pressed her fist to her mouth in an attempt to keep things in place.

Zach eased to a stop and draped his arm over her seat, brushing her shoulder with his fingertips until she opened her eyes.

"Are you all right?"

The compassion in his eyes slithered under her skin.

"I'll be fine," she muttered behind her hand. "We have to leave. What choice do we have?"

"We could stay an extra night until you're well enough to travel."

It is a tempting idea, but... Claudia shook her head. "I want to get back. I'll be all right."

Zach nodded and pulled away. "Rest. I'll get us there as quickly as I can. If you need to stop, tell me."

Leaning back, she braced herself for movement. Even as gently as he drove, it still didn't help her queasiness. Two blocks later, she almost slid to the floor in relief when Zach stopped for gas. With shaking hands, she fumbled for the window button and opened it. The only air drifting in was hot and dry.

"Please don't let me get sick in my brother's minivan," she quietly begged, then dropped her head back onto the headrest.

She dozed in a state of twilight sleep, aware of her surroundings yet incapable of reacting to them. The door opened, another rush of hot air smothered her and they were on their way once more. Seconds later, Zach stopped.

Claudia raised up. They were still in the parking lot of the convenience store where they'd filled up.

"What's going on?"

Zach shoved a packet of motion sickness pills and a can of cola in front of her. "Here. This should help a little. You're sick, dehydrated. The pills should tame your stomach. I took two myself." He popped two from the packet and offered them to her.

She accepted and wrapped her hands around the cola. "It's warm."

"Best thing for an upset stomach. A cold soda might make your stomach cramp."

She popped the top, tossed the pills into her mouth and let the liquid slip down her throat like the welcome breeze she had sought minutes before.

"When you're sure that has settled, I've got some saltines for you to nibble on."

She cast a wary eye toward the package and put her defenses on full alert. "Why are you being so nice to me? You know I can't stand you."

He shrugged back into his seat. "Contrary to your opinion of me, I am the gentleman my parents raised me to be. I can't ignore a lady in distress, even when that lady is you."

It was a cruel jab, but it was nothing less than she expected from him and nothing she was too ill to counter.

"What's the matter, Captain? Not reveling in your conquest? You've been after me for years. Now that you've got what you wanted — "

"Don't start with me, Princess."

His tone was cold, setting her heart racing. Zach teasing and taunting she could take. Indifference, no.

"I don't seduce the unwilling. I don't seduce at all. When I have sex with a woman, I make sure it's one who wants me as much as I want her." He leaned forward, his brown eyes glinting with a cross between humor and desire. "Last night you made your want very clear. That much I'll never forget. How that led to marriage is fuzzy. But here we are, so quit playing innocent." A smirk lit his eyes. "Although if you want one for the road, I'll take you to the nearest hotel, lift your dress and — "

"You wouldn't," she said.

Zach chuckled and twisted the key. The engine roared to life. "What a contradiction you are, Princess — accusing me in one breath, defending me the next. Eat some crackers and try to rest. I'd like to get back before dark and it's going to be a long drive."

The longest in history as far as Claudia was concerned. Much as she hated to admit it, the cola, pills and crackers did help her stomach, but she'd be damned if she'd let Zach know that. He was already too cock-sure for his own good.

Determined to keep quiet, she sat beside him with grim determination to not utter a word throughout the three-and-a-half-hour desert drive. Instead, she focused on the scenery, so different from her coastal California home.

The sun shone with white brilliance. The rocky landscape dotted with cacti and Joshua trees was like a set from an old Western movie. With each mile that ticked by, her eyelids drooped.

* * * *

Claudia sighed and snuggled deeper into sleep when she felt someone's arm drift over her shoulders.

"Wake up, Princess. We're almost to Phillip's house."

She flashed her eyes open. Not only had she slept the entire trip but she'd also toppled to one side, using the console between the bucket seats as a headrest.

"Looks like we've got judge, jury and executioner waiting for us on the front porch."

She shoved herself upright. At least the sleep had done her some good. She didn't feel as bad. A good thing, since she was going to need all her faculties to face the trio ahead—her sister-in-law, her brother and... *Franklin? What the hell is he doing at Phillip's house?*

"Who's the pretty boy?" Zach asked.

"Franklin Delacourte, San Francisco news anchor extraordinaire." She adopted the mocking tone normally reserved for breakroom jibes. Franklin was a pretty man and knew it. He couldn't pass a mirror without taking the time to smooth his two-hundred-dollar haircut.

"Boyfriend?"

"Absolutely not. Occasional forced-upon-me escort when there are social events we're required to attend for the television station. Nothing more."

"Is that feeling mutual?"

She grimaced. "He seems unable to grasp the concept of the word 'no'. He's searching for a trophy wife. I'm not willing to be mounted."

Claudia regretted the double entendre the instant it left her lips. Before he could jump on it, she flashed Zach the evilest glare she could muster. "Don't even touch it. What business is it of yours, anyway?"

Devilment danced in his eyes. "Just curious. I suppose he's the evening news anchor?"

"The most wonderful one who ever walked the earth. If anyone doubts that, he's quick to set them straight."

"I like him already." His sarcasm echoed hers. "He's got balls showing up here."

"Not when I get through with him," she replied.

Zach chuckled. "You get the knife, baby. I'll hold him down for you."

Claudia smirked and let the warm camaraderie of his words seep into her veins.

As he pulled into the gravel driveway, the trio stepped as one from the porch.

"I think they might know," Zach said.

Claudia had to agree. Franklin's mouth was pursed, as if he'd gotten hold of a lemon. Rowan, pushed to the forefront, her golden-brown eyes caught between confusion and joy. Then there was her brother…

Phillip towered behind the other two, waiting to pass judgment. His arms were parked across his chest, while his gaze traveled a slow path between Claudia and Zach. He appeared cautious, curious and determined to have an explanation.

"I feel like I've broken curfew," she mumbled.

"Yeah, and I'm the son of a bitch responsible." He slipped the minivan into park. "Let's get this over with."

Franklin barreled down on her the second she opened the door. He had no right to even be here, much less to be angry. Claudia held her ground. If intimidation was his intent, she could give as good as she got.

"What the hell is *this* all about? I go through all the trouble of coming down here to join you and I find that you've gone traipsing off with this soldier."

Beside her, Zach cleared his throat. "Excuse me. That's Marine, not soldier."

Franklin ignored him. "I want answers."

Claudia lifted her eyebrow and leveled an icy stare his way. "Number one, I do not recall asking nor did I wish you to join me. Number two, no one, especially me, *wanted* you to come here. Number three, I don't answer to you or anyone else. Number four, I did not go traipsing off. I was doing my brother a favor."

"By marrying this…this…"

Zach stepped between them. "The next word better be *gentleman*, Frank."

A beet-red flush mottled Franklin's cheeks.

Rowan tugged Claudia away from the men. "What's going on?"

"It was a mistake. That's all. Just a silly little mistake."

"So, you and Zach aren't married?" Phillip asked.

She rubbed the new ache growing in her head. "Yes, we're married, but it's a little more complicated than that. We were gambling and had way too much to drink. I guess we…" The words faded. What more could she say? The whole situation was ridiculous.

Franklin cornered her once more, pressing his face so close Claudia could count the pores on his nose. "Who would have guessed that it would only take a few drinks to pry open those pretty legs of yours?"

Zach caught her hand before she could zing it across Franklin's cheek. He laced his fingers through hers and tugged them against his chest.

"Look, Frank. I've spent the last several hours convincing my lovely bride that I really am a gentleman. Don't prove me a liar. Leave now before I plow my fist into that perfect profile of yours."

As if sizing up his chances, Franklin gave Zach the once-over then backed toward the red Jaguar parked beside Zach's Jeep. "You're finished, Claudia Stuart. I'll see to it. By the time I'm through with you, there won't be a news team in San Francisco who will hire you as weather girl, much less as an investigative reporter. Ciao, baby."

"San Francisco isn't the only city in the world, Frank," Zach shot back. "And her last name is Taylor." Then, without warning, he swung Claudia close and covered her lips with a kiss.

She wedged her free hand between them, furious that he would take advantage of Franklin's ire. Yet each flick of his tongue across hers tumbled her further into oblivion. She caved with a soft sigh, sagged into his arms and kissed him back. Her body came alive, craving skin-to-skin contact.

The sportscar's engine rev broke the spell. Franklin scattered gravel before he sped away.

She shoved Zach back. "How dare you."

Zach yanked her back and pressed his lips close to her ear. "Don't tell me you didn't like getting the best of him, Princess. Think of it as my wedding gift to you."

"The only present I want from you is a divorce," she whispered through clenched teeth.

"My pleasure. I'll call you when the papers are ready." He nipped her earlobe then jumped back before she could smack him. With a mock salute, he hopped into his Jeep and left.

"Interesting," her brother muttered.

Too interesting. Claudia dusted the goosebumps from her arms. She didn't trust him. Zach undermined her control. Yet here she was succumbing to a kiss best left to the bedroom, leaving her aching for more.

Rowan draped an arm around her shoulders. "Come on. You must be hungry. Let me fix you something to eat and we can talk."

Claudia shook her head. Her nerves were stretched to the breaking point. Food was the last thing on her mind. The tingling remnants of Zach's kiss shoved all other thoughts aside. She tried to focus on something else besides him.

"Rowan, shouldn't you be in the hospital? You just had a baby."

"They released us this morning with a clean bill of health. Come on. There's some leftover pasta inside with your name on it."

Claudia shook her head once more. "I need to be alone for a while. I'm going for a run."

Phillip jerked his chin toward the sky. "It's almost sunset. I'm not sure that's a good idea."

Pushing by him, she stepped toward the house. "I'll be fine."

"Then I'll go with you."

She jerked to a stop. "No. I want to be alone."

"Maybe this isn't as big a mistake as you think. Zach isn't Todd, Claudia," Phillip said.

A punch to the gut would have had less impact. She pointed a finger at him. "I refuse to open *that* topic for discussion. Please, just leave me alone for a little while."

"Later, then. Don't forget your cell phone."

She acknowledged his request with a nod. A truce was declared, even if only temporarily. Claudia hurried to the guest room, hauled on her running gear and dashed from the house.

The sun was gone, painting the surrounding mountains in shades of rose and purple. With the night, the heat dissipated. A gentle breeze stirred the brush.

That was what she needed — freedom. Here she could run the aches in her muscles away. Here her turmoil was lost in the exhilaration of exercise. Confusion no longer existed. Everything was clear. Too clear.

It was a kiss. That was all. Designed to rattle Franklin. Zach had kissed hundreds of women...millions of them. She'd kissed her share of men. This meant nothing to either of them. *So why are you letting it bother you?*

"Shut up," she snapped and picked up her speed.

Claudia ran until her breath gave out then slowed to a walk. Stars twinkled in the pale dusk, like diamonds on deep blue velvet. A full yellow moon was perched on the eastern horizon, giving more peace for her troubled thoughts.

The sound of a car caught her attention. Glancing around, she realized she was more than three miles from the house. Suddenly, headlights blinded her.

Ducking into the creosote bushes on the shoulder of the road, Claudia waited for the car to pass. To her surprise, the driver pulled off the road onto a rutted track. She craned her neck for a better view and saw the car door open.

The driver was short and lean but that was all she could discern. He was dressed in military desert camouflage from head to toe. He hauled something bulky from the backseat of the white sedan. She couldn't quite make it out. Then he pulled a shovel from the trunk.

Claudia inched closer. A peal from the phone at her waist broke the silence. The man jerked around. She fumbled to silence the noise, sliding and pressing the screen to no avail. Finally, the noise stopped and she was able set it to vibrate.

The car door slammed, tires spun and for a moment she feared he would run her down. She hunkered in her hideaway, praying he would go past. The car veered her way then cut to the road and zoomed off.

Breathe... Just breathe.

Once her shaking subsided, Claudia crept forward, waving aside clouds of dust. Tire tracks made it easy to find the spot. There, in the dim light cast by the full moon, she found a military sleeping bag, and inside it, the body of a man.

She sucked in a gasp. Screaming was for sissies. She was an investigative reporter, for crying out loud, but nothing could have prepared her for the blood-soaked package.

Claudia stood there, trying to decide if she should get closer. Doing so might destroy valuable forensic evidence. But if there was a chance he was still alive, how could she not help?

The phone shuddered against her waist. With shaking fingers, she pulled it up to her ear.

"Care to tell me where you are and why you didn't answer the first time?" Phillip barked.

"There's... I found a dead man. I think he's a Marine. Three miles west of the house. Follow the road. Drive slow and when I know it's you, I'll step out. And, Phillip...please hurry."

A muffled groan came from the bag as she ended the call. Claudia hurried forward. "It's okay," she told him.

He fumbled a bloodied hand for hers but he couldn't lift it. Claudia curled her fingers around his.

"Help—"

"Relax. Help is on the way."

"Allison...secret..." He struggled to say more then was gone.

Claudia saw headlights coming their way and folded his hand onto his chest. She would not cry. She would *not cry*.

Chapter Three

He shouldn't have kissed her. It didn't matter how many excuses he'd made since then, the thought still plagued Zach. He'd spent a fitful night battling hard-ons from hell that no hand job could appease every time he thought of how right she'd felt in his arms when she'd molded her fine body against his and kissed him back.

It had been a show. That was all. Something to get under Franklin Delacourte's skin and help Claudia get a little victory over the jerk.

Zach snorted. That was a lie. It was for no one's benefit but his own. She had been there, her body pressed close to his, those full lips of hers slightly parted. Anger, hurt and shock had all been held in by a will not many people possessed.

He'd seen an opportunity to slip in under her defenses, to taste what she'd denied him all these years for what might be the last time. He'd taken it and somehow damned himself in the process.

He'd expected cold defiance and had thought Claudia would tense, her mouth rigid under the caress. Instead, she'd pressed against him and those lips — full, moist, beckoning — had seared a kiss into his memory that a thousand women could never erase.

What he'd felt before was nothing compared to what he was feeling now. For one second in memorable time, Claudia had wanted him. He wondered how he could keep her with him for a little while longer — or maybe find a way to win her over.

Quit dreaming. It was for show, to piss off Franklin.

Zach pulled into his parking spot outside the offices of the Staff Judge Advocate. He barely remembered the fifteen-minute drive to work.

He draped his forearms over the steering wheel and stared at the building. Even renovated, the dual concrete structures looked more like bomb shelters, which somehow seemed appropriate since he considered the area surrounding the Marine Corps base nothing more than a wasteland. It was nothing like the desert surrounding his family's home in Phoenix. There the soil was alive with color, the landscape sculpted into monuments to nature.

Twentynine Palms had its good points but Zach preferred big city lights and lots of people. To get that while stationed on this base, he had to drive at least an hour to Palm Springs.

It took a special type of person to enjoy the place. Not many did, especially with a shortage of available housing, which soured everyone's dispositions. With so many people forced to find temporary lodgings off-base, there wasn't a day that went by without Zach hearing at least five landlord-tenant complaints.

It wouldn't have mattered all that much if he had a job he liked. There again he'd been sorely disappointed.

After six months of trial work, his colonel had moved him into Legal Assistance.

Family law. Nothing was worse. He grimaced. If he had to listen to one more person whine about not being able to pay debts they shouldn't have run up in the first place or Marines who were fathers of children they swore weren't theirs, he'd go nuts. At least one good thing would come of it. He could prepare his own dissolution of marriage papers with no crap from anyone.

"Another great day. Might as well get it over with."

He slung his bag of exercise gear over his shoulder and trudged inside his office. Already the noise from the waiting room had reached a decibel level equivalent to that of a playground at recess. Zach could never understand why the clients always saw fit to drag their children into their problems and disagreements. Surely they had friends who could watch the kids long enough for their parents to sort out their difficulties. But for him to even suggest such a thing would be paramount to treason.

"I understand congratulations are in order."

Zach jolted at the sight of his fellow Legal Assistance attorney Captain Aaron Howard waiting for him in his office. The man thrived on family law and knew his stuff, but he was also the last person Zach needed to see this morning.

Red-headed, freckled and gangly, the man appeared more suited to comedy theater than law. His demeanor suggested that the priesthood might not have been a bad profession.

Aaron never said much. He didn't have to. Yet there was something about him that begged confidence. People wanted to tell him things, and he instinctively knew how to respond. He should have been a minister, not an attorney, and he brought the peace of the confessional to clients who needed a little more than legal advice.

His presence in Zach's office first thing this morning meant only one thing. Someone was going to spill their guts and that someone was Zach.

"I need coffee."

Aaron slid a steaming mug across the desk. "Thought you might. Here you go. Just the way you like it—hot, black and thick enough to rot a hole in your gut. So, tell me about the new Mrs. Taylor. I didn't know you were seeing someone."

Zach groaned and raked his fingers through his hair. "Aw, for cryin' out loud. Bad news travels fast. Shut the door."

The man listened without interruption, sipping his own coffee from time to time. When Zach was finished, Aaron leaned forward.

"So now the two of you will divorce and go on your merry ways. Right?"

Zach nodded. "It's that simple."

Aaron smiled and stretched to his feet. "If it's that simple, why are you still wearing the wedding ring?"

Mouth agape, Zach jerked his gaze to the gold band on his finger. "I forgot about it. That's all." He yanked the ring off and glanced up, but Aaron was gone and Zach's clerk was standing in the doorway.

"Captain Taylor, your first appointment is here. Mrs. Sorrels."

Zach winced. The corporal snickered and ducked away. He gave the wedding ring a spin, watching it twirl like a top.

Rita Sorrels, divorce client from hell... She was enough to make a man swear off women and the only woman Zach could say frightened him. While in the process of divorcing her third military husband, each higher in rank than the last, she was after her fourth—Zach. A week didn't go by without a visit from her. A hungry tiger was less diligent.

He snapped up the ring and jammed it back on his finger. Maybe that would be enough to make her back off.

Sliding her case file from the cabinet, Zach braced himself to meet his personal nightmare. It was worse than before.

Mrs. Sorrels greeted him in reception with little more than a smile. Her clothing was appropriate for the beach, not a law office. Her shorts were tight and cut high enough to be panties. A halter top almost couldn't contain her ample bosom. Her freshly manicured fingernails were sharpened claws, polished blood red to match the toes peeking from her sandals. At least he presumed it was polish and not the blood of her latest victim.

His front office staff should have turned her away for improper attire, but she scared the piss out of them. Even now, they gave her wide berth. Zach should have done the deed, but following base regulations and ordering her to leave wasn't worth the scene she'd create—although he rather liked the idea of calling military police to escort her off base.

"Captain Taylor, a pleasure. I brought you these." She whipped out a plate of brownies.

"I'm sure my clerks will appreciate them, Mrs. Sorrels."

He slid the treats onto the nearest desk and motioned her to his office. When she tried to shut the door behind them, he opened it wider and blocked it with his copy of *Black's Law Dictionary*.

"How can I help you today, Mrs. Sorrels?" Zach sat behind his desk, hoping the barrier would put her off. Instead, she crossed her legs and leaned forward, offering him a good view of her cleavage—one Zach ignored, although Claudia's came to mind. He shook the image away and focused.

"It's my soon-to-be ex-husband." She punctuated the sentence with a dramatic sigh. "I believe the military says I'm entitled to some measure of support until the divorce is final. He isn't paying me a dime. I've begged. I've pleaded. I've even gone to the command. What can I do? I have bills to pay. I don't have enough for groceries."

For yet more dramatic effect, she pulled out a tissue and dabbed at the corners of her eyes. As far as Zach was concerned, she didn't look like she'd missed many meals.

"Mrs. Sorrels, we've gone over this before. Your husband is paying your marital debts. He's paying your rent. That's adequate support." He folded his hands on the desk, pressing forward. "I appreciate your situation, ma'am. Divorce is difficult." *Especially when you've become such an expert at it.* "But have you given any consideration to searching for a job? Surely you have some skills."

"I have. There's nothing around here. Unless... I do a little house cleaning from time to time. I don't suppose you need a maid? You know, once a week. I could cook and clean—"

"I manage quite well."

"Every bachelor needs a little help from time to time. I could be *very* beneficial. Do you mind if I close this door?" She reached for it.

"Actually, Mrs. Sorrels, I do mind. I'm expecting my wife at any moment."

The fake tears stopped in mid-cycle. She jerked her gaze to his left hand. "Wife? You're married?"

"Over the weekend. Now, about that job. Have you checked with the local hotels about housekeeping positions?"

She shoved the tissue into her purse and vaulted to her feet. "I'm sure that won't be necessary. I'll find something soon. Good day, Captain."

Zach waited until he heard the outer door close. With a chuckle, he kissed the ring and tossed Mrs. Sorrels' file back in the drawer. "If only they were all that easy to get rid of."

Now for the rest of the crowd in the waiting room.

By lunch Zach was emotionally spent and more determined than ever to leave Legal Assistance. He took his frustration out on the racquetball court, making Aaron struggle to keep up.

But there was another frustration driving the power behind each swing of his racquet. If he could exhaust himself enough, maybe he wouldn't have to think about *it*, about Claudia. Although he'd have to be comatose to forget how good she felt in his arms and how much he longed to keep her there.

Work. Concentrate on work.

He had to get out of Legal Assistance or he'd go nuts. With each ball he whacked, he reviewed the case he intended to plead with his colonel. He was tired of being shoved aside. Today he would be heard.

At one o'clock he stood outside Colonel Scott's door, showered, back in uniform, speech memorized.

"You wanted to see me, Captain?"

"Yes, sir." When the colonel motioned him to a nearby chair, Zach sat.

"Problems?" Colonel Scott tapped the end of his pen against the pile of papers on his desk.

"To be blunt…yes, sir. I feel I'm being wasted in Legal Assistance. I was sent there to help during a manpower shortage. That shortage is over. Captain Howard can handle things. I want to go back to trial." Prosecution or defense, he didn't care, as long as it got him back in the courtroom.

Colonel Scott dropped the pen, steepled his fingers and leaned back. "I see."

Yeah? Well, do something about it.

He picked up a file and tossed it to the edge of the desk nearest Zach. "Since you're so ill-used in Legal Assistance, you can take that."

Zach wanted to cheer. *Finally, an honest-to-god case to work on.* Struggling to hide his joy, he opened the folder. His spirits plummeted.

"This is a death investigation. You want me to be the Investigating Officer?"

Colonel Scott beamed a smile. His bald head and wire glasses made him look like a congenial Buddha, but the man could be hard-core when the need presented itself. "That's exactly what I want."

"But this is a 7th Marines case, why—"

"Because the commanding general wants someone outside that command. The deceased was well-respected, very well-known. There's no objectivity. An outsider would be impartial."

"So I get the ball?"

"Unless you feel *ill-used*." Colonel Scott leaned back in his chair, his gaze still and steady while he waited for the only answer he expected to get.

Zach tucked the folder under his arm. "No, sir. I'll get on it right away."

"Good. Dismissed… And, Captain…"

Zach turned in the doorway. "Yes, sir?"

"Do a good job with this and we'll talk again." He smiled. "I hear the general's needing an aide."

Great. From Legal Assistance to valet. Suppressing a groan, Zach slipped away. The colonel's chuckle followed him down the hall. Doing his best to ignore it, Zach returned to his desk.

It could have been worse. Colonel Scott could have assigned him to investigate the band of teenagers creating havoc in housing. A week didn't go by without some form of malicious mischief. So far, it had been harmless — toilet paper around a house, dog poop on the doorstep, using the sidewalk as a chalkboard to scribble vulgarities.

Sighing, Zach settled down and flicked the file open with his finger. "Okay...let's see what we've got here."

Gunnery Sergeant Theodore Sunline, found in the desert at approximately twenty-hundred hours the previous evening by a female jogger.

That didn't set well with Zach. He imagined the poor woman, out for a little exercise when she stumbled across a body. Not nice at all. It was true, though, that most women were strong, independent and able to handle anything tossed at them. His mom was proof of that. Still, Zach felt there were some things women shouldn't have to deal with. Finding dead bodies was one. Of course, a kid finding the guy would have been worse. *Thank God that didn't happen.*

He focused his attention on the file.

Exact cause of death unknown, pending autopsy. Next of kin notified. Remains requested ASAP.

That meant the coroner would be asked to make the autopsy a priority. Zach mulled over a visit to the county morgue then shook his head. He'd let the man work without a nosy attorney peering over his shoulder. Besides, Zach didn't think he had the stomach to watch.

He drew a yellow pad of paper closer and started to make notes—questions to ask, people to interview, a visit to Naval Criminal Investigative Service for a full report.

Zach glanced at his watch. The NCIS agents were probably still at the scene. If he hurried, he could catch them.

Hold it.

Another possibility discounted. Hurried work was sloppy work. He'd start with the command, friends, family and the poor woman who had found Sunline's body in the first place. It wasn't trial work, but it was a hell of a lot better than calculating support payments for deadbeat spouses and a great way to focus his thoughts on something other than a woman he could never have.

* * * *

"Now where are you going?"

Claudia froze, her fingers curled around the doorknob. She had thought she was safe enough. Rowan was napping with the baby and Claudia had assumed Phillip would be, too. Their other son was still at school. She hadn't counted on Phillip's tenacity for ensuring her welfare.

She needed privacy, not a nursemaid. How could she bring herself to be blunt with him?

"I have to go to the base to make a statement to Special Agent Brownell. I won't be long." She tried to duck out the door.

Phillip stopped her again. "Dressed like that? Claudia, it's after Labor Day and you're wearing white?"

The teasing grated against her nerves. In the last forty-eight hours, she'd gotten married, planned a divorce and witnessed the botched disposal of a murdered man and all Phillip could think of was teasing her?

Struggling to control a sarcastic reply, she looked back at him over her shoulder. "Trust me. The farther west you go, the less it matters. I doubt the fashion police are on patrol in Twentynine Palms. And, for your information, wearing white after Labor Day is no longer a *faux pax*."

She swung open the door.

"Do you want me to come with you?"

"It's a simple statement. I don't need you hovering over me like I'm made of porcelain. I am an investigative reporter. Nothing fazes me much anymore."

"Not even Zach Taylor?"

Claudia froze. Finally, a jab under the armor. A good one, too. Everything about Zach rattled her reserve.

"What shall I tell your husband if he calls?"

"There's no chance of that. I doubt he has the divorce papers ready this quickly. If he does, tell him where I am."

"Are you sure you know what you're doing?" Phillip's gray eyes were intent upon her face.

It was too much. "I made a mistake. At least I'm wise enough to realize it from the start. And please don't start in on that business with Todd Willoughby. That's ancient history."

"Yet it still controls your every move to this day."

She walked on before he could launch another barrage of questions.

Even before she drove away, Claudia regretted the spiteful tone in her exchange with her brother. She sat in her car cursing her rudeness. Phillip had only been trying to help. Yet each effort on his part only reminded her of the mistake she'd made.

Apologies could come later, when she wasn't rushed. Maybe she'd take Ian to dinner somewhere and give Phillip and Rowan some privacy with their new baby. In a few days, she'd be back home in San Francisco and all this would be another painful memory to add to the list. At least this time it was her own foolishness that was cause for embarrassment. All those years ago, it had been her father who had ruined her life.

She laughed without humor. "Is that a good thing or a bad thing?" *Not that it matters when people still snicker behind my back.*

Todd's rejection hit her anew. Ten years had gone by and the pain could still rear its ugly head when she least expected it.

Think about something else, damn it.

Claudia sped out of the driveway before the turbulent emotions overwhelmed her.

* * * *

Zach liked 7th Marines' Major Cruz Montoya on sight. The guy had the compact frame of a pilot and the bark of a bulldog but his laughing eyes were windows to his true nature. Command and respect were characteristics every executive officer needed, but without the common sense to carry them through, those qualities were show. Zach didn't doubt for an instant the man could be hell on wheels if the need arose, but Montoya also had the sense to use his authority wisely.

He couldn't say the same for the command's adjutant, Captain Eric Hanson. He was accommodating enough—friendly, eager to please. The term 'brown-noser' came to mind, so did 'weasel'. Zach supposed it was the man's pointy little face that gave him that impression. His kind were always hovering about on the fringes, riding someone else's coattails. Most people like Hanson shrank the second someone said 'boo' to them. This guy was no different.

Montoya walked around his desk, hand extended. "Captain Taylor, pleased to meet you. My Marines speak very highly of you. You've helped many of them over some rough spots. Not an easy job, considering the trouble some of them get into."

Zach smiled and shook the other man's hand. "Young and easily fooled, sir. I've been assigned as investigating officer in the death of Gunnery Sergeant Sunline. Do you have a few minutes to talk?"

Montoya waved Hanson out of the room. Once the door was closed, he motioned Zach to one of the two straight-backed metal chairs in front of his desk. He took the other one.

"A terrible tragedy." He bowed his head, resting elbows on knees. "We're all in a state of shock. I wish I could have notified his family face-to-face, but they live back East in North Carolina. They're coming out to claim the body and hold a memorial service here."

Zach nodded his understanding as he made notes.

"You know, in a war situation you expect death. This makes no sense. I don't understand how someone could kill a man like Sunline."

"Hopefully I can piece together something, sir. I'd like to talk to his friends in the command. If it would be possible to provide a list..."

Montoya gave a soft chuckle. "Not necessary. The man didn't have an enemy anywhere. You want friends? Just walk around. Everyone was his friend. He was a Boy Scout leader, a Toys for Tots organizer. Those were some of his community projects. On field exercises, I've never seen a Marine as ingenious as Teddy. A regular Mr. Fix-It." He squeezed the bridge of his nose. "Sorry. This whole thing is giving me a killer headache."

Zach gave him time to recover. After a few seconds, the major went on, "Here, he was system administrator. I don't know how we'll keep the computers running without him. I know Colonel Sinclair will raise hell about this. He depended on Teddy's skills, even had Gunny Sunline helping him set up his home computer. Sunline spent a lot of his free time trying to teach Mrs. Sinclair the ins and outs of the Internet—e-mail, stuff like that. First time I ever saw her... Never mind."

Zach jotted down more notes. "Gunny Sunline was friends with Mrs. Sinclair, too. Do you know when she might have seen him last?"

"I wouldn't recommend involving Allison Sinclair in this. She's best left alone."

"But she may know something."

"I doubt it. Take my advice. Don't waste your time. Colonel Sinclair is extremely protective of his wife. I'd really hate to see Allison upset any more than she already is."

Zach shoved his pen into his notebook. "Then I take it she knows about Sunline's death."

Montoya nodded. "I called her personally, as one friend to another." He snapped to his feet, a clear indication the interview was over. "Captain Hanson will give you the roster of those who worked directly with Sunline. You can work from that. We'll give you as much cooperation as possible."

As long as I stay away from Allison Sinclair. "Thank you, sir. I'll be in touch later for a statement from you."

Zach had just cleared the door when Hanson zoomed up, roster in hand.

"Thought you'd need this."

Zach tucked the list away. "Did Sunline have a girlfriend?"

Hanson snickered. "Only about a dozen. The guy was a regular lothario. Including... Well, it doesn't matter."

Zach arched his eyebrow then let it fall back down when he realized he was mimicking one of Claudia's actions. "I'd like to get a statement from you if I could."

The captain darted his gaze from side to side then lowered his voice to a whisper. "Not here. I don't want to be overheard. Meet me tonight. There's a bar in town." He scribbled the name and location on a piece of paper, shoved it into Zach's hand then scurried away.

This is getting better and better. Zach tucked the note into his pocket while he studied his next move.

Teddy Sunline, poster Marine and lothario. Things weren't as cut and dried with the man as Major Montoya wanted him to believe. He could spin his wheels talking to one person after the other or hook up with NCIS to see what information they had.

Vic Brownell was the civilian agent in charge of the criminal investigation into Sunline's death. He was new to the base and the Naval Criminal Investigative Service but pretty thorough, from what Zach had heard. They'd even had lunch once or twice with other attorneys from Zach's office.

Vic met Zach in the NCIS waiting room when he arrived. His smile was quick, his handshake even quicker.

"Heard you were assigned as IO. Want to see what I've got?"

"That might be a good start."

Vic jerked his thumb toward the back offices. "Got the woman who found Sunline in my office right now. You can talk to her. I'm done."

Zach glanced in that direction. "How's she holding up?"

"Better than me." Vic downed a swig of scalding coffee. "She's a cool one. Knows her stuff. Pretty detailed description of what she saw last night. And I've got to tell you...she's a hottie."

Zach grinned.

Vic slapped him on the back. "Rein it in, big guy. She's sporting a wedding ring."

He snapped open his notebook. "What's the lady's name?"

"Claudia Stuart."

Zach's pen stopped in mid-air. *It couldn't be.*

"What's the matter? You know the lady?"

With a heavy sigh, he put his pen away. "If you'll excuse the saying... That's no lady. That's my wife."

Chapter Four

Claudia was a cool presence this hot October day, but Zach expected nothing less from her. The white linen suit was perfect, not detracting from her figure, not drawing attention to it. Professional was the image she presented. Sexuality seeped out of its own accord.

She sat in Vic's office, long legs crossed, filing her fingernails, oblivious to the turmoil around her. Every male agent in the building had probably found an excuse to wander past the open doorway more than once. They leered like hungry dogs, tongues dragging in their wake.

Disgusting pigs.

Zach strode into the room and tugged her skirt down a fraction of an inch. Claudia started. Her pulse leaped at her throat. A pink flush dusted her cheeks, her pupils dilated in her wide eyes and those full lips parted ever so slightly, as if she anticipated a kiss. And, damn, he wanted to give her one. Then her mask fell into place. Straightening, she planted her feet on the floor and returned her attention to her nails.

"Sharpening your claws?" he asked.

Her eyebrow arched as she focused her gaze on him. "Is there a need?"

He jerked his head toward the hallway. "There might be, to ward off your admirers."

A glance over his shoulder, a sigh and she tucked the file away. "I see Phillip told you where to find me. I presume you have papers for me to sign."

Zach pulled over the vacant chair across from her and sat. Leaning forward, he rested his forearms on his knees. "Actually, I've been a little busy today and haven't gotten around to it. I'm sure you understand, considering the night you had."

Her body heat surrounded him. He brushed his knee over hers, loving the hitch in her breath. He waited for her sharp rebuke. It didn't come. Instead, she tucked her arms over her chest, leaned back and crossed her legs, pressing one against his.

Zach's thoughts screeched to a halt. Blood roared in his eyes.

Breathe, damn it.

She was touching him on purpose, that long, firm calf burning a brand through his camouflage trousers. If it had been any other woman, he would know she was flirting. But Claudia?

He could call her bluff but knew she'd pull away. Zach rather liked the feel of her leg against him, even if the heavy cotton-poly was between them.

"Why don't you tell me what happened last night, Princess?"

"How did you find out?"

"This morning I was assigned as Investigating Officer for the case."

She cocked her head slightly. "I thought NCIS was investigating. What's your role?"

"NCIS investigates the criminal aspects of the case. I gather basic facts and information to submit to higher command. Investigating officers are assigned every time a Marine is injured or killed. Now, what can you tell me?"

She carefully laid out the events of the previous night. With each word Zach saw a little more of the barrier she'd erected between them fall. This was business. She was a professional—an observant one, too. No detail was too trivial. She'd even managed to recall the make and model of the vehicle.

He'd never given much thought to her work. Watching her now, his admiration grew. She would be tenacious, doggedly pursuing her story with a calm precision that would rattle the most stalwart opposition. Pride in her accomplishments swelled his chest.

He nodded as she finished. "Good thing *you* found him and not some screeching female. I know this is a silly question, but in your opinion, was there any chance this could have been an accident? A military prank gone wrong?"

The last wall fell. Claudia shot a glance to the doorway then mirrored Zach's position. Easing closer, she lowered her voice to that of a conspirator.

"I thought of that. Accidents occur all the time, but to think that one Marine would kill another in a prank and dispose of the body is a bit far-fetched. Pure hypothesis, I know, but—"

"Not at all. Go on."

He liked her this way. Her low voice had a sultry quality that tickled him to the base of his spine. If anyone doubted her seriousness, all they had to do was see the intensity in her deep blue eyes.

"The accident theory didn't last long," she said. "I was careful not to mess with the evidence, but I had to know if he was still alive. There was so much blood, but it *was* possible." She tapped him on the knee. "I was right."

"What—"

"He called out to me. I held his hand. He had massive head wounds. He'd been in one hell of a fight."

"Or a fall?"

Again Claudia cocked her head to one side then nodded. "Yes, that could be it. The autopsy will tell. Are you going down to the coroner to get the results?"

"You working a story, Princess?"

Slam. One wall went back up. The animation and rapport that had existed seconds before faded. As she drew away from him physically and emotionally, Zach longed to grab her shoulders and pull her back. Instead, he reluctantly let her go.

"Why not? It would make a good one. Marine killing Marine then disposing of the body in the desert. A crime of passion? Greed? There are thousands of questions begging to be answered."

"Well, I'll have to agree with you on that one." He scooted his chair back a little. "Other than call to you, did the deceased happen to say anything before he died?" It was her hesitation that told him she was about to lie. "Please, don't lie to me."

Claudia's gaze darted to the floor. "All right...yes."

Curiosity opened Zach's mouth.

Claudia shushed him before he could speak. "You and Phillip are the only ones who know."

"Why?" he whispered.

"Believe me. It wasn't easy convincing Phillip to go along with it."

"What did he say?"

She jerked her chin up, locking her eyes on his and making it feel as if they were a team once more. "He asked for help. I told him help was on the way. He called a woman's name — Allison. Said the word 'secret' then died."

"Why didn't you tell the sheriff or NCIS?" The answer was obvious. "Because the word set off your reporter instincts."

"Yes."

"Yet you told me."

Claudia eased back. "I know you well enough to say that if I'd lied to you, you would have shouted the building down until I told you the truth. Then everyone would know."

Zach grinned. "Well, you finally pegged me right on something."

When he stood, she grabbed the edge of his cammie blouse and tugged him back to his seat. "So now what? Any clue who Allison is? And don't lie to me, either."

"All right, I won't. I do have an idea, but I'm not sure where it's going to lead. I have an interview tonight with a guy from Sunline's office. I'm to meet him at a bar in town. I might learn more then."

"I'm going with you," she declared.

"No, you're not," he responded.

Anger flared in her eyes. He couldn't blame her, but there was a little more at stake than a news story here. He covered her hand in both of his, holding tight so she couldn't pull away.

"I'm not going to go into the obvious you-could-get-killed line. You're street-smart enough to know to be careful. Your career is important to you but so is mine to me. If I'm caught feeding you information, I'm finished. Please try to understand. I can't help you."

"Very well." She slipped her hand from his. "I trust you'll have those papers soon."

Bang. The final door slammed into place.

"Come to my office first thing in the morning. It should only take a few minutes to do them up."

"Tomorrow then."

Zach swore he saw icicles framing the words.

She shoved back her chair, retrieved her purse as she stood and left the room. It took every ounce of will he had to not watch her retreat, to not follow.

* * * *

Claudia kept her chin up and her focus on the exit, barely acknowledging Agent Brownell as he passed her on his way to Zach. Her arguing with Zach would serve no purpose. She understood his position, appreciated it, even respected it. But if he thought she was going to back down, he was mistaken.

A shame. For a while there, she thought she'd found an ally. It had felt good and right, working as a team. Now they were back on opposite ends, even if they were pursuing the same goal.

The day was almost gone, but she still had time to reevaluate her strategy before trying to discover in which bar Zach was to have his secret meeting tonight. With each step toward her vehicle, she ticked off another item on her mental to-do list—evidence she recalled, names of people she had spoken to. But she was a stranger to Twentynine Palms with no resources and no contacts to get her started.

Claudia sagged into the driver's seat once she got into her car. *What's the sense?* People were killed all the time. This case was no different. So there was a secret. People died for secrets and with them. Again, no difference.

All she was doing was delaying her return to San Francisco and her escape from Zach. And why? His very presence unnerved her. Yet, minutes before, in that brief space of time when they were of like mind and purpose...

She willed her heart to stop hammering. The sight of Zach had set her off-kilter. Having him near had been devastating. Her thoughts wandered to the last kiss they'd shared, tempting her to take one more taste. She'd clenched her thighs to quell the ache blossoming between them.

He'd brushed his knee over hers. She'd longed to shove her chair back to the farthest corner of the room in order to find a place where she could breathe without that constricted feeling in her chest. Moving away would have meant giving in, showing him that he had gotten to her. Claudia had refused to allow him the pleasure then had taken a little pleasure of her own. *God, the feel of our legs rubbing. The rhythm so like...*

Claudia shook away the thought. As tempting as it would be to explore a relationship with Zach, she just couldn't set herself up for heartbreak again. Men like Zach didn't play for keeps. They just played. She'd come to Twentynine Palms for a visit, to welcome the birth of Phillip and Rowan's second child. It was time to start enjoying herself and put work behind her for once in her life. Zach had the dead man's last words and could act on that tip. Her responsibility in the matter was over.

As for anything else that may have filtered in during the interview with Zach... Well, she'd become an expert in tamping down *those* types of feelings for him. This was no exception.

The decision lightened her sour disposition. She had plenty of time to do some shopping and buy a present or two for baby James and a little something for Ian. He was bound to start feeling left out in the excitement of a new baby. In fact, cooking dinner for everyone suddenly seemed like a nice treat for them.

As Claudia planned the menu, she headed for the exit and waited to pull into the light flow of traffic. Too late, she saw a white car cutting into the lot. There was nothing she could do to avoid the collision. She forced herself to keep her eyes open, to record every detail.

The other driver jerked his wheel to one side. Tires squealed seconds before he smacked into her, crumpling her car fender like it was paper. He jumped from his car and ran to her door. *Another individual with a crew cut made indistinguishable by his uniform.* His nametag identified him as Hanson. His rank was captain. Claudia rolled down the window.

"Ma'am, I'm so sorry. It's all my fault. I was so preoccupied that I didn't see you."

The door to NCIS swung open before she could reply. Zach ran toward her with Brownell close behind.

"Are you hurt?" Zach called out.

"I'm fine, which is more than I can say for my car," she replied.

He grabbed the handle and jerked it open. She accepted Zach's outstretched hand and stepped out to survey the damage.

Busted headlight, crumpled fender, front-end alignment shot to hell. Total cost twenty-five hundred to three thousand, minimum. Her brand-new, sky blue Camry was ruined. It didn't even have a thousand miles on it.

The culprit fumbled for his wallet. "All my fault. I'll cover everything."

"I sincerely hope so." Claudia refused to look his way. She was angry enough as it was. Anything she said would make matters worse. The man had admitted fault. That should be enough.

But it wasn't. He babbled on, apologizing over and over again until she longed to scream at him to shut the fuck up.

Long fingers curled around her elbow. Claudia stared up at Zach. His presence calmed her and she liked that he appeared as angry as she was. They were allies once more.

"Call your insurance company and arrange for a tow. If you want to leave, I'll take care of this. You can use my Jeep. I'll come over tonight and get it. If you're authorized a rental, we can pick it up then."

It was on the tip of her tongue to tell him that she could call Phillip or Rowan to get her, but the way he brushed his thumb slowly over her elbow consoled her, made her feel protected.

"How will you get around?" she asked.

"I can catch a ride." His smile didn't reach his eyes. "Think of it as one of the benefits of having a husband."

Each time he showed redeeming qualities, he ruined everything by behaving, well…like himself. She would have refused his offer if not for the opportunity it presented to rid herself of him more quickly.

"One of the few, I'm sure." She slipped from his grasp. "You can bring the papers with you tonight then."

"My pleasure…Mrs. Taylor."

"This is your wife?" Hanson's face flushed with the question. "Now I'm even more embarrassed."

He caught her hand, and for one brief, horrifying moment, Claudia thought he was actually going to kiss her knuckles.

Zach slipped her fingers from his sweaty grip. "That'll be enough, Captain."

With Claudia tucked protectively under his arm, Zach escorted her to his Jeep. "Jerk. Reminds me of something that crawled out from under a rock." He opened the door and helped her climb inside.

"For a minute I thought you were going to punch him in the nose."

"For a minute I almost did, Princess."

His smile was genuine this time, doing those crazy things to her insides. Claudia's heart quickened. The fact he appeared ready to champion her appealed to her feminine nature more than Claudia was willing to admit. This was the Zach other women saw — the knight rushing to the aid of the maiden in distress. No wonder they melted in his arms. Heroics were a powerful aphrodisiac. Even she wasn't immune.

"I'll see you tonight."

He leaned toward her as if to kiss her, as if it were a commonplace occurrence. What surprised her was that she found her lips parting of their own accord. Whatever spell possessed them was broken with the arrival of the military police.

Claudia watched Zach return to the accident site, admiring him for his physical traits. No boasting swagger marked his step. His was a confident, determined stride — one that made others aware he was a man who knew his own mind. Lethal, if anyone opposed him. Strong, powerful.

Her breath caught. It was too dangerous to let her mind wander. Zach Taylor was *not* a man to settle on one woman for long. *Never again.* Once burned was plenty for Claudia. After making arrangements with her insurance company, she went shopping, but any joy she might have derived from doing so was gone. Other thoughts intruded while she searched for the perfect presents—the accident, the discovery of the body and Zach. Each time she banished him from her mind, he shouldered his way back in—his consideration, his protectiveness, his kiss, that blasted cocky grin of his.

By the time she returned to her brother's house, her nerves were just holding on. Claudia forced cheerful bravado and walked inside, juggling presents and fixings for dinner.

Smiles were the first thing that greeted her—ten-year-old Ian's, Rowan's. They wrapped her in love, unconditionally. Then she saw Phillip—grim, as he talked on the phone.

He held the receiver out to her. "It's Ed from your news station."

Claudia shifted the grocery bag to Phillip and reluctantly took it, wondering why he hadn't called on her cell. There could be no doubt what the call was about. Franklin had made good his threat.

"Surprise me, Ed. Don't tell me you let him bully you." Her boss sighed.

"Sorry, kid. I don't like it any more than you but he's got us over a barrel."

"Let me guess. He threatened to quit."

"Bingo. You or him. That was his ultimatum to the owner. Our ratings are the highest they've ever been with him as anchorman. Demographics show—"

"Women love him."

"Sorry, Claudia. I hate to lose you."

She squeezed back a sudden flood of tears. "I'm working an angle down here, Ed. It could be something huge."

"It would have to be to change the big guy's mind. You know how he can be. Can you give me anything at all to interest him?"

It was a long shot at best. "It has to do with the military. That's all I can say without compromising the case. Tell him…" Claudia bit the inside of her cheek. She was treading on dangerous ground. "Tell him the marriage was a ruse to get inside. I didn't let Franklin know because he has a big mouth. I don't want to jeopardize anything."

"No shit?"

"No shit." *A lot of shit, all bull.* "I'll keep you posted." She hung up the phone and started to unpack the groceries.

"Not so fast." Phillip caught her arm, forcing her to look at him. "Is that what this is all about?"

"It is now. I just have to figure a way to convince Zach."

"So the original story is still the true one. Any chance we could have a more elaborate version?"

"None." She flashed a false smile and went to the kitchen to make dinner.

* * * *

"Captain Taylor, my office…now."

Zach trailed Colonel Scott down the corridor, wondering what could have riled him this time. The wait wasn't long. They'd just cleared the door when the colonel shut it. He wasted no time on preliminaries.

"Imagine my surprise in learning that the main witness to Sunline's death is your wife. Hell, I didn't even know you were married."

"It was very recently, sir."

"I presume you have a reason for not sharing the information with me when I assigned you as IO?"

"Sir, I didn't know Claudia was a witness."

"Good God, man, don't you talk at night?"

The heat rose to Zach's collar. "Sir, it isn't what you think. The marriage was a mistake. We're planning to dissolve it immediately."

Scott launched into a lecture about duty, responsibility and youth, then zeroed back to the issue. "You're removed as IO. Go back to your regular duties."

"Sir, you can't."

"The hell I can't."

Zach searched for the right words to salvage the situation. Nothing golden came to mind. "Sir, I'm afraid there might be a little more to this case than we thought. I'm only in the preliminary stages, but each time I turn around, I come to the same point. Allison Sinclair."

"Colonel Sinclair's wife?"

Zach nodded. "I believe she may have been having an affair with Sunline."

"Are you talking a crime of passion here?"

"Yes, sir."

The colonel laughed. "Martin Sinclair is top-notch material. He's up for general this year. Most people believe he'll make it. He wouldn't kill —"

"Not Colonel Sinclair...his wife. I think she may have killed Teddy Sunline."

Scott stared at Zach for a full minute then burst out with a laugh. "Allison? Captain, have you ever met Allison Sinclair?"

"Sir, Claudia told me that with his last breath, Sunline spoke her name and the word 'secret.' I'd say that deserves delving into a little more closely."

The colonel sank into his chair. "Does NCIS know this?"

Zach shook his head. "Not yet." He braced his palms on the edge of the desk—a risk all of its own, taking a dominant position over his superior officer. "Take me off as IO if you have to, but I want to pursue this, maybe work undercover with NCIS."

"You'll never be able to get close to Allison. She's a very private woman."

"Not me, sir. My wife. She knows what to look for. She's an investigative reporter. I think she can get information out of Allison Sinclair that NCIS never could."

Colonel Scott groaned and rolled his gaze toward the ceiling.

"Please, sir. We can do this. You and NCIS get us assigned to military housing near the Sinclairs and we'll do the rest."

The colonel shook his head, pushed up his glasses and massaged his eyes. "All right. Let's see what the two of you can dig up. But listen to me, Taylor. At the first sign of anything remotely resembling solid evidence, I want your wife out of the picture and this case turned over to NCIS."

"Yes, sir." *Now all I have to do is convince Claudia.*

Dinner? Flowers? Sweet talk? Zach dismissed them all. She would settle for nothing less than the truth.

* * * *

Claudia tried not to race to the door when she heard Zach pull up in his ride. He mustn't misunderstand her intent. She needed his good will. After all, she wouldn't be in this predicament if it hadn't been for that ill-fated drive to Las Vegas. She was as much at fault for the aftermath as he, but the last thing they needed right now was to rehash that issue.

Phillip opened the door to let him in. Just as quickly, he disappeared, leaving them alone in the dining room.

They stood across from one another, each waiting for the other to speak. Claudia took the initiative. "I was fired today."

Zach snorted and shook his head. "I didn't have such a great afternoon myself. Colonel Scott found out you're my wife and dismissed me from the case."

Claudia's resolve crumbled. It had been her last chance. Without Zach's help and a spouse's identification card, she couldn't get onto the Marine Corps base in order to investigate.

"Let's sit down."

He pulled out a chair and motioned her toward it. They sat much as they had at the NCIS offices, knee to knee.

"I have a plan, but I need your help," he said.

With each phase he detailed, Claudia's spirits soared. Everything was working perfectly and she didn't have to beg for his assistance. He'd never need know what she was gaining by helping him.

Claudia pretended to think it over, nodding at appropriate intervals.

"I know you don't owe me anything, but—"

"Cut the crap," Phillip snapped.

They jerked upright and found him lounging in the doorway, listening to every word. "Claudia, obviously you understand Zach's position, so I'll tell him yours. She needs the scoop on this murder to keep her job. End of story time. If the two of you would quit trying to dance around each other, you might find you have more in common than you realize."

He ducked around the corner and left them alone again.

Zach's gaze caught hers, steady, appraising and strangely unaccusing. "Do we have a deal?"

"Yes."

"Good. Tomorrow we can set up base housing, get you an ID card and put our winnings in the bank—all that happily married stuff. I'll pick you up in the morning."

She stood with him. "Wrong. I'm going with you now. I believe we have a meeting at a bar in town. This is my game now. Let me do what I do best."

"Fine, but I'm front man...always, or we end this now. I don't care whose job is in jeopardy."

"I don't like having things out of my control, Zach."

"Neither do I." Zach smiled. "Interesting... We do have something in common after all."

Chapter Five

Rock music blasted Claudia's eardrums as she and Zach crossed the threshold of The Watering Hole. The bar wasn't as crowded as she'd expected. A few couples jostled against each other on the dance floor. Most people huddled at tables, drinking and talking. The decibel level of the music gave them an extra excuse to be close.

She likened the scene to a tribal watering spot, which made the name all the more appropriate. People gathered to socialize and find mates. She'd never cared to indulge in either activity. It was the lure of the music that drew her. She loved music, lived to dance. The lack of a male partner had never stopped her. She and her girlfriends had never been afraid to step out on any dance floor and cut loose.

Claudia smiled. *That would be a scene to make Zach's jaw drop.* She rather liked the idea of seeing him thrown off his game.

While she stood in the doorway waiting for Zach to do a visual scan of the room, she tapped her foot in time to the music, longing for the chance to join the others. Tonight was business, though, and that was what she had to concentrate on. She'd save her dancing for another time or, failing that, the privacy of her own home was always a reasonable alternative.

"There's a good place over there."

She followed the direction of his point — a table in the dark corner with a good view of the door. He guided her forward with a gentle touch to her back. Warmth spread through her, settling between her thighs. With each step, her arousal grew and her thoughts wandered to how she'd deal with this ache once they were cohabitating. Her suitcases were in his vehicle. She and Zach would be heading to his house after this meeting then into base housing tomorrow — them alone, pretending a relationship that didn't exist and her certainly wanting him more with every second they would play house.

He skimmed his hand lower when they reached the table. The impact of him grazing her ass set her libido on hyperdrive. She'd never make it at this rate.

So what? Do it. What's the harm? Show him who's in charge.

Claudia damned her bossy conscience. It knew the harm yet refused to get onboard.

Zach moved the chairs so they were facing the door. Anyone watching would think they were getting cozy. The strategic position would be missed. She fed off the power he'd shared with her, showing they were equals. There might be hope for them after all.

A waitress breezed forward. "Drink?"

"Club soda with a lime twist." The reply came out in unison.

"Please save the comment on the similarity between us," she said. "I never drink when I work and I'm still trying to recover from the weekend."

"Same here, Princess. I never want to see another glass of champagne, much less drink one." He glanced at his watch. "Hanson should be here any minute."

"*He's* your contact?" She nestled her arms under her bosom. "Can you trust what he tells you? He seems overly eager to please."

"I noticed that and intend to keep it in mind."

"I'd feel better if you were wired," she told him

Zach unfolded her arms and tugged her hands to her lap. "And I'd feel better if you'd stayed at the house. Guess we can't always have what we want. Don't worry. I have a recorder in my jacket pocket."

"Then you'd better turn it on because he just walked in."

"Already taken care of." He caught her chin on the tips of his fingers. "A kiss for luck? There *is* an illusion we're supposed to keep up."

Before she could reply, Zach dropped a peck to her lips, gave her a wink and left, snagging his drink from the waitress as he walked off. He might as well have licked her with fire. Her head buzzed and the warmth his presence stoked double throughout her body.

This is never going to work. They'd be in close quarters for who knew how long. With each second she spent in Zach's presence, a little more of her resolve faded. Common sense and desire battled for possession of her body while Zach Taylor waited on the sidelines to claim her soul.

She found herself wondering what it would feel like to toss restraint aside and have at it. What harm could there be in going for it? It'd been a while since she'd been with a man, the Vegas debacle notwithstanding. She was due. It wasn't as if she was inexperienced. She was older now and well-versed in how to give and receive pleasure...and walk away. But Claudia knew all too well that the harm would come, because one day he would leave. As much as she wanted to hate Zach, her feelings swung in the opposite direction. *Scary stuff.*

Her hand shook as she lifted her drink. Men like Zach just weren't interested in women like her, except for one thing. She could respect that. She'd fucked and run for ten years.

She couldn't keep her gaze from straying to the table across the room, to the intensity on his face, to the way his long fingers curled around his glass, to the gaze that drifted her way every so often. It had nothing to do with love. It'd be sex, pure and simple — rough and raw, fast and slow. If she could only remove her emotions as she'd done with past liaisons... Maybe, just maybe...

A pair of impossibly long and shapely female legs blocked her view. Claudia pulled back and looked up. The legs supported a tall woman — at least that was the impression the person meant to give. A short leather skirt came to mid-thigh while the red silk blouse was tied at the waist to accentuate the bosom. Inch-long nails painted flaming red set off the hands. Long chestnut hair had every curl in place. Makeup, perfection. There was just one, small, tiny, minor problem.

The visitor waved to the empty seat. "Mind if I join you?"

Claudia couldn't help but smile. "Not at all."

Extending one hand, she slid into the chair. "Hello there. I'm Kiki LaRue."

"Hello, Kiki LaRue. I'm Claudia." Claudia slowly shook the proffered hand. There was no doubt now. Laughter bubbled to her throat. "So tell me," she lowered her voice, "what's your real name?"

Kiki's smile faded and so did her sultry voice. "Kurt Davidson. You won't tell anyone, will you?"

Claudia leaned back. "Your secret is safe with me."

"How could you tell? Is it my Adam's apple?"

She smirked. "Actually, your Adam's apple isn't that noticeable. Your neckerchief disguises it well and makes a nice fashion statement."

He brushed his fingers over his chin. "Did I miss a spot?"

She laughed. "No. Your *bosom* is off."

Kiki looked down. "Darn tissues." He tsked. "The things they don't teach in Theater Arts." After darting a glance from side to side, he dived his hand inside his blouse and made the adjustment. "Better?"

With a small laugh, Claudia nodded. "Perfect. Next time try a plastic bag of birdseed or rice. It will appear more natural."

"I won't ask how you know that."

"We all have our secrets. Let's just say I used to be twelve and craved a large bust. I take it Theater Arts is your specialty?"

"My minor in college, although I never dreamed I'd be using it to my own advantage."

Claudia braced her chin on the pedestal of her arm and smiled. "There's a story in you, Kiki. Tell me about it."

Persona back in place, Kiki draped one long leg over the other. "Are you writing a book?"

Claudia laughed. "I might be. I'm a reporter and always love an interesting story. Come on. What's yours?"

"I'll make you a deal. I'll tell you all if you tell me two things."

"And those are?"

Kiki pointed to Zach's table. "Who is that gorgeous-looking man?"

Claudia's humor faded. "My husband." *Goodness, a bit territorial, aren't we?*

"No, no. I know the dangerous-looking one is yours. The two of you have been undressing each other with your eyes since he sat over there." She touched Claudia's forearm. "Girl, I don't know how you manage him so well. I meant the man with him, the little one."

She followed Kiki's lustful gaze then shrugged a shoulder. *Beauty is in the eye of the beholder. Kiki must be nearsighted.* "His last name is Hanson. He's a captain in the Marine Corps. That's about all I know." *Besides the fact that he's a reckless driver.*

Kiki fanned her fingers at the base of her throat. "Pity. If you find out more, do share."

"And the second thing you wanted to ask?"

Her smile beamed. There was another touch to her forearm. "You're beautiful—your looks, your demeanor, your entire aura. I must know how you do it."

Claudia didn't know whether to laugh or cry. How did one act when one became an icon to a cross-dresser? Insulted or complimented? Both were a matter of opinion. Kiki-Kurt certainly meant no harm. She liked him…her.

She shrugged. "Why not? It could be an interesting collaboration."

Kiki clapped her hands. "Oh, goody. How wonderful."

Leaning forward, Claudia rested her chin on her fist. "Now, about that story, Kiki."

* * * *

Zach tried to concentrate on Hanson's ramblings. All he could think about was Claudia. He'd never seen a pair of blue jeans look so good. And her feet... She had the most beautiful feet of any woman he'd ever seen, with each toenail painted to pink perfection. She knew how to wear a pair of sandals.

But neither compared to the ribbed bodysuit hugging her torso. A V-neck accentuated her main assets enough to tease, not to display. *Is she wearing a bra or not?* Zach was obsessed with knowing. Neither a wrinkle nor a bulge anywhere divulged the information.

Her white-blonde hair was still slicked back in a twist, adding to the illusion of a Grecian goddess. It was no wonder he couldn't keep his hands off her. He used every excuse he could muster for the brief opportunity it gave him to touch her—her hand cupped in his at the house, the scant caress to the back as he'd guided her into the bar. And the kiss for luck? The only luck he wanted right now was any that could put her in his arms and between her thighs. Zach didn't know how he was going to endure her constant presence.

He almost laughed out loud. Here he'd been worried about their propensity for flinging barbs at each other. Now, with each hour he spent at her side, his obsession grew, along with his dick. The more he saw, the more he loved her, wanted her. Hints of the real Claudia peeked through, but he wanted to see all the woman behind the ice wall. He wanted to see the pleasure of orgasm wash over her face as she writhed beneath him.

Had she been any other woman, Zach would have gathered her against him and kissed her until the ice melted. But Claudia? If he wanted her — body, heart and soul — it was going to have to be by her rules, whatever those were. Hell, he bet she didn't even know.

What's the use? In five years he hadn't been able to get beyond her venomous frostbite. The Vegas fiasco had fueled her ire, made it deadlier. He'd never thought he'd have a chance as a love interest. Yet here she was, his wife, on his mind, under his skin and stirring his libido.

She didn't even give a damn. She sat at the table engaged in an intimate conversation with a brassy bimbo who had been a total stranger minutes before. Why couldn't she be that relaxed with him? What would she do if he coerced a few kisses from her once they got back to his house?

This time, Zach did chuckle. She'd cut him to ribbons then leave the pieces for Phillip to sweep up. Not only would he lose any chance of ever being near her again but he'd also lose a best friend in the process.

"I see you brought your wife."

Zach swiveled his gaze to Hanson. Was the man finally done with his prelude of small talk?

"I didn't have much of a choice. She's really pissed about the accident this afternoon. I didn't take a chance on telling her I was going out by myself tonight. I knew she'd pitch a fit, so I brought her out for a drink instead."

Zach lifted his glass in mock toast to Claudia then smiled when she arched that eyebrow of hers. "You got a wife?" he asked.

Hanson flicked the sweat off his glass. "She couldn't handle military life. Our divorce was final a year ago this month. I understand she's happily married to some accountant and has a baby. Wouldn't surprise me to find out she'd been screwing him all along."

His tone was dry, unemotional—an obvious sore point. Zach shifted the conversation back on track.

"Well, my wife's starting to get a little testy, Hanson, so I'd appreciate it if you would get to the point."

Hanson sucked down his drink. "She doesn't know why I'm talking to you, does she? If this got out—"

"She thinks I'm talking to you about the accident."

Hanson eased back into his seat then leaned forward once more. "At least I provided you with a good excuse."

"I wouldn't need any if you'd been watching where the hell you were going this afternoon. Your point?"

"Yes...well." He took another long draw on his beer.

Zach had never seen a man drink so fast.

Hanson set the glass aside and motioned to the waitress to bring another. "I don't like to say. In fact, it doesn't seem plausible but things are nagging at me, and with a good man dead..." He shrugged a bony shoulder.

Zach longed to shake the information out of him. *Why tiptoe around the subject? Why doesn't he spit it out?* He drummed his fingers on the table while he waited. From the corner of his eye, he saw Vic Brownell walk into the bar. Someone else was getting impatient, too.

"You said Sunline had a lot of girlfriends — one in particular," he prompted.

"He had women calling him all the time, coming around the office."

"Was Allison Sinclair one of those women?"

"With her husband right there?" He snorted. "No. She didn't have to. Sunline went to her."

"For computer instruction, from what I understand."

Hanson gave another snort. "For months on end? How stupid could a person be? There isn't that much involved. You would think she would take notes, call him or at least use e-mail for her questions. But he was over there every night and sometimes during the day."

Zach set his drink aside and leaned back to peruse the man more carefully. "What do you think happened?"

Hanson crooked his finger again for the waitress. "Where's that beer, toots?" He missed the glare she shot back.

"I think things got out of hand," he told Zach. "She started to get possessive and he didn't like it. He probably tried to end the affair. She got violent and offed him."

The scenario made sense. It happened all the time. "How?"

He shrugged. "How should I know? Hit him over the head with a frying pan?"

"And dragged the body to the car? From what I understand, she's a petite woman."

"Hell, maybe she had Teddy meet her in the desert and ran him over in the car. Maybe she had an accomplice."

"Like her husband?"

Hanson froze then snickered. "Colonel Sinclair wouldn't waste his time on murder, not when ruining the guy's career would be more satisfying."

"You'd think a man would be a little more volatile about his wife screwing another guy."

"I don't know. You tell me."

Zach followed Hanson's jerk of the head and saw Vic breezing over to Claudia's table.

"Good evening, ladies. Mind if I join you?"

Claudia and Kiki had been so deep in conversation that they hadn't noticed Brownell's approach. His mere presence sparked a myriad of questions for Claudia, none of which she could ask. It made introductions awkward.

"Kiki, I'd like you to meet…" What *was* the man's first name?

Brownell stuck his hand out. "Vic."

With a flirtatious smile, Kiki accepted. "Charmed."

Still holding her hand, he slipped into the vacant chair. "Kiki, I hate to be rude to such a lovely lady but I need to speak with Claudia alone. Do you mind?"

"Not at all." She blew Claudia a kiss. "Call me, darling."

Vic waited until the woman was out of earshot then moved to her chair. "I'm still trying to decide if I'm surprised that this marriage of yours is a sham."

Claudia let her gaze settle on his. Naturally, Zach would have a law enforcement official working with him but something about the man's approach felt unsettling. "I can't see where that's any concern of yours, Mr. Brownell."

"Please, call me Vic."

She conceded to the request with a tilt of her head.

"It really isn't a concern, but it makes our job even easier," he said.

"How so?"

A wide smile spread across his sun-tanned features.

"If our suspect has a propensity for other men, wouldn't it be easier if she thought she had a comrade in whom to confess?"

Claudia laced her fingers together. "I'm sorry. I don't follow you."

"Tomorrow you and Zach will move into base housing across the street from the Sinclairs."

She snapped her fingers. "Just like that."

His smile widened. "You'd be surprised what NCIS can do. Besides, with all the housing renovation turmoil, no one will notice. People are constantly being shuffled from one house to the other."

"If you're that good, why not move us next door?"

His smile faded. "No vacancy. It was hard enough to get you in across the street as it was. We were lucky it was vacant. If anyone questions why a captain was housed near a colonel, we'll say it was an emergency situation of some kind and stress that it's temporary. In any event" — he leaned closer — "Allison is our suspect, an alleged adulteress. If she thought you played around, too…"

He left the words hanging, expecting Claudia to pick up the hint. It wasn't hard. Her deliberate lack of response forced him to spell it out.

"You and I. We can begin tonight. Let everyone, including your loving husband, see us together. A few not-so-discreet visits to your house in the daytime and we're in."

It made sense. When working undercover, all angles had to be worked in the event something fell through. Zach was doing his part. She should do hers.

"How do you propose we begin?"

He extended his hand, palm up. "The music's slow. Dance with me."

Telling herself it was for show was the only way Claudia could force herself to walk onto the dance floor with Vic. He made it look smooth, drawing her into his arms, pulling her close — too close.

Claudia bit back her disgust. He was aroused and made no secret about it, nor did he make any apologies. He shuffled in time to the music, anchoring her against him with his arm.

"Get your hands off my wife."

The words were measured, spoken through clenched teeth, and for a few seconds, Claudia didn't recognize them as coming from Zach. He grabbed Vic's shoulder and yanked him back. This was no game, no front for the public. Zach was furious, his eyes hard with anger.

Claudia curled her fingers around his biceps. She'd never wanted a man more. "Zach, please — "

He spun around on her. "Get in the Jeep. I want you as far away from him as possible."

He cupped her elbow and steered her toward the door. Claudia held her tongue — not that anything could pierce his anger. He had the courtesy to open the door of his vehicle for her but slammed it closed once she was settled.

It was too much. She waited until he slipped into the driver's seat then snatched his keys from the ignition before he could turn the engine.

"What's the matter with you?" she snapped.

Zach splayed his fingers across his chest. "Me? What's the matter with *me*? What's the matter with *you*?" He jabbed his index finger toward her. "For five years I haven't gotten so much as a civil word from you, and in less than five minutes, you're pressed so tight against Brownell that an ant couldn't squeeze between you. If I'd done something like that, you would have had me castrated and hung from the nearest tree."

"He said it was part of the ruse to flush out the killer."

"W-What?" he sputtered.

His jaw tightened with every word as Claudia relayed their conversation.

"He lied," he ground out.

"It's a good idea, though. Why would he lie?"

His laughter held no humor. "Why do you think? He used it as an excuse to hold you. He wants you—or couldn't you tell?"

Her cheeks heated. Vic had used her for his own gain, slipping under her defenses and taking advantage of her professionalism. "He made it quite apparent to me."

"He made it apparent to everyone in the room, Princess."

Claudia narrowed her eyes and tossed him the keys. "Had it been a normal situation, I would have dealt with it."

This time, Zach's chuckle wasn't forced. "I've no doubt you would. I'll take care of Vic in the morning."

She crossed her arms, a defense against the chill of the night and the vulnerability at having been betrayed. The last place she wanted to be tonight was at Zach's house. She longed to be where she was most safe—her own bed, or at least back at Phillip's house. Nothing could hurt her there and no one would lie to her.

Zach leaned into her space and gently pried her arms apart. "Please, no more of this. I've had to watch you shut me out for five years. I can't bear another second of it."

His face was inches from hers. Not only did he sound pained, but he also looked it. Claudia knew Zach wanted her. He'd made that very clear over the years. But did he care for her, as well? Was his anger now jealousy?

"If you do this when others are around, they'll know this is a farce," he added.

Of course. Our mission. She should have known better.

"I'll be watchful of that," she quietly replied then turned her head away to hide the inexplicable rush of tears.

Zach's sigh whispered down her neck, setting off tremors of want. Finally, he settled in the driver's seat and started the engine. She gripped the edges of her seat to keep from hugging herself.

It took little time to reach Zach's small rental house. From the outside, there was nothing unique about the place. It was set in a neighborhood much like any other, row upon row. Some yards were landscaped with desert vegetation, while others were scraggly with brush and cacti. Zach took care to keep neat the few bushes and one fruitless mulberry tree the owners had planted.

He pulled into the driveway and made no attempt to use the garage.

"I wasn't expecting company, so it might look a little lived in." He gave the keys to her, singling out the one for the house. "Just thought I'd warn you. Go on in. I'll get your luggage."

She accepted the keys and exited the vehicle. As she made her way up the short sidewalk, the porchlight clicked on, guiding her last few steps. The vehicle door shut behind her. She thrust the key into the lock and pushed the door open.

'Lived in' was an understatement at best. Knowing to expect something unusual wasn't enough to prepare her for the mess she'd walked into.

A pile of shoes and socks were inside the front door, which looked like the collection point for Zach's dirty clothes. Despite the fact there was a laundry basket nearby, most items were littering the floor.

The living room was designed for male comfort, with an overwhelming big screen television and entertainment system against one wall. Newspapers drifted from the recliner in the corner. The surface of the coffee table was invisible under a pile of magazines and books. One of the end tables was overloaded with peanut shells and empty soda cans. The other was miraculously clear—its glass top gleaming.

Claudia attributed its tidiness to the fact that it was farthest from Zach's reach. She picked her way across the debris field to peek into the kitchen then wished she hadn't. Dirty dishes were everywhere—sink, counter, stove, table. Trash overflowed the can. She shuddered in disgust.

Against her better judgment, she wandered down the short hall toward the bathroom. Not daring to walk inside, she reached around the doorjamb and flicked on the light. This time she was surprised. The room was immaculate.

"I have four brothers," Zach said from behind her. "Mom hates a dirty bathroom. She drummed it into us at an early age to keep it sparkling clean. She said our wives would appreciate it one day."

"I'll have to remember to thank her."

"The rest of the place isn't all that dirty, just cluttered. I usually clean up over the weekend, but…"

"The kitchen is filthy. I'm surprised vermin haven't set up house in there."

Zach flinched, making her regret her tone.

"It'll be cleaned by morning. I put your luggage in my room. The other bedroom doesn't have a bed. I'll sleep on the couch."

"I wouldn't dream of putting you out."

"I'm trying to make you more comfortable."

"I'm sure you are."

"The sheets are clean. I promise you won't get cooties."

"Clean and cool. Waiting for your next liaison."

He smacked his palm against the wall. "Damn it to hell. I'm sick and tired of you judging me. I don't have a revolving door on my bedroom. In fact, I can't remember the last time I slept with someone."

Claudia willed her racing heart to calm. "I believe that would be me."

He faced her, gaze sweeping over her face. "And I really wish I had a clear memory of it. I'll bet it was the sweetest sex I've ever known. To be with you…to have you in my arms…loving you," he finished on a whisper.

What is he really saying? Oh, hell, she knew what he was saying. She just wasn't sure she could trust it. Emotion overwhelmed her. Tears she thought long buried clouded her vision. She was conscious of Zach reaching for her, caressing her upper arm.

"Claudia—"

She jerked away. "I'll be in the shower. I need to wash the stench of that man from my body."

Before the tears could become a torrent, before she could give in to the unrelenting ache for him, she grabbed her smaller bag and walked to the bathroom, shutting the door firmly behind her. The door to her emotions remained wide open.

Zach slumped to the floor. *What was I thinking to smack the wall?* She wouldn't know he'd done so out of frustration, not anger. He'd let her get under his skin again. At the bar she'd been cool, calm and appraising when all he could think about was Vic's body pressed against hers, then to have her lift her nose in royal disdain and pronounce his house filthy.

Granted, most of the place *was* a mess. He'd meant to straighten up before he picked her up but had run out of time. *Nothing like being put in my place.* Not that he didn't deserve it, but he resented her making him feel like he was being scolded by his mother.

Now he'd gone too far. Those tears shimmering in her dark blue eyes had destroyed him. *And I claim that I love her?*

Zach glanced at the bathroom door. He was tired of the sniping, the taunts. This had to end. Their relationship was too tenuous for him to offer comfort or apologies. For the first time in his life, he was at a loss as to what to do and he wanted to do something to make all the bickering go away.

He heard a slight sound off to his right and looked up. "Hello, Miss Kitty. Did we wake you from your beauty sleep?"

The orange and white cat padded out from underneath the coffee table and brushed a greeting against his side.

"I've really made a mess of things this time."

She offered a meow then crawled in his lap.

"ish I knew what to do. Mom would know." He scratched the cat behind the ears, smiling when she leaned into his fingers. "She would have a field day with me on this one. I can almost hear her saying, 'Just clean up the damn house, Zachary.'"

Miss Kitty opened one eye and meowed as if to say, "Well…clean it then."

Zach nodded. "Yeah, I know. Come on. Let's get to work."

* * * *

Claudia tugged her pajama tank top over her head. The shower had given her time to calm down and stop crying but the evidence was still there in her reddened eyes. She hated Zach for the emotion he dragged out of her but hated herself more for letting him. Her life was about control. It was the only way she could function — with cool, calm control. Then this cocky, overbearing man with a killer smile and body to melt icebergs had thrown himself directly into her path.

She stepped into the matching blue shorts then reached for her blow dryer. Zach made her think, want and feel. All were things Claudia had been fighting to suppress. His mere presence clouded all rational thought and set her nerves on edge. His admission coiled deep inside her, making her want to believe that all he'd said was true. She'd spent great energy avoiding him. Now there was no way to do so. *How could I have thought this charade would work, knowing what his presence does to me?*

It didn't matter what was at stake. She had to leave. There was no other choice for her peace of mind. Her resistance caved a little more with every second she was with him. If she could take the lead and throw him off-guard, she might survive their time together. But she trembled inside whenever he was near, wanting...*needing* him to be the dominant one, to prove he was truly for her. The thought made her laugh. For all his sweet words, she still felt like she was nothing more than a conquest. That was what gorgeous men like him did — took what they wanted and walked away. She'd learn to do the same, so why couldn't she be that way with Zach?

But leaving wasn't possible, not if she hoped to salvage her job. The charade of marriage was vital to the investigation and her future as an investigative reporter. He needed her for similar reasons. Without her, Zach couldn't get an 'in' with Allison Sinclair. There had been glimpses of how well they worked as a team. Each of them had something to gain by seeing this through and something to lose if she walked out. It was time to set some ground rules, to take control.

She fluffed her hair and checked her appearance. Once he saw her, Claudia knew he'd latch on to the fact that she wore nothing under the pajamas, but she refused to cover up with a robe. She was already on edge. There was no sense making herself uncomfortable as well. In reality, the pajama set was no different from her workout clothes. She packed her bag and opened the door. Low tones of conversation reached her from the kitchen. *Is someone here? Is he on the phone?* She second-guessed her need for a robe and crept forward.

"I know. I love you, too, Miss Kitty."

A meow-purr answered. *Zach has a cat?*

She set the suitcase down and continued on, noting that he'd tidied up while she'd been in the shower. She peeked around the corner of the kitchen. Zach sat in the middle of the floor wiggling a ball of string for a small orange-and-white cat. The cat swatted it with lightning-fast speed then crawled into his lap. The kitchen was pristine, as if it had never seen a dirty dish. There went her heart, skipping with an emotion that had nothing to do with hate and everything to do with love. Her hard nipples rubbed against the cotton tank. Lower, her clit kissed the seam of her shorts. *I am so screwed.*

Zach looking up, nailing her in place with the intensity in his eyes. *One of us should say something, shouldn't we?* After what seemed an eternity, he stretched to his feet, the cat still cradled in his arms.

Claudia urged her feet to move. Those dark brown eyes of his had captured her. Then he was standing before her, his body so close. *Too close. Not close enough.* The cat jumped down. Zach braced his palms on the wall on either side of her head.

"I'm sorry I was an ass," he told her.

His gaze drifted to her mouth. She licked her lips, parting them for the kiss she knew he was planning...or the one she was going to take but deciding that it hadn't prepared her for how soft his mouth was against hers or his gentle nips as he laid claim to her.

Claudia's breath caught with the first flick of his tongue over hers. She couldn't fight him anymore. She couldn't fight herself. She craved him and had since that first kiss under the mistletoe. Now she could admit it. Her body signaled defeat with a soft sound that was more like a thunderclap in the room. She fisted his shirt and dragged him against her, gliding her tongue deep into his mouth.

Zach's victory grunt matched hers, yet his conquest was slow.

He broke the kiss and nuzzled the corners of her mouth, traced his tongue over her jaw, down her neck. Claudia thought she'd die from need. She arched her neck on a soft sigh that turned to a low moan when he kneaded his lips down the column of her throat. Over and over again Zach mapped a route around her half-parted lips, preying on her breathless wonder, melting her into his arms. At last he returned to her mouth, slipping in to claim his prize.

Claudia ached for more, and in the fuzzy recesses of her mind, she recalled it was another wondrous kiss that had put them in their current situation. Pressed against the slot machine, body to body, mouth to mouth, his kiss had ripped away her restraints layer by layer—just as it was doing now.

That delicious kiss, the hardness pressed against her and the wall behind her... She might as well have been naked on his bed. If she'd been a little bit coherent, she would have maneuvered them in that direction. But he'd crawled one hand up her neck and into her hair. He planted his other hand on her ass and dragged her close until their bodies were flush and she was anchored against the wall.

Claudia raked her nails over his ribs, loving how he shivered under her touch. She yanked his shirt from his jeans, reveling in his low moan. He released her long enough to haul the shirt over his head and toss it aside then dived into her mouth again. This kiss was harder, more desperate, as if his life depended on having her. Hers did. Heat bathed her palms as she brushed them over his back. His muscles rippled beneath her fingers. Claudia cupped his ass and writhed over his erection. A low groan rumbled from his throat. He broke the kiss and pulled her top off. She reached for his fly button. Zach cupped her breasts and thumbed her hard nipples while he circled his tongue around her ear. A flick of her fingers released the button. She shoved her hands under the waistband, forcing the zipper down until she reached her target. The warmth before was a pale shadow to the fire greeting her touch. The damn jeans and the way he wandered his mouth toward her breasts made it impossible to reach what she wanted. She grabbed the waistband of his jeans and boxers, yanking them down. His cock sprang free, the moist tip kissing her midriff. She cupped his erection at the same moment he sucked her breast into his mouth. They stood there, frozen in an erotic pose, joint moans filling the air.

"Damn, baby," he mumbled around her breast.

"I know," she whispered back, diving for his sac.

Zach broke his hold on a groan, thrusting his erection against her as she kneaded his hard balls. He made her feel powerful, as if he were the one vulnerable to this crazy attraction instead of her. He released his hold on her long enough to pull himself free of clothing. When he wrapped his arms around her again, Claudia hooked her leg over his hip. He cupped her ass and pulled her higher. She swung her other leg up and locked her ankles around his waist. He pressed his pelvis into her heat. Only her shorts stood between them.

Zach rocked into her, stealing the words tumbling through her head. She latched her arms around his neck, slammed her mouth over his and kissed him hard. He growled and thrust against her, pushing the seam of her shorts over her swollen clit. His cock was hot and rigid and his determination to please her seemingly relentless. She knew it was to please her, knew he wanted to strip that last barrier away and be inside her. *Knew it.* He wouldn't stop until she came.

Then what?

Claudia built fantasies in her head as her body inched higher toward climax. He'd carry her to his bed, drag those pajama bottoms away and take her. Her pussy clenched at the image. She tightened her hold around his waist and ground into his thrusts. Or maybe he'd wait for a cue from her that she wanted him. *As if this doesn't scream that?*

She broke their kiss on a groan. Zach buried his face against her neck and raked his teeth over her skin.

"Oh, God," she gasped. "I want you inside me. I need you so much." So much she couldn't bear the wait any longer.

"Damn, baby." He pressed harder and rolled against her clit.

Her breath caught, her body tensed and her orgasm exploded, leaving her gasping for air. He dotted kisses over her face. "I want you in my bed," he told her.

She traced her finger along his jaw. "I agree."

He scooped her into his arms. Her heart did crazy somersaults.

Claudia slipped her arms around his neck. "No one has ever carried me before."

"Good."

She'd seen that hunger in his eyes before, only now she appreciated it.

His long strides ate up the short distance. He placed her gently in the center of his bed then reached for the nightstand drawer. She removed her bottoms, pulled the bedcovers down and knelt there waiting, watching him cover up, envying his hand. When Zach reached for her, Claudia pushed him down instead. She flicked her fingers through his chest hair until she reached his nipples then twirled one between her thumb and forefinger.

"It's time I fucked you. Don't you agree?" She crawled astride his hips.

"Past time." His voice shook a little. He fisted his erection, holding it in place for her.

She nudged his hand away from his cock then put a mild chokehold around it. Zach groaned and thrust his hips up.

"That's it," she whispered. "Show me what I've been missing."

He grasped her hips, helping guide her in place. She rubbed his erection over her slit then pushed his cock deep inside. His eyes rolled back in his head.

"Yes, it feels so good," she whispered. Leaning forward, she brushed her breasts over his chest, rolling her hips.

He glided his hands up her spine, trying to bring her closer.

"Uh-uh," she said, righting herself. "Eyes open, hotshot."

When he complied, she cupped her breast in one hand and circled her clit with the other. His eyes glazed over and his jaw went slack.

"That's it," she whispered. "Take a good, long, hard look at what a real woman can do for you."

She set the pace, determined to undo him the way he'd undone her.

"Who's the boss of you, Zachary?" She pivoted on his erection.

He gasped, gripped her hips and thrust wildly.

Claudia fought his demand with a smile. "Don't you dare come before me, mister."

"Fuck, woman," he muttered, tossing his hands over his head and closing his eyes.

"Eyes open." She landed a playful smack against his thigh.

His eyes flashed open. "Do you really want to open *that* door, Princess?"

Claudia giggled. "Merely attempting to gain your attention."

Mischief danced in his eyes. "Oh, baby, you have it." He laced his hands behind his head. "I'm all yours."

"I thought as much."

She rode him slowly at first, building herself to the peak quicker than she expected. Damn, he was a beautiful man, hers to do with as she pleased. His hungry gaze remained on her, crowning her as his queen, giving over power to her with every moan that fell from his lips, sounds that twined around her heart and pulled her under his spell.

Orgasm rushed in to claim her. She braced her free hand on his chest and whispered, "Now. Come with me *now*."

He thrust up and let go. The bed shuddered with the impact of their release, threatening to break. She collapsed atop him, loving how he wrapped his arms around her and kissed her head. *Oh yes...I am so screwed.*

Chapter Six

"Here's the tape from my meeting with Hanson."

It was all Zach could do to keep from throwing the small recorder at Vic. Whatever seeds of friendship the two had sowed were gone, destroyed by Vic's lecherous actions the previous night.

"Anything interesting?" Vic didn't bother to look up. He just pulled the recorder his way and popped out the tiny tape — antiquated, but it had served its purpose.

"He points a finger directly at Allison Sinclair."

"Now we have to prove it." Vic levered an appreciative leer toward Claudia. "Guess that's where you come in, according to Colonel Scott."

Zach watched her tense under the man's lustful gaze. He felt insulted on her behalf. The anger built with each second Vic raked his gaze over her. To her credit, Claudia put on her professional manners. Only someone intimately acquainted with her would know she was ready to lower the boom.

"You said Zach and I will be provided with a house across the street from the Sinclairs?"

Vic glanced at his watch. "It should be ready for you now, and we can have you moved in by this evening."

She lifted her chin in a haughty tilt. "I don't believe we will be requiring your assistance."

Tipping back his chair, he laced his hands behind his head. "It's important for you both to move quickly. The sooner you're settled, the sooner you can get to know your neighbors."

"How quickly do you think I'll be able to do that if the neighbors in question see NCIS helping us move in? Or is that a common service for your organization? Something to supplement your income, perhaps?"

He loved that wicked sarcasm in her voice, loved how she paused for effect.

"Zach and I are supposed to be presenting the appearance of a normal couple — or did last night's disgusting display cause you to forget that? A randy schoolboy would have been subtler."

Zach would swear he saw the man flinch. In less than thirty seconds she had verbally flayed Vic for his lack of manners and pointed out glaring flaws in his plan.

Taken down a notch, Vic studied her — whether in admiration or loathing, Zach couldn't begin to guess. He was proud of Claudia at that moment. No screeching. No tears. No displays. Simple, calm, rational and no nonsense. *His* woman. *His* wife.

He loved her authority now and had loved it even more last night. He didn't know what had changed to have her finally let him in, but he was going to do his damnedest to keep her. Pride had filled his chest. Lust had followed. She'd fucked him six ways to Sunday the previous night. He didn't know what he'd unleashed, but he was damn glad about it. He wished they'd had time for a repeat performance this morning.

Vic settled his chair forward, his cocky demeanor subdued. "You'll have to admit the plan to make Allison think you're having an affair is a good one."

"It isn't bad," Claudia admitted, "but you aren't the one to help create the illusion. Someone else can be found."

"If too many people are let in on the secret, word is bound to leak out," he countered.

"We don't have to let the man know what his purpose is. Gossip is gossip. Simply having a strange man over in the middle of the day is enough to fuel it. If that isn't sufficient, then I'm certain someone from Zach's office would be willing to assist us." She curved her eyebrow at him. "Unless, of course, you feel military attorneys can't be trusted."

She had him cornered. Zach imagined her thinking that the male animal was never much of a challenge.

Vic shuffled the papers on his desk, avoiding her laser-eyed stare. "Fine. Point taken. The sooner we get started, the sooner we finish."

"Do you have any new information for us?" Zach asked.

He glanced up. "No word yet on exactly what killed Sunline. Deputy sheriffs found his car in the desert five miles from base. It's being processed now. A quick once-over didn't reveal anything. It's a silver-gray Stratus four-door. It wasn't the vehicle you saw the night his body was dumped."

"He either met someone out in the desert or he was followed," Zach said.

"For whatever reason, the murderer put him in the back seat. Maybe that person was physically unable to lift him," Claudia said. "If we're presuming a woman was the killer, she might not have had the strength to haul him into the trunk. It would have been easier to open the back doors and drag him onto the seat. The person I saw was small in stature. It could have been a woman."

Zach's chest puffed with pride as she thought aloud, jotting notes into a small spiral notebook and keeping their full attention.

"Lady, if you ever want to work for NCIS, you've got my recommendation," Vic said.

Claudia's business-face didn't crack. With calm precision, she stood. "I don't think that's likely to happen, Agent Brownell." She swiveled her head and looked down her nose at Zach. "We should get started, shouldn't we? You indicated there was a lot to do."

Zach dug his keys from his pocket and handed them to her. "You go on. I'll be out in a minute."

He waited until she cleared the door then glared across the desk. Vic's gaze was focused on the doorway, as if he were still able to see Claudia.

"God, she's a beautiful woman," Vic said in a rush of breath.

It was too much for Zach. Vic kept crossing one line after the other. "What you did last night was uncalled for."

Vic tore his gaze from the doorway. "You can't blame a man for how his body reacts when he's dancing with a woman built like that."

Zach tightened his jaw. "She's not a piece of meat for you to drool over."

A smirk lifted one corner of Vic's mouth. "Why should you care? You said you were only keeping up with this marriage for the sake of finding a killer. That you'd both—"

"I know what I said," Zach snapped, "and I know what I'm saying now. Stay away from my wife."

Again the smirk. "I thought the two of you couldn't stand each other. Why should it matter to you?"

"We might not get along, but in all the years I've known her, I've never treated Claudia with the disrespect you did last night." No, they'd just hurled barbs at each other.

Zach forced himself to stand with the same cool precision Claudia had used. He stared a hole through Vic, letting the tension between them build before adding one final, quiet warning.

"If you try to pull a stunt like that again, I'll... Well, let's just say I'll see that you regret it."

* * * *

Claudia leaned against the side of Zach's Jeep and stared at the plastic identification card in her hand. She didn't know whether she felt like a possession of the government or a member of an exclusive club. The tan, laminated card proved she was Zach's wife, a military dependent and entitled to all the privileges that position afforded. It was to be carried with her at all times and presented upon demand or whenever she used the base's facilities. If she shopped at the stores, she showed it. If she needed medical care, out it came. *Free medical care. What a concept.* Even if they went bowling or to the movies, it was necessary to prove her identity. Claudia Taylor, dependent of and upon Captain Zachary Taylor. *In more ways than one.*

Sighing, she glanced up when she heard Zach leave the NCIS building. With two fingers, she flashed the card. "Are you certain there isn't a secret handshake or password to go with this?"

His smile sank beneath her skin, igniting images of the way they'd made each other come the night before. She wanted more. Had he beaten off in the shower this morning, wishing it was her hand and not his around his cock? She'd certainly gotten herself off in the shower wishing for him. She made it something for their 'to-do together' list. Their association might not be long-lived, but she was determined to take advantage of every second.

He reached the passenger side and opened the door for her. "I'm sure we could arrange something if you feel you need more of an initiation."

She pushed away from her perch. "I'm content, thank you. I think I've had enough bureaucracy to satisfy me for the moment."

"Good. Next stop is Housing."

"Can't we go directly to the house?"

"We have to make it official, remember? They'll give us the keys. We do a walk-through and bless it, then I have to sign for it." He waved her to the seat. "Shall we?"

Claudia slipped into place, loving his proprietorial touch to the small of her back. She was tempted to drag him down for a kiss that would set the world on fire. Zach moved away before she could do so.

He parked himself behind the Jeep's wheel and clicked his seat belt in place. "After we sign for the house, we'll deposit the Vegas money in the bank, check on your car at the body shop and see if your rental car is ready. By the time that's done, the movers should be at my place."

"My insurance covers a rental. It should be ready."

He twisted the key, cranking the engine. "If not, or if they drag their heels, we've got twenty thousand dollars between us, courtesy of Vegas. Hell, we'll pay for it ourselves."

She had to admit she liked this new peace between them, the way he'd let her put Vic in his place and that he'd made all they had to do today easy. If only it were real and not because of the investigation. She could let herself love this Zach, the one who loved his family and cats.

She waited in the Jeep while Zach retrieved the keys to the house they'd share. Once he had them, they were on the move again. Five minutes later, he pulled into a short driveway in front of a duplex townhouse.

It was a brownish-beige color, matching all those surrounding it in typical box-on-the-hillside fashion, and like the residences in the city of Twentynine Palms, the front yards were desert landscape.

"That must be Allison Sinclair," Zach said.

Claudia followed the direction of his gaze. She'd been so absorbed with the house that she hadn't looked elsewhere.

Class, that was her first impression of Allison Sinclair. Even while washing her light gold Cadillac, the woman didn't dress down. She wore canary yellow twill slacks with a long-sleeve camp shirt, all topped with a straw hat to keep the sun off her face. She even wore gloves. So they were rubber. It didn't matter. This was a woman who took care of herself and her appearance.

She was trim, compact. No more than five-two and barely one hundred pounds, if Claudia guessed right.

The very thought of this woman wielding a weapon powerful enough to kill a man was ridiculous. *Of course, jealousy and rage often give people super-human strength.*

As they stepped from the Jeep, Allison glanced up from under the brim of her hat. Claudia smiled and waved. Zach followed suit. The woman's response was hesitant then she gave them a nod.

"Not very friendly, is she?" Zach said under his breath.

"Why should she be? We're strangers."

"No, we're not. We're neighbors. Shall we take a look around inside for the heck of it?"

With a sweeping motion of his arm, he waved her forward then dropped his palm to her back. Claudia leaned in to his touch. Affection overwhelmed her. She felt giddy inside, over-the-top happy.

Rein it in, girl.

Zach gave her the honor of unlocking the door. When she pushed it open, he scooped her into his arms and carried her over the threshold.

"It's tradition, yes?" His smile beamed over her.

Claudia laughed. "It is." Even if it was pretend, she made up her mind to live in the moment with Zach and worry about the consequences to her heart later.

He set her on her feet and kissed her quickly. "Let's check it out."

The interior was another surprise. An open and spacious living room blended into a dining area. There was a bathroom near the base of the staircase. Blinds and drapes covered every window. It was carpeted throughout with a looped pile of variegated beige and brown. Not her first choice for a floor covering, but then it really didn't matter since this wasn't going to be a permanent arrangement.

Around the corner of the wall, she caught a glimpse of the kitchen but explored no farther. Upstairs they discovered two bedrooms and a second bathroom.

Claudia parted the master bedroom curtains with her index finger and discovered she would have gotten a clear shot of the Sinclair bedroom across the street had those drapes been open. Every window was sealed against the day, keeping the world and prying eyes out.

Allison was still at her post, meticulously scrubbing her car, using a toothbrush to clean around the edges of the windshield. Claudia was all for being neat and clean, but toothbrushing the windshield seemed a bit obsessive.

"Won't people think it odd that a captain and a colonel are living across the street from each other?" she asked.

"Not on this base. This is the only officer housing we have. Granted, we would normally not be placed here. If the colonel makes waves about it, he'll be told it was an emergency situation and that it's temporary. The commanding general will back us on that." He peeked over her shoulder to the scene across the street then stepped back. "Well, Mrs. Taylor, for the record, do you love the house and can't wait to move in?"

"I'm breathless with anticipation." She let the curtain fall back into place and faced him. "If we're going to play this out for a while, there will be some things I'll need from my apartment in San Francisco. I only brought clothes for a week."

"Fine. We'll go up this weekend."

"That won't be necessary. I'll see if Phillip will go with me. Everything I need should fit in their minivan."

It'd give her a cooling off period where she could evaluate all of whatever was happening between them.

"I'm devastated you don't want my presence."

"I'm sure." Sarcasm. That was what she was used to with Zach. It was easier to deal with, not the Zach who awakened parts of her better left alone. Claudia was weary of this insane game they'd been playing. It took too much energy to maintain, the peace had been so nice—and the sex was off the charts.

"Once we're back at your place, I'll pack up the kitchen and return here while you deal with the movers. It might give me and Allison a chance to bond."

A smile dimpled his cheeks. "From the look of her, I'd say the two of you have a lot in common, Princess."

Prissy and snooty?

"Both beautiful women oozing culture and class."

He'd rendered her speechless. There was nothing snide in his remarks, no duplicity of any kind in his eyes, no sarcasm framing 'princess.' In fact, the term had an endearing quality to it that tugged at her heart. Claudia parted her lips, craving his kiss, his arms.

Then take one.

With the muffled sound of a car door slamming, they broke eye contact and turned to the window. Zach peeled the drape back with one finger. In the Sinclair driveway, four women got out of a silver Toyota now parked behind Allison's car. They greeted her with waves and hellos while she peeled the rubber gloves from her tapered fingers. Her expression was devoid of emotion. No joy, no irritation…nothing. There was a brief conversation, a bit of cajoling then the women piled back into their car and drove away. Allison watched until they were out of sight then returned to her task.

"I suppose those are some of the infamous officers' spouses?" she asked of Zach.

"I'd say that's a yes. And she didn't seem happy to see them."

"She didn't seem *anything*, Zach. I don't know if her lack of emotion was sad or scary."

"It's something to keep in mind when you deal with her. You're going to have to get beyond her defenses."

Like you're trying to do with me? Claudia left the question unasked. "Any idea how I'll be able to infiltrate their club?"

Zach snickered. "Don't worry. From what I've heard, they'll be coming for you."

"Lovely. I'll gird my loins."

His full-out laughter tripped her heart. It was a wonderful, uplifting sound. Contagious.

"Come on." He cupped her shoulder. "Let's get your rental car."

Claudia aimed for the stairs with Zach close behind, jiggling his keys.

"Here's the key to my place in case you get there before me." He held it out when they hit the first floor. "I have a spare."

"Where will you be?" She plucked the key from his fingers.

"I have to square things with my landlord. I don't want him thinking I'm skipping out on him. I shouldn't be long."

"When will the movers get there?"

He glanced at his watch as he opened the front door. "Ninety minutes. Make sure they don't leave the doors wide open. I don't want Miss Kitty to run out into the desert and become a coyote snack."

"Oh my goodness, no." The thought horrified her. "She's very pretty and certainly adores you. I hope we get along."

"You will." He blessed her with one of those unguarded smiles that devastated her senses. "Just don't leave her food bowl empty. She likes the comfort of seeing it full. She'll thank you by taking a single bite before sauntering off. Heaven forbid she can see the bottom of it."

Claudia laughed and stepped outside.

Allison ducked behind the front of her vehicle. At least that was the impression Claudia got, although she could be cleaning microscopic road scum from her headlights with that toothbrush of hers.

"It's going to take a lot of skill trying to cozy up to a woman who obviously has no interest in socializing with others."

Zach skimmed his hand down her back, coming to rest at the curve of her butt.

"I've been watching you schmooze people for years. You're a pro." He leaned in. "And that's a compliment." He stole a quick kiss, gave a light pat to her rear then led her to his Jeep.

It's all for show, right? But what if it isn't? She really needed to stop dissecting his actions. They had a job to do and hers was the task of extracting information from a remote woman. The sex was an added benefit.

"Strangers I can understand, but her own friends?" she said when they were in the vehicle.

"I know." He backed from the driveway and headed for town.

"Allison didn't even crack a smile when they appeared."

And Claudia was supposed to find a way to prove the woman killed Teddy Sunline? She shook her head. *How could anyone pierce an exterior as icy as* —

She stopped herself short. The comparison hit her in the gut. She glanced at Zach from the corner of her eye to see if he had somehow read her thoughts. His gaze was focused on the road.

I'm not like Allison Sinclair, am I? Pristine, cold, remote. *No,* she decided. Allison was that way with everyone. Claudia was only so with men — and for good reason. There was a difference. She took what she needed physically then sent them on their way, cold and calculated. She deserved the moniker Ice Princess and Zach wasn't the first man who'd called her that.

She and Zach parted ways at the rental car agency once he knew she had what she needed. Twenty minutes later, she pulled into Zach's driveway. Miss Kitty greeted her at the front door with a lazy mew.

"That's more of a response than I'll ever get from Allison." Claudia gave the cat a scratch behind the ears and heard her healthy purr.

"Come on, pretty girl. We've got some packing to do."

Claudia smiled. The cat followed her into the kitchen. *Opportunist.*

Food-wise there wasn't much to pack. Zach's primary source of nutrition appeared to be cereal and peanut butter. She spent most of her time making a list of what they needed. As for cookware and dinnerware, they needed enough to get by until the rest was unloaded. Everything fit into ten grocery sacks in the trunk of Claudia's rental car — a duplicate of her own.

The rumble of a truck announced the movers' arrival. She saw Zach pull to a stop on the street behind them. Claudia cracked open the door. Miss Kitty's ears perked up, her body tense for flight. Claudia picked her up before she could dart for the exit.

"Oh, no you don't, you little sneak. You're coming with me."

She cradled the cat in her arms and toted her to the car. Deep purrs of contentment rewarded her efforts.

* * * *

Zach waved to Claudia as she drove away, Miss Kitty draped around the back of her neck. They'd truly bounded. *One little happy family – for now.* Until they caught a killer. But, damn, he wanted forever. He always had. But Claudia?

His need for her had tripled now that they'd had at each other. *Who knew she'd be so fucking hot in bed?* Sure, he'd imagined she would be, but reality made his fantasies pale in comparison. Every second he was away from her, she was on his mind. Whenever she was by his side, all he wanted was to drag her against him and love on her until they collapsed into exhaustion. At this rate, he'd go insane before their undercover work was finished.

"Mind if we get started on packing you up now?" the lead mover asked.

Zach nodded and let them inside. They swarmed the house like ants.

Hours later his possessions were at the new house on base.

Claudia greeted their arrival with Miss Kitty cradled in her arms. The cat seemed to be in no hurry to leave. Zach couldn't blame her.

More time ticked away while the movers unloaded and set up the furniture. Neighbors peeked from their windows. A few came up to introduce themselves. There was nothing from the Sinclair residence — until the colonel himself drove up.

Martin Sinclair made six feet look like seven. He gave them a hearty hello as his long strides took him into his house.

Zach glanced at Claudia. Her eyebrow lifted as if to say, 'Curious.' He acknowledged her with a nod and wondered how long Sinclair's friendliness would last once he discovered Zach was a captain.

The lead mover shoved a clipboard under Zach's nose. He scribbled his signature, verifying the job was done. NCIS would handle the bill and everything else associated with the transition. His one priority had been an immediate landline connection and that the number remain the same. That was his family's primary form of communication whenever he was stateside, since they never were sure when he'd be at work and didn't want to disturb him. Brownell had assured him it would be ready.

Zach waved the movers off and shut the door. His gaze fell on the answering machine sitting on the floor, attached to the wall. A check of the phone confirmed it worked. *At least something has gone right today.* Actually, many things had gone right, all dealing with Claudia.

"Neither of us has eaten all day. I'm starved. How about you?"

"I have dinner planned. It shouldn't take more than thirty minutes." Miss Kitty leaped from her arms, padded toward the kitchen then peered over her shoulder to see if Claudia was following.

"We can go out if you like," he told her.

"As I said, I have something planned. If you want to help, you can make the bed and put towels in the bathroom, providing you have any that are clean."

"If not, I'll take some outside and squirt the hose over them."

His comment was meant to be funny, and he applauded his efforts when he saw the hint of laughter tugging at Claudia's lips. "Or you could hook up the washer and dryer."

"Smart *and* beautiful."

"Thanks. I think you're pretty, too." She flashed him a grin that lit his heart on fire and followed Miss Kitty into the kitchen.

Zach did an about-face and trotted upstairs to put the bedroom and bathroom in shape. Since she'd said nothing about sleeping arrangements, he presumed they were still going to share his. *Score one for me.* Or maybe she would remedy that situation with her weekend trip to San Francisco.

That brought his thoughts to a halt. He hated she'd chosen Phillip to go with her and didn't relish the idea of being without her. Funny, he'd spent night after night alone, but one night with Claudia by his side and he was spoiled. That little taste of domesticity now had him craving more, even if it was only temporary. Maybe the peace and quiet would give him time to get his head on straight and figure out where this was leading, if it was leading anywhere. Hell, he didn't want peace and quiet. He wanted her. He wanted forever.

The scent of dinner wafting to him rumbled his stomach as he worked. At least it smelled like she could cook. That was a plus, since who knew how long they'd be cooped up together?

He opened the window to let the evening breeze drift in. Sounds of the neighborhood reached him. Children shouted at the playground nearby. Dogs barked. A television blared. Two kids argued over a basketball.

"Dinner," Claudia called up.

Zach shoved away from his perch and loped downstairs, his mouth watering with each step. Whatever she'd fixed, it smelled delicious. He rounded the corner to the dining area and saw spaghetti and salad waiting for him. Without further prompting, he piled his plate high then froze.

"What *is* this?"

Claudia slid her chair from the table and slipped onto her throne. "Jicama salad with vinaigrette dressing."

"No...in the spaghetti."

"Tofu meatballs."

Zach's stomach turned. "Tofu?"

"It's high in protein and very good for you. It takes on the taste of the food you're eating. Try it."

"No meat?"

"I don't eat red meat."

"But I do," he said.

"But I cooked. The least you could do is try it."

Resigned to his fate, Zach pierced a minuscule portion with his fork and lifted it to his mouth. With his eyes closed, he shoved it in.

"Chew," she ordered.

He opened them. She sat across from him, arms tucked under her bosom, giving him a luscious hint of cleavage. A light smile lifted one corner of her shapely mouth. *Damn*. He wanted to kiss her. He conceded defeat and chewed. "This is good." He speared a larger bite.

"I told you so."

He half-expected her to stick out her tongue. Instead, she devoted attention to her salad. Zach twirled up a mouthful of pasta.

"What's your opinion of Martin Sinclair?"

Claudia shrugged a shoulder. "I was initially struck with how handsome a man he is. His personality leaps out at you. He has a ready smile, all of which makes me wonder why a woman would want someone else."

"He may look movie-star perfect, but we don't know what goes on in their marriage. Maybe he's the devoted husband but she's the one with the problem. Some people play around no matter how great they have it with their spouse. It's in their nature."

"If that's the case, I feel sorry for her and her husband."

"I see it all the time in Legal Assistance. It's almost like an epidemic. Husbands deploy, and before their side of the bed can get cold, their young, lonely wives are seeking a replacement. It's enough for the most romantic person to give up on having a happily-ever-after."

"Marriage isn't about the happily-ever-after, Zach. It's about compromise and commitment. It's about being a team, even when you don't want to be. It's about being strong when the other person can't be or isn't. Sometimes you're happy. Sometimes you're not. Sometimes you can't live without that certain someone and other times you wish them dead, but you stay together through thick and thin."

Richer and poorer. Sickness and health.

He didn't know how to respond. They ate in silence while Miss Kitty picked at her food. Two servings later and after polishing off the salad, he watched Claudia carry their dishes to the sink. He followed her to dry while she washed, which left him with the task of figuring out where she'd put everything.

"It's staggering the amount of work we've put into catching a killer," he told her.

"I'll help you put everything back once this is done."

"Thanks." He put the last pot away and turned in time to see her attack a spot on the faucet with the washcloth.

Zach watched her scrub, look, then scrub again. "Well, it isn't a toothbrush, but I suppose it's just as effective." The words were out before he could stop them.

Claudia froze, eyes wide, staring at the cloth in her hand. He wished he'd kept his fucking mouth shut. She slowly set it aside and turned his way. For the first time in their relationship, he couldn't decipher the look in her eyes. Her having one hand on her hip didn't help, nor did the way she gave him a thorough once-over. Zach wasn't sure whether to be afraid or turned on.

Time ticked away with them locked in position, focused on each other. If he'd been confident enough in his reception, Zach would have pulled her to him and kissed her. But this was Claudia and last night's truce didn't mean the war was won. And he sure as hell hadn't helped matters by opening his mouth. "I'm sorry. That was uncalled for," he finally said.

"Are we done for the night?" she asked. "We have no other obligations? Vic isn't going to be coming by for any reason?"

"Not that I'm aware."

"Good." Slow steps brought her closer. "I'm going to take a shower." She wiggled her finger down his chest, stopping when she reached the button on his jeans. "Would you like to join me? You can bring your friend with you."

She pressed her palm over his cock. It swelled into her grip. *Damn.* He loved the twinkle in her eyes.

"Are you needing your back scrubbed?"

"And other things."

He grinned. "I live to please."

"You are so self-sacrificing."

"It's my claim to fame."

She stepped away, running a lascivious gaze over his body. "I would disagree."

"I'll lock up, draw the curtains and meet you there."

"Do hurry. I'd hate to have to start without you." She flashed him a come-fuck-me smile and walked off, putting a little extra sway in her hips.

Zach hurried through his tasks and was ready to vault the stairs two at a time when he saw her sandal four steps up. He picked it up and found its mate a little higher. Jeans, shirt, bra and panties followed, the latter ending at the bathroom door. She had the shower running, and visions of water sluicing over her body in homage to the goddess she was filled his head. He dropped her clothes to the floor and added his to the heap after pulling a condom from his jeans pocket.

"I hope I'm not too late," he said when he opened the door. "I was distracted by the enticing trail of clothing left in your wake. I picked it up for you, by the way."

"Goodness, there's hope for you yet." Claudia peeked around the edge of the shower curtain. "I see your friend is awake."

"He always is whenever he's around you."

He slapped the condom onto the vanity counter and stepped in next to her. She skimmed her hand down his erection in what felt like slow motion. He squeezed her ass, dragging her closer.

"I like how you're all wet for me."

Claudia giggled. A first for him. The sound trickled over his body, landing hard down below. She tightened her grip and wriggled her free hand to his balls. Breath hissed through his clenched teeth and he swore part of his brain shut down. Zach shook away the haze and tried to focus. She didn't make it easy, the way she tugged, rolled and tried to separate them. He loved every second. Then he spied the array of bath products in the corner — shampoo, conditioner, liquid soap, body oil.

Oh yeah.

"Care to make things interesting?" he asked.

Her hold loosened as she drew back. "How so?"

He gently pushed her against the wall and reached for the body oil. Keeping his gaze locked on hers, he squirted a liberal amount over her breasts then offered the bottle. When she raised her palms, he filled them with oil. She dived her hands to his groin, smearing oil over his cock and balls, rubbing her breasts over his chest. Zach lost his grip on the bottle. It thunked to the tub. Claudia kicked it aside and started to kneel.

"My turn first." Grasping her elbows, he pulled her up and pressed her to the wall.

She glided her hands up his chest, rolling his nipples in her palms. He reciprocated, tweaking before he sucked one into his mouth. Claudia sighed and arched into him, draping her arms over his shoulders, digging her fingers into his hair, rubbing her stomach over his cock. He slid his hands down her back and clamped one hand over her ass. Groaning, she tried to hook her leg over his hip. Zach pulled away.

"Not yet, sweetheart."

He worked his way downward a lick at a time, kneading her buttocks until she writhed against him. When he neared his goal, she locked her muscles.

"What's wrong?" he asked, looking up. Anxiety stole the pleasure from her beautiful face.

"I don't do this." Her cheeks flushed.

"You were going to do it to me." He ran his hands over her bottom and down her thighs, trying to soothe her concern.

"Yes…but not to completion."

Step at a time. "I don't blame you. I wouldn't want to suck a man off, either."

She laughed a little and some of her tension ebbed.

He dropped a kiss to her belly. "You don't like it or you've never tried it?"

"I tried it…long ago. I just never wanted a man to—"

"Get that close and intimate with you?" He twirled his tongue into her navel. She gasped and flexed her fingers in his hair.

"Yes," she replied.

Zach circled his thumbs up her inner thighs. "Were there problems this other time? Was it too rough?"

She huffed out a sigh. "He was bothered by"—another blush covered her cheeks—"the hair. He wanted it removed. I refused, but the incident still made me feel…dirty."

"Then he was an ass."

Another laugh. "Yes, he was."

"Hair doesn't bother me and I love the scent of you. I want to taste you. I want to feel the tremble of your orgasm on my tongue. I want all of you, Claudia, but not at the expense of your comfort. No means no and I will always respect that." Even while he was trying to tempt her to take a chance on him.

She toyed with his hair while they stared at each other. He'd stopped his thumbs right below her pussy. The choice was hers. He couldn't stress that enough.

"Have you done this before?" she asked.

"This?" He slid his thumbs through her labia.

Claudia tensed in a good way. "Shower."

"No one has ever asked me. They've demanded it of me, but they never asked."

"Good." She combed her fingers through his hair again. "No means no?"

"Yes." Her eyes glazed over with every pass he made.

"You may proceed."

A little formal, but he'd take it and did so without hesitation, flicking his tongue around her swollen clit. Moaning, she opened herself up to the caress. He grunted in response and caught her labia between his lips, kneading one then the other until her fingers tightened against his head and she tried to maneuver him right where she wanted. He allowed himself a self-satisfied grin and pulled her clit between his lips, holding it in place while he flashed his tongue over it. He reached for her breasts, gathering the oil from her skin, then spread it over her anus and rolled his finger over it. She clamped her thighs around his head and fisted his hair. He paused, waiting for her refusal. It never came.

He danced his thumb over her pussy while he licked through her labia and urged her to open to him. She relaxed by slow degrees, relinquishing her grip on his hair. Her heat warmed his face. He found her clit again, slipped his thumb into her pussy and breached the muscle guarding her ass.

Claudia smacked her palm on the wall with her groan, body quaking under the onslaught of her climax. She slumped, panting for breath. Zach eased from her then kissed his way up her body, stopping when he reached her mouth. There was the look of a well-satisfied woman about her. She tickled her fingers to his nape, cupped his neck and kissed him, slow and deep.

"My turn."

Claudia traded places with him, pushing him against the wall. She dragged her hands down his body with her descent. Once she reached his erection, she tucked it between her breasts, pushed them closer with her biceps and fucked him. Zach grappled for a handhold, but she was on the move again, this time ducking her head between his legs. She locked one hand around his cock and sucked one of his balls into her mouth.

"Goddamn," he gasped.

He hit his head into the wall and spread wider. She flashed her tongue over his sac then sucked the other one while she pumped his dick slowly — too slowly. Her finger wandered to *his* hole — virgin territory. As he had, she spread oil around and around, her tongue doing sinfully sweet things to his balls while she maintained a death grip on his erection. When she crawled her hot lips over the underside of his cock, Zach was pretty sure he'd died and gone to heaven.

He started to cup her head then planted his hands on the wall. If he grabbed her head, he'd be trying not to deep-throat her. This was her game now. A flick of her tongue over his frenulum had his head buzzing. Gasping, he pumped his hips into the caress. Her finger at his anus pressed harder as she worked her wrist over his sac. She tightened her grip on his dick. He looked down to find her poised at the crown, her devilish gaze on him. Then she went down on him at the same time that she thrust her finger up his ass.

"Damn, honey. I'm going to come."

He half-heartedly tried to free himself. Claudia only sucked harder, pushing her finger against his prostate. Zach thrashed against her, fighting the oncoming rush yet needing relief more than he could bear. He gave her another warning. Still, she refused to release him. She went deeper, brushing her breasts over his thighs. After releasing her grip on him, she clutched his sac and rolled his balls. Jets of fire spewed from his cock. She took it all.

He sank to the tub, pulled her into his arms and kissed her. Then he kissed her again — and again. And one more time, before he gave in and told her how much he loved her.

Chapter Seven

Claudia stretched her muscles, trying to ignore the smell of breakfast cooking. Her rumbling stomach demanded to be fed.

"Run first then eat," she ordered it, even though going about her morning routine was the last thing she wanted.

They'd put each other through their paces last night after their shower. It seemed they couldn't get enough of one another. Her body ached in places she didn't know she had. Deliciously so. She wondered how Zach was faring. *Clearly, well enough to cook breakfast.* Her stomach rumbled again.

"Not going to happen."

She was dressed to run, and run she would. She couldn't miss a workout two days in a row. After drawing her hair into a ponytail, she left the room.

She trotted down the stairs, hoping to give herself a good warm up. With each step, the breakfast scents grew stronger. Her stomach protested.

I've got to get out of here.

"I'm going for a run," she called to Zach.

"You'd better drink some water before you go and take a bottle," Zach shouted from the kitchen. "The desert will dehydrate you in minutes."

"On it." The fact she'd forgotten proved she had no business running.

She strode into the kitchen, determined to stay on task. Zach turned from the stove. He stopped in mid-action, sizzling skillet poised in his hand. His gaze took her in with one sweep. His subsequent smile did a number on her insides. Giddiness threatened to escape. Her heart fluttered. And here she'd thought she could fuck Zach with no emotional fallout.

"You look cute," he told her.

Claudia did her own quick perusal, noting the erection swelling his cargo shorts. Her body tightened in response.

"What have you got there?" She pointed to the pan.

Zach swiveled his hips back to the counter. "Omelet. I also made hash browns and bacon. Want some?"

The heat of his nearness as she ran a glass of tap water overwhelmed her. Then he leaned over her shoulder and she went all fluttery inside.

"What's in it?"

"Onion, mushrooms, a touch of salsa and a sprinkle of mozzarella cheese."

"No green peppers?"

He screwed up his face. "I hate green peppers."

Claudia nodded. "Me, too."

Zach slid the finished omelet onto a plate, cut off a bite and pierced it with his fork. "Sure you don't want a bite?"

He waved the tempting morsel in front of her face. She followed the tidbit much as Miss Kitty would an interesting toy.

"Maybe a taste." She slipped the fork from his hand and guided it to her mouth. Tilting her head to one side, she nodded. "Not bad. Delicious, in fact."

"Have another bite." He motioned to the plate.

Claudia twirled the fork between her fingers and studied her target. It *was* perfect, just the right combination of ingredients to make it mouth-watering. She carved off another bite.

"Would you like me to make you one?" he asked.

She shook her head and sampled another piece. "I really can't. I have to go run."

"Well, you won't mind if I make myself one, then?"

She drew back in surprise, stared at the almost empty plate and laughed.

"There's no harm in a good breakfast." He grinned and kissed her cheek. "Finish the rest of the omelet and I'll make another for myself. We can work it off at the gym later."

"But my..." She grabbed the plate, shrugged and dived in again. "I'll run tonight."

With a broad smile, he braced his backside against the counter and leaned closer to her. "I'll run with you."

Claudia winked. "You couldn't keep up with me."

Zach laughed. "We'll see about that, Princess."

God. She wanted to wrap her arms around his neck and kiss him. Better yet, drag him upstairs and back to bed. She watched him whip up another omelet while she finished off the remains of the first. The man knew his way around a kitchen. That alone garnered him some level of respect. The fact that he didn't render any blistering comments over her healthy appetite earned him even more. Or was all that in the past after the last two nights wrapped in each other's arms? There was that tug to her heart again.

"My hands are full," he said. "How about shoving some of those hash browns in my mouth?"

With a fresh fork, she lifted a serving to Zach, almost missing her target. He caught all but a smidgen that landed on his chin.

"Oops." She laughed. "We goofed. Here...let me." She brushed him clear with her thumb.

Zach's gaze met hers. Gone was the light-hearted camaraderie. In its place was an emotion too common whenever she was near him—unbridled lust. It overwhelmed her. If he kissed her now, they'd be back in the bedroom soon after. Hell, they might not even make it to the bedroom. She couldn't get enough of him.

"Bacon," he rasped.

Claudia shook her thoughts clear. "What?"

"I'll have a piece of bacon now."

"Of course." But she didn't move.

She was conscious of him moving the skillet to a different burner, of him facing her more fully, bracing his hands on the counter on either side of her and never once breaking eye contact while he did so. She willed him to pull her against him and do what they craved.

A blast from the doorbell startled them.

"The joys of neighborhood living." He shoved away from her. "You'd better get it. We don't want to intimidate any wives by having me show up at the door right at this moment."

"What could you possibly do to intimidate them?"

He motioned to his groin.

Claudia arched her eyebrow. "Lust after it would be a better term—and I don't share."

"Good to know." He reached for her…or she for him. The doorbell pealed on.

"I'll change into more appropriate clothes." He took the stairs two at a time.

The impatient visitor switched to pounding at the door. Whoever it was thrived on persistence. Had this been a normal situation, Claudia would have wasted no time giving her—or him—a strong piece of her mind. But they were here to make contacts, even annoying ones.

That attitude faded when she opened the door and saw Vic standing on the other side dressed as a cable installer. A truck parked in the driveway added to the illusion.

"Cable man," he sang out, then dropped his voice a couple of decibels. "You gonna let me in or do I have to stand here all morning?"

"You should be careful about giving me a choice. You might not like the answer." She shoved the door wider, waved him in and shouted for Zach.

He thundered down the steps seconds later in jeans and a pullover shirt. "You're taking a chance coming here, don't you think?"

Vic shrugged. "Everyone needs the cable installed when they move in. Your neighbors won't suspect a thing."

"Until the real cable man shows up," Zach replied. "I can only presume you have information?"

"I do."

Vic's demeanor turned from cocky to businesslike. It was an improvement, but Claudia still didn't trust the man to remain professional for very long.

"Have a seat at the table. You can tell us over coffee while Zach and I finish breakfast. After all, you do have to stay here long enough to give the illusion of having actually worked."

Vic chuckled. "You sure you don't want a job with us?"

"Positive." Claudia walked away.

Vic waited until they were seated around the kitchen table then curled his fingers around his steaming coffee mug.

"We got the preliminary autopsy back on Teddy Sunline this morning. He died of injuries consistent with blunt force trauma."

Zach swallowed a mouthful of omelet. "You mean he was hit over the head."

"More like he was hit all over his body," Vic replied. "The coroner said it looked like someone ran over him with a car."

Claudia leaned forward. "The one I saw that night?"

Vic shook his head and sipped his coffee. "Well, we know it wasn't Sunline's car. As you recall, it was found deserted a couple of miles from his house. There's no damage to it. No bloodstains. No residual blood or tissue. When a car hits someone, it's obvious."

Zach tapped his finger on his fork. "What about fingerprints?"

"The forensics team is going over it now, but it's fairly clean. The only fingerprints so far were on the steering wheel. The car looked like it had just been detailed."

"Sounds like a professional job."

"Or someone who thought very carefully before carrying out the murder. Someone very meticulous."

Claudia and Zach caught each other's gaze. It was a strike against Allison.

"We saw Allison Sinclair washing her car yesterday when we arrived...with a toothbrush." Zach polished off his last bite of toast.

Vic snorted. "Well, I guess it doesn't get any more meticulous than that."

"But there's no damage to it from what we could see." Claudia dabbed her napkin at the corners of her mouth. "What about Sunline's house? Any clues there?"

"We're still waiting for permission from the family to search it."

"If you like, I'll speak to them. They might respond more favorably to a woman."

"Pushy, aren't you?"

"Whatever it takes to get the job done. In the meantime" — Claudia shoved her chair back — "I think it's time for a little neighborly visit with Allison Sinclair."

"Excellent idea." Vic drained the last of his coffee. "Here's what you do..."

In less time than she cared to think about, Claudia was standing before the Sinclair door, armed with several excuses with which to worm her way into the house. Wearing a polished confidence she didn't feel, she pressed the doorbell.

But it wasn't Allison who answered. It was her husband. Claudia did a double-take, overwhelmed with a combination of surprise and awe.

She was five-nine, but Martin Sinclair towered over her at a good six feet. He had the looks of a movie star and a ready smile to go with them. For a Marine colonel, his salt-and-pepper hair was just shy of being too long. Claudia imagined there wasn't an officer higher than him willing to point that out, and if they did, Sinclair would smooth his way around that slight infraction of Marine Corps policy.

"Good morning. This is a pleasant surprise."

There was a hint of accent in his voice, but Claudia couldn't place its origin. "I'm sorry to bother you. I thought you'd be at work."

"My wife's a bit under the weather, so I stayed to make sure she was going to be all right. What can I do for you?"

If the woman was sick, Claudia didn't want to bother her. Still, she couldn't stand here looking stupid. "We moved in across the street yesterday. In all the craziness, neither of us can find our chargers. Our cell phones are dead. I was wondering if I might use your phone to call my brother. Our landline won't be turned on until sometime tomorrow and I wanted him to know our new address. I'm sorry. I didn't realize your wife was ill. I can come back later." Lie after lie. She hoped it wasn't obvious.

"Nonsense."

He caught her arm before she could step back and drew her into the house.

Claudia resented the grip he had on her. It was too personal, much too harsh and too forceful. Just as she was about to point that out to him, he released her.

"What are neighbors for if we can't help each other? Allison's up and around. I'm on my way out. Our landline is over there." He pointed to the kitchen.

Claudia was afraid to set one foot on the carpet. It was the same style and color as that in her house but here it was pristine. Each pile was upright and perfect, the only footsteps those of the man who had answered the door.

Everything about the house was impeccable, like a picture from a magazine. No dust or fingerprints marred the cherrywood tables. The cushions on the white sofa were wedged in place with a precision a bricklayer would envy. Each book on the tall case was arranged by height and width. Not one of the spines was cracked or looked used.

Allison glided down the stairs dressed in khaki capris and an oversized camp shirt. A silk scarf in shades of cream and gold was arranged at her throat. If Sinclair hadn't mentioned it, Claudia would never have guessed the woman was ill.

"I'm sorry to intrude. I'm Claudia, your new neighbor. I needed to use your phone."

Allison shot her husband a glance then nodded. "Of course. May I offer you a cool drink?"

"No, thank you. But I was wondering if you would be able to tell me where I can do some shopping. My husband tells me I'll need a formal dress for the Marine Corps Ball next weekend."

"Not a problem," Sinclair said. "Allison will be glad to take you down to Palm Springs tomorrow. Won't you, dear?"

Her faced remained expressionless. "Of course... tomorrow."

"That's certainly one way to get to know your neighbors." Claudia gave a soft laugh to cover the awkwardness she felt. "I wouldn't want to impose."

Sinclair waved the comment away. "No imposition at all. Allison has nothing better to do with her time. And if you *really* want to get to know the neighbors around here, you can offer up your place for the next football gathering."

She'd rather chew glass. "We can do that. I'll let Zach know."

"Monday it is. Ladies..." He dropped a kiss to Allison's cheek and left.

Allison folded her hands in front of her. "The telephone is in the kitchen."

Claudia dared a peek over her shoulder as she crossed the sacred carpet. Behind her, Allison refreshed the carpet pile, wiped a nonexistent speck of dust from the table, adjusted the drapes and fluffed the cushions. Claudia had never felt more out of place in her life.

She punched in Phillip's number as fast as she could then counted the seconds until Rowan answered. Rowan played her part, receiving information that didn't matter without any questions. The entire conversation lasted less than a minute, yet Allison's constant fussing made it seem like an hour.

Claudia slipped the receiver into its cradle but refused to set foot on the carpet. "Thank you. I'll let myself out the back door."

"Come over when you're ready to leave tomorrow morning. I'd like to get an early start. I need to be home before Marty gets off work."

It was her job. She swore she'd get to the bottom of Sunline's murder, but if she had to spend one more minute with Allison... "Tomorrow then."

Zach was waiting for Claudia by the door when she walked back into their house. Vic was nursing a second cup of coffee at the kitchen table.

"That was quick," Zach said.

She sank into the nearest chair. "We're going shopping tomorrow morning. Plus, you and I get to host the neighborhood football party next week."

"That *was* quick." Vic laughed.

She traced the point of her chin with her hand. "A little too quick. Orchestrated primarily by Sinclair, not me. Either he's one hell of a nice guy or…"

Zach propped himself against the counter. "Or what?"

Away from the Sinclairs, more questions than answers arose. Allison's actions were automatic, not by rote or routine but by something more. She was a puppet whose strings were yanked. If so, by what force — guilt? Or her husband?

Claudia shook the thought away. It was premature and unprofessional to jump to conclusions. "It's nothing I can put my finger on. It just feels odd over there."

"How so?"

"I don't know. Regimented. Claustrophobic. Maybe tomorrow I'll get some clues. I need to get out of here for a while. I'm going to the gym." Claudia jumped up and grabbed her purse.

Zach snagged the strap and yanked her to a halt. "If you'll wait, I'll go with you."

"I'd rather be alone."

He released his hold and held up his hands. "I understand."

The expression on his face said differently. Claudia couldn't find a way to tell him that this wasn't about him. She hoped the palm she placed on his chest spoke for her. He pressed his hand over it and squeezed then kissed her. Relief seeped through her bones.

* * * *

Claudia stood inside the entrance to one of the base's gyms. Every machine she could want to try was before her and free to use. A rare treat. A glorious opportunity. Her heart wasn't in it.

From the corner of her eye she saw a man approach her. She turned the other way. Conversation was also not on her list of priorities for now. She wanted time to think, to clear the image of Allison flicking her pale, thin fingers over the carpet pile.

"Need some help?"

She narrowed her gaze at the sandy-haired intruder, ready to blast him with a frosty rejection. His friendly smile stopped her. There was a familiarity, yet Claudia couldn't recall having met him before.

His grin widened, pale blue eyes sparkling with laughter. After a quick glance around, he leaned closer. "Girlfriend?" His voice was low, for her ears only.

"Kiki?" she whispered, trying not to laugh. "Or should I stick with Kurt?"

"In the flesh. I work here. I teach aerobics, self-defense and help people use the machines." He winked. "It's glorious. All these men. You would be surprised at how many husbands get jealous of me being around their women. If only they knew."

Claudia laughed until her sides ached. It was the medicine her fractured soul needed. Kiki...Kurt just smiled.

"So"—he tucked his arms over his well-defined chest—"here to relieve a little stress? You look a little fried."

Is it that obvious? If they had been old friends and not new, Claudia might have confided in him...her... whichever.

"We've been moving into our new place here on base, and I decided I needed some stress relief. Some time on a stair climber should do it."

"Great. Once you're done, I'll treat you to lunch."

She rolled her eyes. "Please, no more food. I'm here to work off a breakfast you wouldn't believe. Cold water will do just fine."

"Great." He lowered his voice once more. "Maybe we can trade secrets. Even dressed to sweat, you have that certain *je ne sais quoi* that I'm dying to learn."

Kiki-Kurt had that certain something, too — no matter which persona he portrayed. Two hours later, sitting outside the gym talking over liter-bottles of cold water, Claudia marveled over the masculine side of her newfound friend. It was an amazing transition from the night before, and no one but she was the wiser. He was a fine-looking man with a narrow waist and lithe, hardened muscles. Not as well-built as Zach, but fine nonetheless.

"I'm curious," he admitted.

Claudia smiled. "About what?"

"You. You're an attentive listener. You ask all the right questions to keep a person talking, but what about you? Who is Claudia? Who is this calm goddess in the eye of storm?"

Her smile faltered. She traced circles in the perspiration on her bottle. "She's a fraud, Kurt."

By slow degrees, the words tumbled out. Claudia found herself telling Kiki-Kurt things in detail that she had never discussed with anyone — about Todd, her father, the pain of betrayal, her first meeting with Zach, the ridiculous farce of a marriage, her parallel to Allison, even the killer sex. When the final words spilled out, she was exhausted, drained. All she longed to do was curl up somewhere and sleep.

"So now, knowing all this, what does Claudia want? Answer quick, without thinking."

"To be with Zach. To keep him with me once this is over"

Kiki-Kurt covered her hands with his. "But, girlfriend, you're *married* to the man. You're already with him."

Claudia jerked upright then slumped once more. "He's going to break my heart and leave."

"You don't know that. Life is about taking chances. Enjoy the good while it lasts. Deal with the bad *if* it comes. Live life. That's what it was meant for."

It was good advice, but playing house to catch a killer wasn't going to last forever. Once they had the information needed, they'd go back to their separate lives. She had a job she'd fought hard to get and was now working even harder to keep. It was why she was here. Zach was a career Marine. She'd known that from the start, listening to him and Phillip talk. His goal was to make colonel. God only knew how many places he'd be stationed during his twenty- or thirty-year military career. She had goals, as well. How could she set those aside and follow him from one place to the other?

She'd told Zach that marriage was about compromise and commitment. It was also about trust. She hadn't trusted a man in ten years, yet here she was, ready to place her heart in his hands. Signs of trust had to start somewhere. The question was, where?

Kiki-Kurt chucked her under the chin. "Quit thinking so hard or that line between your eyebrows will be permanently etched there. Live in the moment and make it all it can be. Sometimes it's all we've got."

Chapter Eight

On the surface, Teddy Sunline's house was no different from the dozens of others surrounding it. That in itself drew Zach's suspicions. By all accounts, Sunline was a bachelor, yet his front yard said otherwise.

Rose bushes danced alongside the house with beds of alyssum weaving between them like giant swatches of lace. Tulips, lilies and irises anchored a winding sidewalk. Pots of marigolds were nestled on the front porch next to the door. Near the stoop, hummingbirds darted to a feeder.

Vic pulled two pair of disposable gloves from his pocket and handed one to Zach. "We don't want to taint any evidence we find."

Behind him, Zach heard the other two agents snap theirs into place. "Are you sure this is the right house? I keep expecting to see a wife and kids any minute."

Vic scanned the yard then slowly shook his head. "I've been asking myself that same question, but this is the address he gave his office. Guess we'll find out in a second or two." He jangled the keys then slipped one into the lock. The door whipped open before he could turn the knob.

The young woman on the other side glared at them and Zach didn't doubt she was one step away from calling nine-one-one.

"Can I help you?" A frosty challenge, not a question.

Vic fumbled for his identification then flipped the wallet open for her to see. "NCIS. Sorry, ma'am. We were told this was Teddy Sunline's house."

Her brown eyes flicked to each man. "It is. Is Teddy in some sort of trouble?"

"Who are you, ma'am? His girlfriend?"

She blinked wide, confused eyes. "Janie Brighton. I'm Teddy's maid."

"Perhaps we should go inside." Vic didn't give her time to decide. He cupped her elbow and maneuvered past the front door.

The interior was as striking as the outside—neat, orderly, comfortable. An aura of welcome embraced Zach. He hated to disturb that by watching Vic tell the woman Teddy was dead.

She crumbled into tears before their eyes, emitting a low, animal wail that reverberated through the house as she doubled over, clutching her midriff. The cry brought another woman to the sliding patio doors at the rear of the house. Dressed in jeans, T-shirt and gardening gloves, she shoved back the door and raced to Janie's side, her eyes accusing.

"What did you do to her?" She wrapped her arms around the smaller woman.

Janie fell against her. "Oh, Helen, Teddy's dead."

Helen stiffened. Her shocked gaze demanded answers. "Who are you people? What are you doing here?"

Taken aback, Vic closed his jaw and attempted to gain control of the situation. "And who are you, ma'am?"

"Helen Moore."

Zach leaned forward. "And let me guess… You're the gardener."

"I am. What's it to you? What's happened to Teddy? What are you doing here? And I'm going to ask you again… Who are you people?"

In painstaking detail, Vic gave up enough information to satisfy the women without compromising anything about the case. While Janie cried, Helen remained stone-faced, defensive and angry.

"I suppose you've come here to search for clues," she said when Vic was finished.

He nodded. "That was the plan. Although from the looks of the place, I'd say anything we'd find has been wiped clean."

Helen jerked up her chin. "Janie's very good at her job. If you're half as good at yours, you'll find Teddy's killer." She squeezed her friend's shoulders. "Come on. We need to call the others."

"Oh, Helen, what are we going to do now? Who's going to take care of us?"

"Hush now. It'll be all right. We'll take care of ourselves. That's what Teddy was trying to help us learn." She flashed angry eyes at the men. "You'd better dust the phone for any fingerprints now because I'm getting ready to use it."

"To call…?" Vic waited for her to fill in the blank.

Again, her eyes narrowed. "The others." The flat tone of her voice discouraged any further questions.

Others turned out to be more women. One by one they showed up at the house. Each performed a separate task for Teddy Sunline — cook, laundry, mechanic, car washer, groceries, mending, even one to tend the hundreds of houseplants. Sunline had never had to lift a finger for himself. His harem saw to his every need.

Vic gathered them all on the patio. There, the other two agents separated them out one by one for interviews. The answers were all the same. Teddy Sunline was a wonderful friend. No, they didn't think it was odd that he wasn't around. They usually never saw him during the week because of his work schedule, and he was to have spent the weekend at Big Bear Lake.

All took offense when asked if they had more than a friendship with Sunline. Every one of them hesitated over, *'Do you know of anyone who would want to harm Teddy Sunline?'*

The reply was always a firm, *'No.'* But the delay, the glance away and the whitened knuckles said otherwise. Whatever it was they were hiding, they weren't divulging it to military investigators.

Zach found himself wondering if Claudia's presence would have made a difference. He flirted with the idea of calling her, then he remembered she was at the gym. Asking her to come help them now might generate friction over why they'd left her behind in the first place.

Vic tapped his pen on his notepad when the last interview was complete. "Well, that was a wash. I've never seen a more tight-lipped bunch of women. Look at them out there, all huddled together and none of them saying a word except to plan the memorial service."

Zach glanced their way. *Like frightened animals.* No, that was the wrong analogy. Animals fought when frightened. 'Frightened children' was more appropriate.

"Maybe we'll find something around this place." Zach clicked his tongue. "Although I think the best we can hope for is clues, not evidence."

Vic agreed. Zach read disillusionment in his face. Dead ends, everywhere they turned.

Leaving the two agents outside to finish interviewing, Zach and Vic split up, each selecting a specific portion of the house. A cursory search revealed nothing — as they expected. There were three bedrooms — one Sunline's, one devoted to an extensive computer setup and the third a guest room.

"All ready for company," Vic said.

Female company. Closets and dresser drawers were filled with women's clothing — all in various sizes. The adjoining bathroom was decked out with soaps, shampoos and bubble baths. Both clothes and toiletries were neatly organized and indicated a wide range of tastes.

"Still nothing to tie Allison Sinclair to Teddy Sunline." Vic shoved the dresser drawer closed. "The place looks like a damned used clothing store."

"Actually, there's nothing to tie him to any of these women other than their 'employment'." Zach drew air quotes. "You know, Cruz Montoya mentioned Teddy was teaching Allison how to use the computer. Maybe that's an avenue we can explore."

Vic pinched the bridge of his nose, closing his eyes in exasperation. "If there is, I wouldn't know how to find it. I'll have to get the computer guys up here."

"Not necessary." Zach pivoted on his heel and ducked into the middle bedroom. With a tap of his finger, he brought the electronic beast to life.

He felt Vic watching from the doorway, either afraid to approach or in awe of the process. The screen demanded a password.

"Hah." Vic barked out a short laugh. "Get past that, cybernerd."

Zach's cockiness faded. The damn thing wanted Sunline's password. He drummed his fingers on the wrist support then peeked under the mousepad.

Julieanne.

With a broad smile, Zach punched in the name. "There we go."

"Impressive," Vic muttered. "How did you know to look under the mousepad?"

"That's where my password is at work."

Vic ventured farther into the room until he hovered over Zach's shoulder. "So, what do we have?"

"A lot." Zach scrolled through the icons. "Bills, taxes, Christmas card lists, property inventory."

"What about e-mail?"

Zach clicked on the mail icon. Ten messages waited for Sunline—the most recent from Allison Sinclair. With one touch of the Enter key, the message appeared on the screen.

I'm scared.

"Not exactly the confession we were hoping for, is it?" Vic asked.

"No, but this is." Zach scrolled down the letter. Each piece of correspondence had been tacked to the previous one, building a lengthy history of the relationship between Teddy Sunline and Allison Sinclair.

Starting at the bottom and working back up, the words between the two left no doubt a friendship existed. Yet there was nothing obvious enough to show something more—only hints, until an alarming series of entries appeared.

We really should delete the rest of this e-mail. This is getting huge.

I know, but your words give me strength when I really need it.

It happened again, didn't it?

Yes.

Why don't you call the MPs?

They'd never believe it. He's got them fooled.

You can't continue to live this way. Leave. There's room for you here until you can get on your feet.

I can't. I'm afraid. There's no hiding from him. He'll find me and it will be worse than ever.

So you stay with him until he kills you? You think it won't happen. My sister didn't think so, either. When she realized the truth, it was too late for her. It's not too late for you.

Days passed without an answer, then Allison sent him two words.

I'm pregnant.

Sunline's response?

Leave now! *If your life means so little to you, think of the child. He'll hurt you both!*

Still, it had taken another month of coercion and planning before Allison had made her decision. The date had been set. Both Zach and Vic knew the outcome of that particular evening.

Disbelief... Stunned and absolute disbelief... That was what struck Zach when the last word sank in. He wanted to protest, say it was all a lie. Sinclair was a stellar officer, up for promotion to general. To be guilty of spousal abuse would be the kiss of death to his career. But would he have killed Sunline to keep his nasty secret quiet?

It didn't seem plausible. None of it. In the back of his mind, Zach wondered if it wasn't a sympathetic bid for attention on Allison's part to attract a lover. The only problem with that scenario was the circle of women huddled on the back patio.

Vic drew back. "Shut it down. I'm taking the computer as evidence."

"You don't believe what's hinted at here, do you?"

"I don't believe or disbelieve. My job is to get to the truth. This is the first solid lead I've got, even if it does open up a lot of other questions."

Business-like and professional—qualities Zach had seen in Vic when they'd first met weeks ago. That was why he'd liked the man at first. It was Claudia's appearance that had made those traits in Vic disappear. As long as Vic kept his lascivious nature under control where she was concerned, Zach could respect him. But one step over that line...

"What do you intend to do, take each woman aside and grill her about Allison and Sunline?"

Vic shook his head. "They're too tight-lipped, especially when they're talking to military investigators. We'll leave that up to your beautiful wife."

Zach shoved away from the desk and faced Vic full on. "She has a name. It's Claudia. Not 'toots', not 'cutey', not 'babe', not 'good-lookin'. *Claudia*. Use it."

Vic's jaw set. He gave a deliberate nod then walked from the room, snapping instructions to the other two agents.

So much for professional respect. They returned to Zach's house in silence.

The rock-and-roll music reached them first when they walked up to his door — one of his favorite CDs. He pushed open the front door with Vic on his heels.

Miss Kitty lounged on the back of the sofa, tail twitching in slow motion along with the rhythm. In the center of the room, oblivious to everything else, Claudia danced in wild abandon.

She was gloriously free, filled with grace and uninhibited and hot as hell in a pink tank top and shorts. Had they been alone, Zach would have jumped in with her. Would have moved from one dance to another until he could sweep her into his arms and they fell into an embrace that matched the pace of the song.

Then she whirled around and stopped, flushing. Her gaze fell to them...to him. For a brief second Zach thought he caught a flash in her blue eyes — a longing, a desire, a look he could only describe as intimate, and his body responded, his cock swelling to painful proportions.

Embarrassed, Zach glanced at Vic. The lust in the man's eyes mirrored his own and he felt a surge of anger. He strode to the stereo and clicked the switch off. Silence descended.

Miss Kitty hopped from her perch. He expected his usual greeting from her. Instead, the cat twined herself around Claudia's legs. It was the last indignity he intended to take.

"If you're done prancing around, we've got work to do." He regretted the words and tone the instant they left his mouth, but it was too late to take them back.

Claudia didn't know whether she wanted to cry or break the nearest lamp over Zach's head. An hour before, she'd agonized how to set aside her fear of rejection and build a life with him. Now she wondered how she could have been so stupid, so blind.

Zach was arrogant, obnoxious and too handsome for his own good, not to mention hers. When she compared him to the man standing beside him, there *was* no comparison. Vic's gaze stripped her naked every time, making her feel soiled. His whole manner screamed that he believed he was God's gift to women. But Zach...

Just looking at him, no matter how annoying he could be, swelled her heart with affection. True, they'd had their run-ins over the last five years, yet in these few days with him Claudia had seen a different Zach, caring and protective. She'd seen him champion her against Franklin's snide comments and play with Miss

Kitty. He'd kissed her as she had never been kissed before, fiercely...passionately.

And the sex. Let's not forget the sex.

As if she could. It was etched on her soul.

"Charming as usual." She raised her chin, fighting the litany of barbs that had been so much a part of their relationship. If she wanted to move beyond that, someone had to make the effort. "Welcome home, *my love*." She laced the words with sarcasm. He deserved that much after his prancing remark.

Zach fought a smile and shoved a document into her hands.

"What's this?" A silly question, since she could obviously see it was an e-mail printout. "Between Allison and Teddy?"

Zach flopped onto the sofa and motioned Vic to the recliner. "You might want to read it back to front."

Claudia shuffled the papers in that order and tucked herself into the far corner opposite him. "Where did you get this?"

"Off Sunline's computer."

"Sneaking around behind my back. I should have known." She tsked.

While she scanned the correspondence, Zach told her about the search of Sunline's house and of the strange collection of women. With each word she read and heard, Claudia's heart broke a little more. When she was finished, she set the last sheet with the others on the end table and closed her eyes to shut away the tears.

"You believe her." Vic's statement was to the point, but his tone was laced with disbelief.

Claudia forced herself to look at him. "Of course, I believe her. Why shouldn't I?"

Zach leaned forward, resting his forearms on his knees. "Because her husband is one of the most well-respected officers in the Marine Corps. He's guaranteed a promotion to general. You've met him. You've seen what a great guy he is. How could you possibly —"

"We don't live with him. We don't sleep with him. We only see what he wants us to see." She massaged the ache in her forehead. "I suppose Julieanne is Teddy Sunline's sister?"

Vic shrugged. "That's as good a guess as any. There's nothing in his record to indicate he had a sister. His next of kin is listed as his parents, and he left his life insurance to a niece and nephew. The Casualty Assistance Officer is picking up Sunline's relatives at the Palm Springs airport today. I'm going to have to find a way to interview them tomorrow."

At least the man has some semblance of a conscience. "Now what?"

Zach's deep sigh brought her head up. It was Vic who answered.

"Those women are a tight-lipped bunch...except with each other. We thought if you attended the funeral on Friday, they might see you as less threatening — a friend of Sunline's. You could get some information."

"So, infiltrating the Officers' Spouses' Club is out?"

"I imagine they'll come for you soon enough." Zach chuckled. "From what I've been told, they are a persistent bunch. No telling what you might learn from them."

"Since you've already met Allison, this might be another, better way to earn her confidence," Vic told her.

"In the meantime, I would hope you'll start looking more closely at her illustrious husband," she told him.

Vic stared at his hands. "As you've already pointed out, if he is guilty of spousal abuse, we can't find out what the Sinclairs want to hide. It's up to you."

"Then I'd better get started." They swiveled their heads in her direction as Claudia walked to the front door.

"Where are you going?" Zach asked.

Without turning, she replied, "To see if Allison will go to Teddy's funeral with me." She swung open the door, letting it click shut behind her, and started across the lawn.

Claudia's distress was no act. All she needed to do was remember Allison shying away from the other women, scrubbing the car with a toothbrush, dusting the pile of the carpet with her fingertips. It all made sense—spousal abuse. Put in context, it made Claudia ill. By the time she reached Allison's door, tears obscured her vision.

The door opened on the first ring.

"I'm sorry to bother you again."

Allison placed herself in the entrance. The oversized camp shirts she always wore made sense. She was pregnant and hiding it from her husband. "Is something wrong?"

Claudia gave a solemn nod and a tear slipped down her cheek. "I've just learned that an old friend of mine is dead. While I was at the gym, I called his office to tell him I was living here now, and they told me he had been killed. This is all such a shock. I don't know any other women in the area, and I needed someone to talk to."

"Of course." She hesitated before opening the door wider. "Come in. I'll fix us some tea...unless you'd prefer coffee."

"I don't want to trouble you. I just wanted to talk."

"No trouble. I always have a pot of tea ready."

The house was as immaculate as it had been earlier that day. Knowing what Allison would go through once Claudia walked across the carpet made the trip agony. She forced herself to be nonchalant, then fought the urge to fluff the damn pile herself to keep Allison from having to do it later.

The kitchen was gold and white with yellow checked curtains dancing in the gentle breeze that came through the window. Allison waved Claudia to the table with matching placemats then set out the pot of tea and two china cups.

"I'm sure it was quite a shock to hear of your friend's death," she said as she poured.

"All I can feel is guilt for not having kept in better touch with him. It wasn't hard to do, to send a quick e-mail. I kept putting it off. Then, when I learned we would be coming to Twentynine Palms, I figured I'd surprise him. Only I was too late. Now Teddy's dead."

Allison paused, her cup halfway to her lips. The only sign she was shaken was in the rattle of the cup as she slipped it back onto the saucer. "What did you say his name was?"

"Teddy Sunline. Did you know him? He was a gunnery sergeant somewhere here on base."

For some reason, Claudia expected Allison to deny it. Instead, she let her gaze travel to those bright curtains and gave a nod.

"He was a member of Marty's command. He was helping me learn how to use the computer. I didn't realize..." She closed her eyes and gave a quick shake of her head. "I heard he was killed. I couldn't believe it myself. Odd that you would know him, too. Such a small world."

Allison's emotions were held in by a strength of will that broke Claudia's heart. All Claudia knew of the man were the few words he'd uttered before he died. Yet the more she discovered, the more she wanted to bawl her eyes out.

She slipped her hand over Allison's. It was small, dainty, fragile. When she squeezed it, Allison grabbed hold. *A lifeline? A cry for help?* She couldn't ask, couldn't force the issue now, but with time, maybe... "Let's go to the funeral together. It's at one o'clock Friday afternoon." She pressed Allison's hand in parting comfort. "He's helped so many of us."

For the first time, fear clouded Allison's eyes. Then she nodded. "Pink roses. We mustn't forget the pink roses...for Julieanne. You do know about Julieanne, don't you?"

Claudia forced a smile. She felt like a fraud. "Don't all of us who have been in that situation? Yes, Teddy would like that we remembered. He loved his sister so much."

"Very much," Allison choked out. "We'll have to buy them soon, before the florists in town run out."

"I'll take care of it for both of us."

Gratitude eased the tension in Allison's face. The sound of a car in the garage brought it back. She leaped from the table so suddenly that her cup toppled over.

"Marty's home early."

Claudia grabbed her hand and pulled her back into her seat. "Relax. We're just two new friends visiting."

"But I haven't started dinner...and the carpet."

"I'll fix the carpet. You've been invited to my house for dinner."

"No. No. He won't accept."

"But you don't know that."

"Yes, I do. He knows I know that. Please just go. I'll see you in the morning."

There was little more Claudia could do. Reluctantly, she eased away. "I'll fix the carpet for you on the way out."

Heartbreaking. That was the only word for it, and it was all Claudia could do to keep from dragging Allison to her house. A whirlwind of emotions surrounded her. She was angry at herself because there was no way to help the woman and confused that Allison continued to live in terror year after year. But nothing matched her fury at Sinclair for abusing her and the Marine Corps for elevating him to a god-like position of authority.

She forced a casual stride home. Sinclair could be watching every move she made. Nothing could give away the anger boiling beneath her skin. She was ready to pummel the first object she could get her hands on.

The front door opened when she reached it. Judging from Zach's scowl, he'd most likely guessed she was upset. To his credit, he said nothing when she stepped inside. She bypassed Vic when he stood and headed for the kitchen. Miss Kitty hopped from her perch atop the sofa and followed.

Grabbing a head of lettuce from the refrigerator, Claudia smacked it on the counter and whipped out a butcher knife. From the corner of her eye, she saw Zach braced against the door frame watching her. Vic didn't have the sense to give her space. He came to a stop much too close, fists on his hips.

"Well? What did you find out?"

She whacked her target into bite-sized pieces. "Julieanne is Teddy's sister. Allison admitted to knowing Teddy. We're going to the funeral together."

"Did she tell you that her husband beats her?"

She tossed the knife onto the counter and whirled around to face him. "You insensitive son of a bitch. You'd better go back to life school and do a little more studying. This is a secret even her own parents wouldn't know and you expect her to confide in me in less than a day? She's a victim, not a murderer." One stride forward brought her nose-to-nose with him. "I don't need her to tell me. I saw for myself the fear in her eyes when he came home today and she hadn't started dinner and the carpet was unfluffed."

"Sinclair's home?"

Claudia parked her hands at her waist. "Yes."

Vic muttered a curse. "How the hell am I going to leave here now? He can't see me."

He stomped toward the living room. He was the last person she cared to spend any more time with and knew Zach felt the same way. For the integrity of the investigation, there was little choice.

While Vic paced a circuit in the living room, Claudia mutilated the rest of the lettuce. Zach stepped up behind her, slid his hand over her wrist and relieved her of the weapon.

"Put the lettuce away for now. We could probably both do with a good run. You set the pace. I'll do my best to keep up," he added with a small smile.

Five minutes later they were pounding the pavement in unison, taking out their frustrations and confusions in a desert ridge run that wound up being five miles.

But it wasn't until well after midnight, once Vic had finally slipped away under the cover of night, that the one question bothering them was broached.

"Do you still think Sinclair's innocent?" Claudia stroked Miss Kitty's fur, taking in the comfort her flexing paws and deep purr provided.

Zach traced the pattern in the arm of the sofa. "I honestly don't know what to believe at this point. He's a top-notch Marine officer, yet everything you pointed out earlier today is true. We can't know what they are both determined to hide."

"I keep straining to hear if anything is going on at their house."

He snorted. "In a neighborhood this close, you'd think someone would have heard long before now."

"Maybe they did and didn't dare interfere because of his rank."

Sinclair was the highest-ranking officer in their base housing area. He could easily ruin anyone of lesser rank with a word or suggestion, a criticism whispered to the right person. Just like in the big cities where victims were raped and mugged while frightened witnesses looked the other way, Sinclair got away with spousal abuse.

"Would you report him?" she asked.

"Yes." Zach answered without hesitation.

He took Miss Kitty, set her on feet then leaned closer to Claudia. "Shopping with her tomorrow's going to be tough for you."

"I can manage."

Zach chuckled. "I don't doubt that for a minute. Just don't do anything crazy, like try to whisk her away from it all. I don't want to be scraping up your remains from the desert floor."

"I won't be foolish. I've been in tighter situations than this."

"Maybe so, but none more emotional."

He was right about that. Everywhere she turned, Claudia was assaulted by one emotion after another. Dealing with them drained her more than she thought possible.

"I didn't appreciate your prancing remark this afternoon."

Surprise covered his face. Before he could defend his actions—whatever they might have been—she went on.

"I love dancing. I love dancing in my home. I love dancing naked." *Let him absorb that image.* "This is my home for now. I will be comfortable in my home. I will dance. You will not be snide about it."

"I'm sorry." He had the courtesy to look shamed. "I've never seen that unrestrained side of you before. I loved it. Seeing you made me want to join in. Then I saw Vic ogling you, all eyes and tongue hanging out. It pissed me off. Made me jealous. Unfortunately, I took it out on you."

The admission of jealousy swelled her chest. "I can't help how men ogle me. I don't care for their lecherous glares either, but I'm not going to ugly myself up as a result. I also don't like being the brunt of your sharp tongue when I haven't done anything wrong. Don't do it again."

"I'll do my best. Would dancing naked with you help make up for my idiocy?"

"Though I am intrigued, the very thought of seeing you naked is so distracting that I doubt we'd get much dancing done." She slipped her arms around his shoulders, stretched out and pulled him atop her. "Let's skip to the main event."

He slid his hand under her tank top and traced his thumb over the underside of her bra. "In that case, let's move to the bedroom."

She hooked her leg over his thigh and rocked her pelvis over his erection. "What's wrong with sex on the sofa?"

He muffled a groan and pressed his cock against her pussy. "I don't have any condoms down here."

Claudia traced her tongue over his lips. "I'm on the pill. We don't need to use them." It was the biggest leap of trust she had to offer.

There was a moment where Zach was very still. She wondered what was going through his mind. Did he understand what she was doing? Did he trust *her* enough to go without?

"In that case, we're definitely moving to the bed." He pushed to his feet and extended his hand to her. "I do *not* want cum stains on my sofa."

She laughed. "I had no idea you were so fastidious."

He raised one finger. "Not a word about my lack of housekeeping skills."

"Heavens no." She rolled her eyes. "I hope I'm still in the mood by the time you turn off all the lights and check all the locks. At least the curtains are already closed."

"The doors are locked and I don't give a damn about the lights right now." He clapped his hands. "Come on. Let's go."

"Your execution leaves much to be desired. I feel the mood fading." She stretched out, wiggling into the cushions, and grinned. "No. I want to have sex on the sofa. It's all I dreamt of all day."

"Seriously?" He jammed his fists on his hips. "Why are you messing with me?"

She giggled. "Because you're fun to mess with." Claudia ran her finger up his thigh and over his erection. It thrummed beneath her touch, demanding more attention. "Your friend wants to play with me. I'm crushed that you don't."

"I *do*. In bed, not on my sofa. It's new."

"Ooo, then it deserves to be properly broken in. Now I'm definitely having sex right here. If you want it to remain in pristine condition, I guess you'll have to get inventive"—she jerked her hand away when he reached for it—"because I'm doing this with or without you."

He narrowed his eyes and crossed his arms. "I dare you."

"I love a challenge."

Claudia reached under her top to unhook her bra, her gaze locked on Zach. He followed her actions as she pulled her tank top and bra off. She cupped her breasts and thumbed her nipples, trying not to laugh when he licked his lips. Spreading her legs, she brushed her hand down her body until she reached her pussy. His nostrils flared, his jaw tightened and he twitched when she slid her hands into her shorts. She dragged them and her panties down slowly, monitoring the leap of his pulse at his throat. Once free, Claudia tossed the garments aside.

"This shouldn't take long"—she slid her fingers over her clit—"then we can wander up the stairs and do"—she feigned a gasp of pleasure—"whatever you wish." She added an enthusiastic groan to her repertoire. "You may have to carry me because—oh, God, that's good—I might be too spent."

Zach scooped her up. Claudia squealed with laughter. "Oh, dear God, don't kill us going up the stairs."

"We're not going that far." He set her down behind the sofa and pushed her facedown. "Don't worry, Princess. I'll be quick."

"Now that's a fib and we both know it." Straightening, she draped her arm up and around his neck, turning until their lips met. Then, when they parted, she said, "There's nothing quick about the way you fuck me. I've never been more thoroughly loved on in my life."

"Damn, baby." He covered her mouth and danced his tongue with hers.

Her breathing grew ragged. One part of her wanted to take command and strip Zach bare. The other part was content to see what his next move would be.

He broke the kiss and guided her back into place over the back of the sofa. "I missed showering with you earlier."

He ran his hot hands down her back until he reached her ass. He clamped his hands over her buttocks and kneaded his fingers deep. Heat crawled over her body and slithered to a stop between her legs.

"Keep your hands out of your pussy while I undress. I want to be the one who makes you come this time, though the thought of watching you rub off drives me insane."

"Later?" Her voice quivered with the word.

"We'll put it on our to-do list. It's getting longer by the minute."

"The list? Or your cock?"

He chuckled and rubbed his erection over her ass. The rough jeans made her want to spread wider, but she remained as he'd requested. He kissed his way down her spine then stepped back. The whisper of clothes coming off filled her senses. Heat from his body radiated her way. Then he was naked and hard — so hard. He wedged his cock between her legs, maneuvered her higher and slipped inside.

Claudia jerked her head up on a gasp. She flexed her fingers into the cushion to keep from stuffing them in her pussy. Zach leaned over her, dropping kisses across her shoulders. He pulled her hair to one side and nibbled her neck. She moaned and turned her head to one side to give him better access. He wasted little time slipping his fingers to her clit.

"This feels so damn good." His words feathered over her ear. "I've never been bare inside a woman before."

The words coiled around her heart. She shut down the analysis in her head and let herself feel everything — physically and emotionally.

"This might be quicker than I intended." He nipped her earlobe. "But don't worry, sweetheart. I'll make sure you're coming with me. I'd never leave you hanging."

He started a slow glide in and out. The intensity built with every sweep of his fingers. Claudia fell into his rhythm, straining with him to both come yet hold on for him. Their movements grew frantic the closer they neared the goal. He grew harder inside her, hotter. Her clit felt like a marble. Then she was there, as was he, exploding as one and letting the climax wash over them.

Before she could recover, Zach scooped her in his arms once more and headed for the stairs. She draped her arms around his neck, cuddled deep and clamped her lips tight to keep from telling him how much she loved him.

Chapter Nine

They stood peeking through a slit in the bedroom drapes, enjoying their morning coffee while they monitored the Sinclair house for activity. He'd gunned his 1965 Corvette Stingray once already this morning as he'd backed down the driveway then took off. Fifteen minutes later he'd returned home, only to leave again. They were biding their time, waiting to see if he was gone for good.

Zach loved the fresh-washed scent of Claudia standing in front of him, all tucked up nice and cozy. Forty-five minutes before, they'd blotted each other dry after a shared shower that had left him feeling decadently spoiled. He hoped she felt the same way.

He slid his hand over her hip and kissed her temple. She sighed and snuggled closer. His heart begged him to tell her that he loved her. His brain told him to shut the fuck up and not risk losing a good thing. There had to be logic in there somewhere, but he'd be damned if he could figure it out. Things were great between them and the sex was life-altering. But when this was over, she'd go back to her life in San Francisco. Wasn't that the point of all this? She was trying to save her job. He was trying to keep her. Together they were trying to find a killer.

"Have you ever lived with anyone before?" he asked.

She turned to him. "Never. You?"

He took a sip of his coffee and kept his gaze on the house across the street. "Nope."

"Ever been in love?" she asked.

With you. Zach didn't think that would wash well. "I really don't know how to answer the question. I've always been very goal-oriented and determined. Once I know what I want, I go for it, no matter how long it takes. Women—no, that's not fair. People in general don't understand my diligence. Many have told me to give it up."

Yet here she was, in his arms. Goals were worth fighting for.

"You don't need those types of people in your life." She turned toward the window, sipping her coffee.

"Have you ever been in love before?" He wasn't sure he wanted the answer.

"I was." She shrugged. "It didn't work out."

"The guy with the hair issue?"

"That would be the one."

"Asshole."

"That was the general consensus of opinion."

Zach didn't want to know any more. "You seemed restless last night."

"Sorry if I kept you awake," she replied. "I kept rehearsing subtle questions to ask Allison and made plans if we're followed or harassed. I'm not looking forward to this."

"I can't say I blame you. I wish I could come up with a good excuse to go along. But then, she'd never speak up."

"No, she wouldn't. Do you think it's safe to go over there now?" she asked. "I do," he replied. "Besides, he's the one who thought of this shopping trip. You have every reason to be there."

"Somehow that doesn't make me feel better.

Claudia handed him her cup and left. Zach remained at the window, monitoring her progress down the steps and through the door. A long, loose stride took her to the Sinclairs' doorstep. She pressed the doorbell but received no answer. He could see the furrow between her eyebrows, even from this distance. She punched the button again. Allison opened the door only as far as the chain lock allowed. From what he could see, the room beyond was dark.

She and Claudia talked for a few moments then Allison shoved a piece of paper through the opening to Claudia and shut the door in her face. She stared at the paper, crumbled it in her hand and headed back. Anger tightened her features. He braced himself for a door slam that didn't come, but she did take the staircase at a hard, pounding run.

"What was her excuse?" he asked when she stepped into the room.

"She says she's sick."

A flash of movement in the backyard caught his attention. Cruz Montoya hurried away. "Hmm...I'll bet. Look."

Claudia ducked in front of him. "Who's that?"

"Major Cruz Montoya." He let the drape fall into place and cocked his head her way. "*Now* what do you think of our alleged victim?"

He didn't stick around for her answer. He had to cut across six yards and two blocks before he caught up with Montoya. Zach didn't bother to pass off his breathlessness with the excuse of being out for a run. It was time for answers.

He grabbed Montoya's car door before the man could shut it, wedging himself in the opening. "Sir, I think it's time we talked."

"Do you have a break in the investigation?"

"Not one I expected."

"Then perhaps you'd better run it through NCIS." He curled his fingers around the handle.

Zach refused to move. "I need to talk to you. I'd rather it be privately without witnesses for now. But if I have to, I'll spit it out right here."

Montoya scanned the area. "I don't see anyone. Spit it out."

"Very well, sir. Are you having an affair with Allison Sinclair?"

"She *is* a beautiful woman, isn't she?" Montoya made a second attempt to pull the door closed.

Zach shoved hard with his hip, widening the gap between door and car. "I saw you leave her house a few minutes ago."

Anger flickered across the man's face. "I thought I made it clear that Allison was not to be involved in your investigation. There's no reason to stake out her house."

"I'm trying to uncover a murderer. All my clues lead to her — and now to you." He met Montoya's narrowed glare. "Forbidding me to look out my windows isn't within your authority. So, tell me, sir...are you an accomplice or her next victim?"

"Aren't you taking a chance in either event? Now stand away from the car, Captain. I have to get back to work." He gave another tug at the handle, harder this time.

Zach held the door in place. "Is her husband knocking her around?"

It was a dangerous path to take, but Zach felt he was safe enough. Montoya's silence had been bought the instant he'd been caught sneaking out of the Sinclair house.

"Your job, Captain Taylor, is to investigate the murder of Gunnery Sergeant Sunline, not delve into the personal lives of Allison and Martin Sinclair."

"For some reason, Major Montoya, I get the feeling both events are related."

For the first time since Zach had cornered him, Montoya broke eye contact. Staring at the range of low mountains behind the base, he tapped his index finger on the steering wheel. Zach held his breath, wondering what strategy he could use next if this last one failed. Finally, Montoya released his hold on the door.

"Get in. I'll buy you a cup of coffee."

Bingo. Now, maybe, he'd get some definitive answers. Unfortunately, the coffee shop was also one of the most popular places on base for breakfast. Zach and Montoya tagged on to the end of a long line, then each had to endure a round of pleasantries when one acquaintance after another greeted them.

It was a place to see and be seen. Even the Commanding General had his hair cut in the barbershop next door. It wasn't exactly the type of atmosphere for obtaining confidential information.

By the time they had their coffee, a corner booth was empty. Zach claimed the coveted seat, forcing Montoya to sit with his back to the door. Montoya nestled the insulated paper cup between his hands and locked his gaze with Zach's.

"Colonel Sinclair was with me the night Sunline was killed. It was my job to keep him busy while Teddy got Allison away from here." His voice was a controlled whisper, just carrying across the green tabletop.

"So you *knew* Sinclair was abusing her."

Montoya didn't waste a nod. He merely stared. "I couldn't believe it myself when Teddy told me. I didn't *want* to believe it. But the proof was there once I looked—once Teddy forced me to look. He asked for my help and I gave it to him."

"Why not report Sinclair to the general?"

"Spousal abuse is a dirty little secret. You'd be surprised at the lengths some women go to hide it. It's almost like they can't admit it to themselves, much less someone else. Allison's no different. She thought it was her fault. It took her a long time to admit to herself that she had to leave. Teddy was willing to help but it had to be on her terms. She asked for silence. We agreed."

Those terms had gotten her nowhere. "You seem to know a lot about the subject."

"Only because of Teddy. Each one of those women at his house is a victim saved from a life of domestic violence. He offered them sanctuary, escape. He tried to help them build confidence, self-esteem, even invented jobs for them when they couldn't find work elsewhere."

Zach only had one question. "Why?"

Montoya narrowed his eyes. "His sister was killed by her husband, beaten to death while their two children slept in the next room."

How can I respond to such a revelation? The thought made Zach's stomach churn. He'd been raised in love and tolerance. A bad day for him meant whiny clients, forced marches and pesky telephone solicitors.

Even when Claudia had voiced her suspicions, he hadn't truly believed. *Why?* Because the entire concept of abuse was alien to him? Or because he couldn't believe that the Marine Corps would harbor such a high-ranking individual?

Zach sipped his coffee. It went down sour and burned his stomach. He slid the cup aside.

"Now what happens to Allison?"

Montoya snorted. "What do you think happens? The poor woman is scared to death. She's convinced that Sinclair somehow managed to kill Teddy and now she's in fear for her own life."

"And her baby?"

The man's back stiffened as he drew away. "How did you know about that?"

"Is it yours?"

"You little prick," Montoya spat out through clenched teeth. "Who the hell do you think you are?"

"I'm an investigator...investigating."

"No, it's not mine," he snapped. "Allison is a lady. She has class and dignity. The baby is hers and Sinclair's. Now how the hell did you find out?"

Zach hesitated. *What do I have to lose at this point?* "Agent Brownell and I found e-mail between her and Teddy stored on his computer."

Montoya covered his eyes with his hand. "I pray to God Sinclair doesn't think to go through the e-mail on her computer."

"Do you think he killed Teddy?"

He shook his head. "I'm telling you, Captain, that there's no way. He was with me. Teddy had a lot of friends, but helping those women made him a lot of enemies, too."

"Their husbands and boyfriends."

Montoya pulled his head up. "I doubt you'd ever get any of the women to admit it. From what Teddy told me, most of them have come a long way, but to have them actually stand up to the men in their lives or turn them in for murder... Well, that's an awfully big step."

That would explain their silence when he and Vic had been at Sunline's house. "I think I may be able to get an in with Sunline's group."

"It's going to have to be a good one. Think of these women as survivors of war."

Zach smiled. "Trust me. They'll be giving up their secrets before they realize it."

Montoya tipped back the rest of his coffee. "Now...let's discuss Allison. Since you've discovered Sinclair's abuse and the baby from your snooping, do you intend to do something to try to help her?"

"I've got an angle on that, too. I trust I can depend on your help in whatever we do?"

Montoya's dark eyes never wavered. "As long as it means Allison will be safe."

* * * *

Claudia worked out her frustration on a stair climber. From the glowers Kiki-Kurt kept giving her, she must have been on the machine too long. She didn't care. She'd do anything to keep her thoughts directed away from what was bothering her. The trouble was that it wasn't working very well.

Had she been pulled into Allison's lies? Claudia prided herself on her ability to read people. So where had she gone wrong with Allison? Or had she? Had she misread what she thought were signals of abuse? Had she not wanted to believe Allison was capable of duplicity and possibly murder? If that were the case, then why had her skills failed her?

The answer came too quick for Claudia's comfort. She saw her own obsessiveness in Allison's actions and was determined to prove there was no correlation between them. Her conscience raised its head and struck.

And what compulsion are you fighting?

Claudia wanted to scream at herself, to throttle the thoughts that nagged at her. She'd decided to go to the gym, realizing that a hard workout was her solution — a compulsion in its own right. But before she could find the solitude of physical exercise, the first contingent of the Officers' Spouses' Club had arrived at her house.

The four ladies were a determined bunch. They'd been pleasant enough, but they'd wriggled their way into the house, scanning their surroundings with the sharp eyes of appraisers, despite the smiles plastered on their faces. They'd commented on the furniture and the neatness of her home, cooed over her few attempts at decorating. The only way Claudia had been able to rid herself of them was to offer her place for a coffee that evening.

Her peace had been temporary. The minute she'd scooted her company out of the door, the body shop had called. Hanson wanted the accident kept off his record and was now willing to foot the bill for all the repairs. Claudia didn't give a damn, as long as her car was repaired as fast as possible. Though she was tempted to report Hanson anyway, she'd never been that petty. It was more evidence of her stress escalating to the boiling point.

Finally, she'd been able to leave the house. The stair climber had beckoned. She'd been on it ever since and was no closer to resolving her questions than when she'd begun.

"Enough." In one firm yank, Kurt pulled the power cord from the wall. "You've been on that thing for over an hour. What are you trying to do to yourself?"

She wanted to cry, to crumble to the floor right there and weep. "I lost track of time. That's all."

"Hmm. I doubt that. I've never seen anyone more determined. To do what, I can't say."

Claudia forced a smile. "I have to host a coffee this evening at my house for the Officers' Spouses' Club. I could use a friendly face there. Do you suppose Kiki can come?"

"Nice change of subject." He smiled and leaned in. "Kiki would love to come. All those women putting on their best faces. What great practice. Do you think they'd suspect?"

Claudia laughed at how easily he'd slipped into Kiki's voice. "They might."

"Even with the birdseed?"

"Even with." She cocked her head to one side. "But why keep them guessing? Why not let them in on the secret?"

He pulled back, eyes hooded with suspicion. "What do you mean?"

Mischief danced around her, making her feel giddy. "You come as Kurt and let them make you into Kiki. It'll be a great ice breaker."

"How are they... Why would they..."

Claudia waved his concerns away. "I'll take care of everything. You just bring your Kiki stuff with you. It'll be fun. Trust me."

"Yeah...right."

Zach's jaw stiffened. He didn't know what alarmed him more — the good-looking guy whose head was bent a little too close to Claudia's or that Sinclair's gaze followed her from across the room.

He stayed in the doorway where he knew the sharp daylight silhouetted him from behind, making it impossible to see who he was while he kept tabs on the two men. He recognized the first as one of the facility's new managers. A friendly sort...helpful. His name was Kurt. Judging from the lack of animosity on Claudia's face, she didn't consider him a threat to her. That was good enough for Zach. The last thing he felt like dealing with was another Vic eyeballing her.

Sinclair was another matter. The fact that he was here at all was disturbing enough. True, it was a public facility open to everyone on base. But all things considered, it seemed odd that the man would choose this time, this moment, to come here. If he were here to exercise, all his efforts should be focused on the dumbbells he was curling, not on Claudia. Sinclair's gaze rarely left her.

By now Sinclair would know Claudia was taking Allison to the funeral. He might have discovered Zach was the investigating officer. Hell, he might have even found a way to read the preliminary report from NCIS — although he doubted Vic was that naïve. Now, he was here, watching. *Studying his next victim?* The thought made Zach more nervous than he cared to be.

Despite Cruz's assurances that Sinclair had been with him the night Sunline was killed, Zach couldn't count on that to make the man innocent. Sinclair had too much to lose. His entire powerful career rested on secrecy. Having Allison leave him would raise too many questions. Having a Marine junior to him assist in her escape only increased Sinclair's vulnerability to exposure and left open the possibility of blackmail.

Now another threat blocked his path to greatness, and Zach didn't doubt for a minute that Sinclair would go to any lengths necessary to protect himself. For Claudia, Zach guessed he would try intimidation. If that was the case, Sinclair was wasting his time. Claudia could stand up to the best of them. For himself and Cruz, their own military careers would be threatened. Somehow the evidence had to be obtained and presented to their commanding general before that could happen.

Without breaking visual contact from his target, Sinclair set aside his weights and walked toward Claudia. Zach didn't like it. There was nothing pleasant in his eyes. Zach cut across his path, getting to Claudia first.

Kurt pointed toward him. Claudia turned, a smile frozen in place. But it was her eyes that took Zach's breath away. They sparkled. She was happy to see him. His heart soared. Kurt leaned close and told her something. Claudia grinned and elbowed him in the ribs. Kurt hip-butted her and walked away. *She's certainly gotten friendly with him fast.* Jealousy shoved his joy aside.

She blotted the sweat from her face and neck with the edges of her towel. The closer Zach got, the more his heart raced and his cock hardened. There wasn't a thing he could do to hide it. *Why should I? She's my wife, damn it. My very hot and beautiful wife.*

"I see you got my note," she said when he neared.

"I did. Nice move, having that coffee at the house tonight. I'll make myself scarce and go hang out with Phillip and Rowan."

"Chicken."

He laughed. "If you're done, I thought we could grab some lunch."

"It will have to be a quick lunch. I have to prep for tonight's coffee."

"I can help with that," he told her.

She slung her towel over her shoulder. "Wow, you might be a keeper after all. I need to run back to the house and shower. It shouldn't take more than thirty minutes."

"They have a locker room. You could shower here."

Claudia cringed. "I didn't bring a change of clothes. Plus, I hate the idea that someone else might see me naked."

"Because they'd be consumed with jealousy and melt into a pool of goo at your feet?"

She laughed and shoved her fingers in his chest playfully.

Zack said, "For the record, I hate the idea, too. Male or female. I want you to be for my eyes only."

The flush in her cheeks deepened, making her irresistible. Zach kissed her. When he pulled away, it was to find a smile lighting her eyes.

"Well, if it isn't the newlyweds."

His erection wilted at the sound of Sinclair's voice. Claudia glanced over Zach's shoulder. He turned, positioning himself between her and Sinclair. His sweat-dampened T-shirt clung to his chest. He was aware it outlined every muscle. Zach's heart went out to Allison. *Is this a friendly greeting or a hint of a warning?* Zach refused to take chances.

"How are you today, sir?"

"Tolerably well." His eyes glazed over as his gaze drifted to Claudia. "I understand you and my wife are going to a funeral tomorrow."

"Yes. Teddy Sunline's. He was a friend of mine long ago"—she slipped her arm around Zach's waist— "before I met Zach. He helped me survive a difficult period of my life. Imagine my surprise when I learned Allison knew him, also."

Sinclair's demeanor shifted. Zach could see it, could feel it and it scared the hell out of him.

He caught the edge of Claudia's T-shirt behind her and tugged it in a pathetic attempt to warn her from saying anything more. "Yes, sweetheart, Teddy was a member of the colonel's command. Now, if you'll excuse us, sir. We're off for lunch."

He steered her toward the exit.

"What was that about?" she whispered when they reached her rental.

"You were right about Sinclair."

Tension left her body. Her eyes widened. "I was?"

Zach nodded. "I'll explain at the house, where we can't be overheard."

She glanced over his shoulder again and he knew Sinclair was watching. She brushed her hand up his chest and kissed him. For show or because she wanted to, Zach didn't care. He wrapped his arm around her waist and pulled her flush against him, deepening the kiss. She broke hold but not contact.

When she clicked the locks open on the car, he got the door for her then leaned in once she sat.

"Last one home is… Well, you know the rest."

"I'll be right behind you."

"Ooo, I do hope so."

She danced her finger down his chest, paused at his waistband then traced his zipper. He caught her wrist before she moved to the ridge swelling his jeans.

"We could save a lot of time by riding together. I can come back for my Jeep after we eat."

Her smile widened. "I like your thinking."

"Hands to yourself?"

"Where's the fun in that?" She winked and patted the passenger seat. "Time's wasting. You can tell me all on the ride home."

He used the cover of her car to adjust his erection then walked around to the other side and got in.

* * * *

She *hadn't* been imagining things or assigning characteristics to Allison in order to appease her own conscience. *I was right.* Agony was listening to confirmation of the proof of Allison's abortive attempt to leave.

She made the turn into their housing area, hands clenched around the wheel. She wanted to give the woman friendship and sanctuary, yet the very nature of their relationship was based on lies. Somehow that had to change. This was no longer about a news story. This was about saving someone's life.

"We have to find a way to help her."

"Agreed, but we also have to get solid proof he's knocking her around. *And* proof that Sinclair killed Teddy."

Puzzled, Claudia screwed up her face.

"You can't believe he's guilty of that, too, can you? How? You said he's got an air-tight alibi—one of the men trying to help Allison leave. I think I'll have to agree with Major Montoya about this one. If Teddy was really responsible for helping all those women, any of their men could have killed him."

"My mom always says to trust your instincts, no matter how crazy they seem. Mine say the man did it. I just haven't figured out how."

He parked his elbow on the armrest and stared ahead, most likely running possible scenarios through his head.

His was logic Claudia couldn't argue with, especially when her own instincts had screamed that Allison was suffering in an abusive relationship. The *how* part of it was a bit tricky. Only one thing came to mind.

"Could he have had an accomplice?"

"Anything's possible, Princess."

She thought it funny how a term she'd hated had turned into an endearment.

"Luther from the body shop called," she told him. "Hanson told Luther that he wanted to keep the insurance companies out of this and that he would pay for all repairs and have them expedited. Luther also indicated that from the look of Hanson's car, he would have expected to see more damage on mine. He said he was surprised I wasn't in the hospital, that Hanson's car was pretty dinged up and he'd seen trucks hit deer with less damage."

"Fuck," he muttered. The answer they'd been seeking was right before their eyes and had been all along. Hanson, who'd fed them false clues… Hanson, who'd covered up the damage Sunline's body had caused to his car by plowing into Claudia's. "No wonder he doesn't want to involve the insurance company. It would mean a thorough investigation," Zach said. "We've got to be careful here. I need to call Vic."

He pulled his phone from his pocket.

Claudia pushed open the door. "When you're done, you *could* meet me in the shower."

Zach chuckled. "You do realize that once this investigation is over and I have to go back to the office, I won't have the luxury of answering your siren's call to passion."

Claudia laughed. "Then I'll do my best to not lead you too far astray." *How can I? Once the investigation is complete, I'll be leaving. Right?*

Chapter Ten

Zach took off before the first contingent of spouses descended upon their home. Unfortunately, he'd driven all the way to Phillip and Rowan's only to find their minivan gone and cursed himself for not calling in advance. Still, he took a chance that one of them was there. He wasn't disappointed. Before he could rap his knuckles on the door, Rowan had it open.

"This is a surprise," she said with a smile.

He stepped into the welcome embrace of their home.

Nestled in Rowan's arms, baby James tried to focus on the new face. Zach dusted his finger against the chubby cheek, laughing when James turned to suckle it.

"I was just getting ready to nurse him, if you don't mind."

"Oh...uhm...sure."

Rowan laughed softly. "Relax. You don't have to watch if it makes you uncomfortable. I'll sit with my back to you."

"It's...uh...I mean..."

She shoved him toward the living room. "Sit and tell me what's up."

"I needed a place to hang out. Claudia's hosting a coffee for the Officers' Spouses' Club tonight."

"Better her than me." She settled into her chair and draped a towel over her shoulder and the baby's head, shielding James from his view. Contented suckling sounds emerged from under the cover.

Zach's tension eased. It was a natural thing. He didn't know why it bothered him. This was Rowan, for crying out loud. She was as close to him as a sister — closer, in fact. They worked together every day.

"You just missed Phillip. He and Ian went to a soccer game. If you hurry, you might be able to catch them at the park."

He stretched back. "No, thanks. Phillip will put me to work helping him coach."

"How's the investigation going?"

Rowan listened while he gave her a detailed account, fueling him on with questions to clarify her perspective of the events. She knew Vic Brownell through her stepfather. Both men worked for Naval Criminal Investigative Service as agents. She respected his work. Zach decided it was best to withhold his and Claudia's personal opinion of the man.

"Was Vic able to find anything at the body shop?"

Zach shook his head. "The car was freshly detailed, even with all the damage."

"Surely a search warrant—"

"Would tip our hand."

"What about probable cause?"

"For now, Hanson says he was in a car accident. We're his witnesses, since Claudia was the other party."

"How convenient." Her tone was heavy with sarcasm.

"Very." He nodded. "Vic managed to convince the body shop owner to delay work on Hanson's car for a few days. Now he's trying to find someone who can verify that the car was wrecked before our accident and find anyone who might have seen Hanson at the time of the murder."

"What about Allison Sinclair?"

Zach's rambling narration squealed to a stop. "What do you mean?"

Rowan shrugged her free shoulder. "Where was she when all this was going on? She's got a small window of opportunity to leave. If she's finally taking the steps to go, she's not going to sit around the house waiting for Sunline to pick her up. Besides, neither of them is going to risk him coming to the house. I'd guess that she met him somewhere. She may have even been in his car or nearby when the accident occurred."

"I doubt that. There wouldn't have been any place for her to hide."

"How do you know? You don't know where he was killed. You only know where he was dumped. Her car could have been left somewhere else, and she was hiding in the bushes. You said she was a small woman. Maybe she was hiding in the back seat. What about fingerprints in Sunline's car?"

"The front was wiped clean."

"The *back*, Zach. Picture it. If she's there, she's scared to death. She'd be curled up on the floor." She glanced down at the baby. "Excuse me. Someone's ready for bed."

Zach went over the information that neither he, Claudia nor Vic had considered. While Rowan tucked the baby in, he called Vic to share her theory with him. The silence on the other end lasted so long that Zach knew Vic was mulling his words over with serious consideration.

"I'll have the team check the back seat again," he replied. "We still need to get Allison's fingerprints without alarming her or tipping her off to our suspicions."

"I'll take care of that."

Claudia was the next call. Zach hated to interrupt her with all those women arriving, but if Allison was in their house, there might not be another chance to get her prints.

"I need you to try to get a good sample of Allison's fingerprints," he told her when she picked up the phone.

"I hope you intend to enlighten me later."

The purr in her voice sent his blood racing. "You can bet on it, Princess."

He ended the call with a broad smile then jumped in surprise when he turned and found Rowan calmly appraising him from the threshold.

"This is certainly a change."

Zach shrugged and returned to the couch. "Yeah, well, we're getting along much better now."

"I see."

Two little words that said a ton. Zach watched Rowan saunter back to her living room chair. She was going to elaborate, no doubt of that. She'd never been one to mince words.

Rowan tucked her feet under her then turned that penetrating bright-eyed gaze his way.

"I think I'm in love with her," he admitted in a rush of breath.

"You *think*? Zach, you'd better know." She braced her elbow on the arm of the chair and leaned forward. "Claudia isn't one of your normal trysts. You're dealing with a fragile heart here."

"I know that."

"No, you don't know that. Until a week ago, you and Claudia couldn't bear to spend more than five minutes in the same room alone with each other. Any conversation between the two of you bordered on war. The constant sniping and undercutting was enough to drive any innocent bystander insane. Now you love her? Excuse me... You *think* you love her."

"You don't get it."

He didn't know how to make her understand. How could he tell her after all these years, after all that had passed, that he'd been in love with Claudia all this time?

"Things have changed."

"Why? Because you're horny?"

Zach sighed and plopped his head on the back of the sofa. "That's not fair. You're making this sound like a dirty act of sex instead of a tender one."

Rowan kept her voice calm and level. "Listen to yourself. This is still sex to you — sex, not making love. There's a huge difference. I know you enjoy being with women and I suspect you *are* a considerate and thoughtful lover, but this is so very different. My God, this is Phillip's sister. Your best friend's sister."

"I know that," he snapped back. "But she's also an adult and she's going into this with her eyes open."

"Don't get angry with me, Zach. I'm only trying to help."

"I want to be with her."

"With her — or will any woman do?"

When he glanced away, she went on. "Ask yourself what this is about. Are you just wanting sex? God knows Claudia must be. Other than your drunken Las Vegas tryst, I don't think she's been with a man in ten years." She pressed her lips together, as if she had said too much.

He wanted to call bullshit on her statement. Claudia knew her way around a man's body.

"Why?" he asked.

Finally...Rowan's turn to fidget. Zach touched her arm and held her in place. "I've got to know."

She closed her eyes and slowly nodded. "Yes, I suppose you do."

Focusing once more on him, Rowan patted his hand. "She was left at the altar, in front of a church filled with hundreds of people, the pillars of society and her peers. She was so brightly in love with Todd Willoughby that the stars couldn't outshine her. Her father deemed it an unsuitable match. He was furious. A Stuart marrying a cop?"

Zach gave a humorless chuckle. He'd met Donald Stuart once and that was more than enough for him. "What did Donald do?"

"He didn't want Claudia married to a blue-collar worker. Claudia refused to listen. With both her mother and Phillip backing her up, Donald was losing — and you know how he hates to lose."

"So I've heard. Go on."

"He offered Todd an obscene amount of money to call off the wedding with the condition that he do so in a manner that would publicly humiliate Claudia. Donald felt that once subdued, Claudia would be under his control once more. End of rebellion."

"But it backfired."

"Yes and no. God, Zach, she was a beautiful bride — vibrant, innocent and so happy, truly like a princess. The pain on her face when Todd turned and walked away from the altar crushed me. You can imagine what it did to Claudia. But she never cried in front of those people, never uttered a sound until everyone had been sent home with apologies and she could collapse in Phillip's arms. He said he'd never seen anyone so grief-stricken. He wanted to kill the guy *and* Donald. The next day we helped Claudia pack and moved her to San Francisco. She's barely spoken to her father since and has guarded that heart of hers like a priceless gem — with good reason, as you can see."

Yes, he could see, and hearing about it was enough to break *his* heart.

Rowan squeezed his hand. "You need to ask yourself what this really is. If this is a whim, it won't be Claudia you have to deal with — or Phillip, or even me. It will be your own conscience."

Zach rubbed the furrows from his forehead. There was no easy way to handle this. Either way, Claudia was going to be hurt. Things had already gone too far to prevent that.

* * * *

Claudia listened to the gaggle of women, adding little more than polite responses to the conversation. As a rule, she abhorred social functions, even when they served a purpose. This gathering was nothing more than a gossip-fest and she had no doubt she'd be the main topic of discussion come morning.

She watched Allison with the other women. Here there was no evidence of the frightened, abused wife.

Allison's façade was in place, presenting the illusion of a fairy-tale life and solid self-confidence.

The young wives were the most pathetic, trying to fit in with the older crowd, not quite knowing how to do so, afraid the wrong word would damage their husbands' careers. There had to be a common ground to ease the way, something that would make them all equals and disperse the traditional roles of leader-follower, mentor-protégé.

That was where Claudia had hoped Kiki-Kurt would come in, only he still hadn't bothered to show. She couldn't blame him. She was asking him to unmask himself. Once this night had passed, he could never be out again as Kiki. Everyone would know his true identity. His job on base might also be jeopardized.

The doorbell rang. No one noticed. Smiling, Claudia excused herself and answered it.

Kiki stood on the other side. Actually, it was a pale imitation of Kiki. Where before Kurt might have passed as a woman, tonight he looked like a man in drag.

He spread his arms wide. "What do you think, doll?"

Heads turned their way. Eyes screamed *intruder alert*. A few fanned their fingers at their throats and feigned silent gasps.

Kurt breezed in. "I'm sorry. I didn't know Claudia had guests tonight. But I've got to say I've never been happier to see a bunch of women in my life."

Then he surprised her further by telling them who he was. Several nodded. They knew him from the gym, but confusion remained.

Claudia linked her arm through his as she had an idea. "Kurt and I went to college then tried our hands at acting in Los Angeles. When I caught up with him here, I told him about a juicy role coming up."

He shrugged, following her lead. "I'd have to dress as a woman. Obviously, I'm not very good at it. Auditions are next week. I hoped Claudia could straighten me out, give me some tips." He held up a small tote bag.

Claudia lifted her eyebrow his way then faced the ladies. "Sounds like a good project. Anyone willing to give this poor man…woman a hand?"

Laughter rippled through the group. All Claudia had to do was step aside and let them have at him. Two women snagged his arms and pushed him into a chair while a third slipped the wig off his head. Not bothering to hide her amusement, Claudia nestled into a chair and sipped her decaf.

This was the icebreaker she'd hoped for. Bound in a common goal to transform Kurt, the women tossed aside age and husbands' ranks. Slowly Kiki emerged in raucous form. Gales of laughter shook the rafters, especially during his inaugural steps in a pair of impossibly high heels. Even Claudia had to dab at the tears in her eyes. Kiki-Kurt was a true clown.

Allison's guard was also down. Although she didn't help in the makeover, she still managed to get caught up in the fun. She drank down the last of her lemonade then set her glass aside.

Claudia snagged it and the empty glasses and cups around her.

"Refills, anyone?"

"I'm sure Claudia could be persuaded to let me add a splash of Kahlua to anyone's coffee," Kiki announced in a high-pitched voice.

More laughter followed, as did a rapid flurry of acceptances.

"We won't be long." Kiki prissed into the kitchen, setting them off once more.

Claudia snapped open a small paper bag and slipped Allison's glass into it.

"Fingerprint sample?" Kiki asked.

Claudia nodded. "Vic Brownell is waiting for it."

"Why don't you let me take it to him?"

"Nonsense." Claudia folded the top down. "He's right on the corner."

"But you're the hostess. You shouldn't leave."

"And you're enjoying their company much more than I am. If they happen to notice I'm gone — and I doubt they will — tell them Miss Kitty mangled a lizard and I had to give it proper burial outside." She ducked out the door before Kiki could argue the point.

The chill of the night air embraced her, reminding her of home. By tomorrow at this time, she'd be back in her San Francisco apartment, if only temporarily. But what about after this? Pining away for Zach? Living with Zach? What was supposed to have been a joint venture to find a killer and put Claudia back in the good graces of her news station had spiraled into something more. Change was coming and she didn't know whether she welcomed it or feared it.

There I go, analyzing everything again. Why can't I take things as they come?

All she had to do was take a chance. *Why is that so hard?*

The question weighed on her mind as she set out to rendezvous with Vic. She saw him in the distance, dressed to run as he'd said he would be. He was in the periphery of the streetlight where his presence was nothing more than a hint among the shadows. But even with that camouflage, she saw him tense and move toward her.

Too late Claudia caught a flicker of movement to her right. She spun around and into the full force of a tackle, knocking the wind out of her. The glass shattered. Her attacker pressed his knee deep into her back, nailing her to the ground, and for one horrifying moment, Claudia thought he meant to rape her. Just as suddenly, she was free, yet still unable to move for lack of air. He jammed his foot on the bag and disappeared into the dark. All she saw of him was his white sneakers, stark against his black attire.

She sucked in a breath and shoved her forearms under her, shaking off a wave of dizziness.

Vic skidded to a stop beside her. "Good God, Claudia, are you all right?" He wrapped his arm around her shoulders and helped her sit.

She nodded. "Fine, I think." Nothing felt broken, but she was still in shock. "The glass is broken. I'm pretty sure it was deliberate. Did you see who it was?"

"Too dark for details—male, slight build, average height. He targeted you. You can see right into your kitchen. Anyone looking saw what you did. I was watching you. I should have been watching the house. Zach is going to fucking kill me."

He slid his arm around her waist and helped her to her feet. "Let's get you back to the house before something else happens."

She accepted his help up then shrugged his arm away. "How do I explain you?"

"I'll take care of explanations."

It took a few steps before Claudia found sure footing. Annoying as Vic could be, he stayed by her side to catch her if needed.

"Do you think he's watching?" she asked.

"I doubt it. He did what he set out to do."

Break the glass. What else would he have done if Vic hadn't shown up?

She glanced at the house. Kiki-Kurt was watching them from the window. She felt like an idiot for not realizing anyone could see inside. *Not one of my better moments.* She'd been too invested in getting the fingerprints for Zach. Kiki rushed Claudia the minute she and Vic crossed the threshold.

"What happened?"

He...she—*Damn, am I'm ever going to get this right?*—caught Claudia around the shoulders with one arm and dragged out a kitchen chair with the other. She sank into it and hugged herself against the shivers now attacking her.

The other women rushed into the room. In minutes, she was surrounded. Their presence didn't help.

"I was out jogging and saw someone rush her," Vic told them. "Probably one of those kids we've been having problems with."

Cries of outrage and disbelief followed. Claudia waved the women back with shaking hands. "I'm all right."

"This happens much too often. Damn teenagers have no respect anymore," one woman declared.

"No telling what they were up to this time," another said. "I don't know what's gotten into them. Maybe gang influence from Los Angeles."

"Whoever it is, by the time the MPs get here, they're long gone. They're getting rougher all the time. How much longer is this going to go on?"

Voices rose in angry agreement, each clamoring to be heard.

Kiki curled a heavy hand over Claudia's shoulder and squeezed, reassuring her. "I say it's time for action.

Why not start a self-defense class for women? Nothing fancy, just the basics. I'd love to teach you. We could use Claudia's backyard." She leaned closer to Claudia.

Heads bobbed around the room.

"Done and done." Kiki clapped her hands and shooed everyone from the kitchen. "Now, ladies, it's been a wonderful night, but Claudia does need to settle a bit. Before you go, let's gather in the living room and make a list of everyone interested in the class. Names, e-mails and phone numbers, please."

Vic waited until the women migrated out under Kiki's careful administrations then he pulled out a chair and sat across from her. "Police, hospital or Zach?"

Claudia didn't bother to look his way. "You *are* the police, and I don't think I need a doctor." She flicked pieces of grass off her cream linen pants, now ruined. "What do we do about fingerprints?"

Vic jerked his head toward the living room. "I think your friend is taking care of that."

Claudia glanced in the direction indicated. Kiki had Allison picking up all the dishes and remaining glassware.

"Do you want me to call Zach?"

She glanced down at her grass-stained blouse. "I think he's going to notice once he walks in the door. I'd rather he hear it from one of us first. He's at my brother's house. Just be careful not to let Phillip know what's happened or he'll start a ruckus. It could make this investigation very public."

She might have well asked for a pot of gold to drop from the sky. Vic spent less than a minute on the phone with Zach. The expression on his face when the call ended warned Claudia of her fate. Ten minutes later

Zach, with Phillip at his heels, stormed through the front door and across the sea of women straight for her.

"What happened?" they barked in unison.

Claudia shushed them, darting warning glances to the room beyond.

Zach stomped toward the living room and swung open the door. "Party's over, ladies. Everyone out."

Allison was the first to leave, darting out the door as if the devil were after her. The others wasted no time following. Only Kiki remained.

Zach jerked his arm toward the exit. "I said 'everyone'."

Kiki smiled and shut the door. "Relax. I'm one of the good guys. I'm on your side."

He didn't argue. Instead, he barreled Claudia's way. "What the hell happened? Are you all right? Did he hurt you? Did he *try* to hurt you? Did he say anything? Do anything?"

The questions came so fast all Claudia could do was stare at him.

"Calm down," Vic told him. "I was there. I had her back."

She didn't think it was wise to tell him that Vic had been too focused on her to see the man in the first place.

Zach cupped her face in his hands. "You could have been killed."

She pressed her hands over his. "I'm okay."

"No, you're not. Your shaking. You've got grass stains all over your clothes and dirt on your face." He wiped his thumb across her chin. "Your hair is all kinds of crazy." He brushed his hand over her hair, cupped her head and kissed her forehead.

From the corner of her eye, she watched Phillip step back. Zach did the same, breaking contact.

"Pack your things. You're going back to San Francisco first thing in the morning and you're staying there."

She forced herself to her feet, to stand up to him, despite her fear and her desire to go where it was safe. "No. We're too close to finishing this. We have an agreement."

He caught her shoulders in a gentle hold, lifting her to her toes, pulling her to him. "Not to have you killed. God only knows what could have happened if Vic hadn't intervened. I couldn't bear it if anything happened to you."

Claudia stared into his eyes, seeing for the first time what was really there deep within those brown depths. *Zach cares for me.*

A veil of tears obscured her view, but she refused to look away. He *cared* for her. *For how long? Years? Months? Days?* It didn't matter. It only counted that he did.

She watched the worry lines fade. His hold loosened, but he didn't let go.

"Don't cry, honey. Please don't cry." He gathered her in the shelter of his arms, whispering soothing words of comfort.

"Well," Phillip said, "I guess I'll be going. I can see I'm not needed here. Claudia, I'll pick you up right after tomorrow's funeral. It's a long drive to San Francisco. Make sure you're ready."

"I should be going, too," Kiki said, gathering her things.

"Not yet," Vic replied. "I need to get those prints you collected for me, but first I need yours and Claudia's fingerprints to eliminate those possibilities."

"Get them and go," Zach told them. "We've had enough for one night. You can dust the glasses in the morning. You've been here overly long as it is. I'm sure you can come up with some disguise to sneak into the house tomorrow."

Zach paced the floor while Vic collected her prints and Kiki's, agitation clear in the set of his tight jaw. In all the years she had known him, Claudia had never seen him so distraught and she prayed she would never cause him worry again, while she gloried in the fact that all this posturing was because he cared for her.

She waited until Zach shut and locked the door behind Kiki and Vic. He braced himself against it, his shoulders hunched as if he could keep all the bad away by standing there.

Claudia dusted her hand across his back. "Zach, I'm fine. Really."

"You could have injuries you don't realize. I need to check your body. Get your clothes off."

If he wasn't so rattled she would have called him on the lousy attempt to get her undressed. She indulged him instead. Zach paced around her.

"Your elbows are scraped."

Claudia rolled her eyes and kicked off her sandals. The slacks were next. She left them in a puddle at her feet and stepped out.

He jerked his finger toward her knees. "You've got an abrasion on your left knee."

She glanced down. "Barely. It's not even bleeding."

He grunted and continued his circuit. With a beleaguered sigh, she unbuttoned the sleeveless top and let it slide from her shoulders.

"Good God! You've got a fucking bruise the size of my hand in the middle of your back!"

He bent her over the back of the sofa. Puffs of hot breath skittered over her flesh as he probed around the injury.

"Did he hit you?"

"He put his knee in the middle of my back."

"I'm gonna kill the fucker. Come on. We're going to the emergency room. He could have injured your kidneys, cracked a vertebra or a rib. Are you in any pain at all?"

"No." *But I am getting a little irritated.* She righted herself and cupped his face. "Enough, Zach. Stop."

His arms were rigid at his sides, fists clenched, but she could feel him shaking.

"You could have been killed. I want you to pack and leave in the morning. Hell, I'll take you back to San Francisco myself right now."

"I'm going to that service, Zach."

"There's no need for you to go to that funeral and certainly no need for you to continue with this investigation. Once it's over, I'll give you the information you need for your story."

"Someone needs to save Allison."

"And who's going to save *you*?" he shouted.

"You are," she whispered and kissed him.

His lips were stiff and unyielding. Claudia refused to back down. She pressed her naked body against him, dropped kisses at the corners of his mouth, nipped at his lips and traced her tongue over the seam. His cock was hard between them, thrumming to be free of his jeans. She trailed one hand down his chest and cupped his neck with the other.

He capitulated with a deep groan, taking control of the kiss — of her. He clamped his arm around her waist and his hand over her ass, kneading her butt cheek and writing into her. She hooked her leg over his but it was Zach who tumbled them over the back of the sofa and onto the cushions.

His sneakers *thunked* to the floor. Claudia grabbed the hem of his shirt and pulled it up. He broke the kiss long enough to lose the shirt then fumbled to unleash his cock.

"I swear I'll die if I don't get inside you right now."

The roughness in his voice was coupled with emotion. He sounded close to tears. Fear did that to people—made them desperate. She was right there with him, helping him shove jeans and boxers down his hips. His erection sprang free, tapping her hot spot. She sucked in a breath.

"I know, baby. I know." He kissed her hard and plunged inside.

She met the lash of his tongue with equal measure, digging her nails into his back. He growled into her mouth and shoved his hand to her clit. Claudia locked her ankles over his calves and tried to keep pace with the frantic strokes he beat into her body. All she could do was hold on and enjoy the ride, feel the pleasure build, fight the tears emotion seemed to insist they share.

They came as hard as they'd fucked. Pants for breath shuddered through them. Zach pressed his forehead to hers and brushed his thumbs over her breasts. Too soon he was pulling away, righting his clothes. She braced herself for the argument to begin again. Instead, he extended his hand. She slipped hers into his and let him help her up.

"I'll lock up and get the lights. It's been a hell of a night. We should probably try to get some rest."

He kissed her, squeezed her ass and stepped away.

"Well, I could use a glass of wine," she told him.

"Pour me one, too. Hell, bring the bottle to the bedroom and we'll just split the sucker. I'll get your clothes."

"Throw the outfit away. I don't think I can ever wear it again without thinking..." she said.

"Trash it is, then."

They met up in the bedroom. Zach uncorked the chardonnay, divided the bottle between two huge wineglasses and gave one to her. They sipped propped against the bed pillows. The wall he'd erected might be invisible, but she could see it all the same. She'd be damned if they were going to go to sleep with this sucker looming over them, but she wasn't ready to discuss it, either.

Claudia set her glass aside, rolled his way and kissed him. He draped his arm around her shoulder and deepened it until the blood beat in her ears. She broke the kiss and traced the curve of his mouth with her thumb. Zach set his glass on the nightstand.

"Rowan told me about Todd," he said.

She hadn't been expecting that. She and Rowan were going to have words. "Rowan has a big mouth."

"Would you have ever told me?" he asked.

"He's irrelevant and has been for ten years. He's the past." *You're the future.*

He sighed and combed his fingers through her hair. "You aren't like any other woman I've ever known."

"I know." She circled her finger over his nipple. "I'm your Ice Princess."

"Yeah, you are."

The words felt like a caress against her cheek. He rolled her earlobe between his lips. She arched her neck and he dragged his mouth down the column. Heat flushed her skin. She wiggled her fingers down his body and found him hard and ready.

He caught her hand before she could wrap it around his cock and pulled her atop him. She sighed the instant his hot mouth covered her nipple. He teased it to a tight peak while piercing jolts of pleasure danced through her. She cupped his head and held him in place. He sucked hard, drawing animal-like cries from her throat. All she wanted was more.

He dusted his hands across her stomach, around her hips and over the backs of her thighs. She spread herself wider, inviting his fingers between her legs. He caught her hips instead, urging her higher until she straddled his chest and her pussy was perched near his mouth. He parted her labia with his thumbs, exposing her hard clit. Watching her, Zach flicked his tongue around it.

She cried out and braced her hands against the headboard, writhing her hips in time with the lazy circuit he made around her clit, through her folds and back again. Her climax was building to such a fierce intensity, Claudia swore she'd die if she didn't reach it soon. She fucked his mouth, trying to take control. Zach evaded her each time.

"You come when I'm ready, Princess," he growled, then latched on to her clit and sucked the orgasm right out of her.

She thrashed against his hold, coming a second time before he rolled her onto the bed and stabbed his cock deep. He dragged her legs over his shoulders, pressed his thumb over her clit and fucked her hard until she came again…and again.

His face contorted into the pleasure-pain that heralded his climax. He seated himself with a final thrust, finally letting go. Then he sagged over her body, kissed her as if his life depended on it and made her want to do it all over again.

Chapter Eleven

She could have been killed.

The words continued to run a torturous circuit through his head at dawn, paralyzing him with images of her lying dead. And for what? A stupid investigation anyone could handle. What did he care about the Sinclairs? Or about who was responsible for killing a Marine he didn't know? Claudia could have lost her life. The horror of that possibility ate a hole in his gut.

Through the night, he'd craved physical contact with her, being deep inside her, holding her against him, watching the pleasure wash over her face and ripple through her body to his. Even as they'd lain sated in bed, wrapped in each other's arms, he'd been hard again and desperate to have her.

Each time he'd pulled Claudia to him, it had felt like his heart was going to explode. Telling her that he loved her couldn't happen. She'd never leave if she knew. He needed her as far away from here as possible, needed her safe. It seemed there was only one way to get her to leave. Zach would have to destroy it all.

Years down the road he knew he'd think back on this moment with regret. Claudia would always be the love of his life that had gotten away, the one he'd forced away. But at least he would know she was alive and hating him, not dead because of an investigation they never should have gotten involved with in the first place.

Claudia stretched awake against him. Zach longed to draw her atop him and fuck her till he dropped. Instead, he tossed back the covers and sat up on the edge of the bed.

"Going for a run? If you wait, I'll go with you."

Sleep made her voice husky, just as passion did. Zach's cock filled, begging to be appeased.

"We need to talk."

The sheets rustled behind him.

"Claudia… This is a mistake."

The bed sagged. He felt her body heat as she neared, but it didn't prepare him for the rush when she wrapped her arms around him. Her nipples were pressed hard against his back, devastating him by slow degrees.

"You mean going for a run when we really should be doing *this*?" She slid her arm around him and fisted his erection.

With a muttered curse, he whipped around, pressed her to the bed and plunged inside her heat. She met him stroke for stroke as he pounded out his passions over and over again—for his pleasure, for hers. It was wild, crazy, intoxicating. He was lost. He was in love. Claudia had to leave.

Zach shoved away after they'd come and slid from the bed. There was no choice. He hated himself for what he was about to do. He wouldn't, *couldn't* look at her. Reaching for his clothes, he laid it all out.

"You should start packing. You and Phillip have a long drive ahead of you."

She sighed. "Phillip's at work, and I have a funeral to go to."

He turned around. It was a mistake. She was propped up on her elbows gloriously displayed with nothing left to the imagination. He dragged his gaze to her face. Another mistake. One eyebrow was arched. A cross between humor and challenge was in her blue eyes.

"It's over, Claudia. There's nothing more for you here. I want you gone."

Claudia cocked her head to one side. *He's afraid. Zach Taylor is afraid.* But of what? Their newfound closeness? Or for her safety in this mixed up investigation?

If it was the former, Claudia could understand it well. She'd spent ten years avoiding any relationship, five years avoiding him. There was no telling where this was going, but she knew what they had was good and she wasn't about to let it go until it had fulfilled its course naturally.

Had she not made this resolution, perhaps she would be the one dressing with haste, ready to head for the hills. She wasn't ready to say her good-byes to Zach but neither was she going to corner him into admissions he was unwilling to make. In time, with patience, he would come to her.

But if it was fear... Well, Claudia had a big surprise for Zach. They'd come too far in this investigation to give up now. Like it or not, she intended to see this through to the end.

Peeling back the rumpled sheets, she draped her legs over the side of the bed. Using her toes, she hooked up the edge of her robe from the floor, arched one leg in a slow-motion tease then pulled it on. From his wide-eyed expression, her bait had worked. She had his full attention.

"We've established the fact that Allison and Teddy were friends. We've established the fact that she's upset by his death. We've established the fact that she's a victim of spousal abuse. Knowing all those things, don't you think she at least deserves the right to say her final good-bye at his funeral?"

Zach looked away.

Claudia pressed on. "I've given her that chance. She can't go unless I take her. Her husband would never allow it. We can't take that from her. We just can't."

She walked on to shower and let him think. He wouldn't protest her stand. She knew that. But she also knew that he would still insist she leave once the funeral was over. She'd give him that victory, but she had no intention of staying away, no matter how big an argument it created. They had a job to do. They had a relationship to explore. And, dammit, they were going to do to both. He'd wanted to know the real Claudia, now he'd found her. He was going to have to learn to deal with her.

Zach was gone by the time she came down the stairs fifteen minutes later. Claudia wasn't surprised. He'd delivered his ultimatum and expected her to follow through. Let him think he had won. Once lulled into a feeling of complacency, she'd show him the full force of her feelings.

She heard dishes rattling in the kitchen and found Vic dusting each cup, glass and plate meticulously for fingerprints. His disguise this morning? Plumber.

"The neighbors are going to think this is the most run-down house on the block. Coffee or tea?"

"Coffee's fine." He kept working.

"Were you able to get an angle on Hanson's car yet?"

"A few people have indicated they saw damage before the accident with you. He passed it off as a fender-bender. It's still not enough to elicit a search warrant. Right now, it seems like a big coincidence. Besides, what motive could he possibly have to involve himself with the Sinclairs to the extent of murder?"

"Maybe hitting Teddy was an accident?"

He shook his head. "Nope. It was murder."

Claudia mulled that over. "Could he have been struck hours before he was dumped? That would eliminate Sinclair's alibi."

"He wasn't dead that long."

"He...uh...was alive when I found him."

Vic didn't bother to look up. "I was wondering when you'd get around to telling me that. Yes, I know. Phillip told me. Anyway, that theory makes more sense than implicating Hanson. He has no motive. No one's *that* loyal to his commanding officer. Do I get that coffee now?"

"Sure. How's it going there?"

He shrugged a shoulder. "We found several good prints in the back of Sunline's car, very low on the seat and door and the same ones on the outside of one of the back doors."

"Have you found a match?"

"Hard to say at this point for sure. We need to process them. Your friend did a good job here, though. Allison's print is the topmost on all these dishes."

Claudia poured the coffee then sat to watch. "It's hard to think of the poor thing, huddled in the backseat while her friend was killed. She was probably scared to death she was going to be next."

"If she's been living under the umbrella of abuse all these years, she probably lives in fear of death every day." Vic *tsked* and shook his head. "It's ironic, isn't it? She's afraid to stay, afraid to leave and the first attempt to escape her fear is reinforced by her rescuer being killed. You've got to wonder why she took the chance in the first place."

It wasn't hard for Claudia to figure out. "Her baby. She wouldn't want to subject her child to that lifestyle."

"You can bet she won't try again."

"I don't know. She was brave enough to chance it with Sunline. She might be again if the right person and opportunity approached her. The baby's life will be more important to her than her own."

Vic turned around, mug clutched in his hand. "I'm beginning to think Zach's right in sending you away. You try something crazy like trying to spirit Allison out from under her husband's nose and you'll wind up dead, too."

Claudia took a slow sip of her coffee then lifted her gaze to his. "First of all, Vic, I'm not a child to be shipped off and Zach will find that out soon enough. Second, my conscience won't allow me to sit back and not help her. I just need the chance."

To her surprise, he tilted his head and gave her a slight bow. "Then I'll try to see you get it. Just keep me informed and I'll watch your back." He raised his mug. "Here's to the liberation of Allison Sinclair."

Claudia hesitated then lifted her own mug in the toast. "To Allison's liberation."

A strange ally, but then a week ago, nothing in this world would have convinced her that she would be sleeping with Zach Taylor, much less married to him…and enjoying every single second, despite the current roadblock.

* * * *

For the first time since Zach had taken over as Legal Assistance Officer, he found he didn't mind listening to the mundane problems of his clients. The problem was, he'd worked through the waiting room full of people in record time. Now there was nothing to keep his thoughts distracted.

"I never thought I'd say this, but today you're a workaholic."

Zach looked up to find Aaron Howard hovering in the doorway. "I know Fridays are hectic. Just thought I'd come in, put in a little extra time and help you out."

Aaron plopped down onto the sofa. "Odd… Legal Assistance never seemed to appeal to you before. You used to be the first out of the door whenever we had liberty. Is your investigation not going well? Or has shacking up with your nemesis taken its toll?"

Neither question was worth answering. Father Aaron was *not* going to wring a confession out of him today.

"Ingrate. See if I bust my chops helping you out again." He shoved away from the desk. "Now, if you'll excuse me, I've got other things to do."

Zach made it as far as outside the entrance to the courtroom building before Colonel Scott swooped down on him.

"What the hell are you doing here? I thought I told you to take the week off and act like a happily married couple. You botch this investigation and I'll make damn sure you're working as the general's aide."

"Sir, things have gotten a little more complicated than we expected."

"That's what happens when you start uncovering the truth. Now get the hell out of here." He glanced beyond Zach's shoulder. "Staff Sergeant Stuart, nice to see you up and about. Here to pick up your maternity leave papers?"

Zach inwardly groaned. *Not Rowan, not now.* With dread in his heart, he turned around. She stood there calmly appraising him, the baby bundled in a pouch before her.

"I am, sir."

Colonel Scott cooed over the baby for a few seconds then walked into the building, leaving them alone.

"Do you want to talk?" she asked.

"No." He hurried by before his emotions could pull him into conversation and ran right into the object of his distress as he rounded the corner.

Claudia had used the three-mile distance from the house to his office to work in a run. Her cheeks were flushed from the exertion and sweat glistened on her skin. Both were a disturbing reminder of hot sex with her, something Zach preferred not to recall.

"Hi." She drew in a breath and bent to stretch out her legs and calves. "I tried to call but you didn't answer and I didn't know your work number. I need the Jeep to go to the funeral. The tires on my rental were slashed."

Neighborhood kids or Sinclair trying to keep Allison away from that funeral? He'd guess the latter.

"Did you report it?"

"I did. Military police came by and the rental company is being pissy about replacing the tires."

He dug the keys from his pocket and tossed them her way. "Take it and go."

Claudia caught the key ring in one hand and watched him storm off in the opposite direction. "What the hell's wrong with him?"

Rowan turned her toward the parking lot. "Oh, I suspect you know. Come on. I'll follow you home and let you fix me lunch."

They returned to Claudia's house and settled in the kitchen with drinks and vegetable pita sandwiches.

Her sister-in-law was the most nonintrusive person Claudia knew. A true friend, never offering her opinion or butting in unless asked to do so. With Rowan she could relax and not worry about being judged. Claudia had always treasured that about their relationship — until now. She was busting to tell Rowan all she was feeling. She could keep quiet no longer.

"Zach and I have been sleeping together."

Rowan stirred the ice in her water with a forefinger, avoiding her gaze. "Yes, I know."

Claudia drew back. "How? Did Zach—"

"Because—for lack of a better term—you're glowing." She picked at her pita and cuddled baby James. "I'd be lying if I said I wasn't concerned. I'm not going to insult you by asking how you feel about him.

I know you well enough to know that you must feel something or you wouldn't have taken that step."

"Oh, puleese. You act as if I haven't had sex in ten years. I assure you I have."

"Yes, but there's sex, then there's *sex*." She focused on Claudia, her eyes filled with compassion, friendship and concern. "Are you prepared for all the emotions involved here, good and bad?"

Claudia pulled in a deep breath. "Is anyone ever prepared? All I know is that I'm tired of hiding from them. I'll deal with whatever comes." She took a decisive bite of her sandwich.

"That's all anyone can hope for." Rowan smiled. "Be patient with Zach. He's dealing with a few strange emotions of his own right now."

Zach was dealing with something, of that she was certain when he barreled through the house and into the kitchen before Rowan's words had died.

"How did you get—"

"Montoya drove me home," he replied. "He told me Sinclair is planning to attend Sunline's funeral this afternoon in his capacity as commanding officer."

"But you think he's going there to watch me and Allison?"

"That's exactly what I think. I'm going with you."

Claudia laughed softly. "What could he possibly do in a church filled with people?"

"Nothing, because I'll be there with you."

"Zach, I doubt Allison will feel comfortable with you—"

He beat his fist onto the countertop, rattling the dishes in the cupboard. "I don't give a *damn* about how Allison Sinclair feels! This is about you...*your* safety. The discussion is *closed*."

Claudia clamped her mouth shut. There was no reasoning with him.

He did a crisp about-face and headed for the bedroom, bounding up the stairs.

A slow sigh lifted Rowan's shoulders. "As I said, Claudia…patience, lots of it."

They finished their lunches in silence.

* * * *

It was standing room only at the base chapel. Claudia was glad they'd arrived early. She sat with Allison at the front with the rows of other women who had come to pay their last respects. Each clasped a pink rose.

Zach remained in the rear. She wasn't certain if that was out of respect for Allison or his need to play watchdog. She'd glanced back in time to see Sinclair arrive. He was surrounded by an entourage of Marines from his unit, one of whom was Hanson.

The Hispanic major by his side glanced toward them then directed Sinclair's attention elsewhere. Claudia guessed him to be Cruz Montoya. They were too far away for her to read his nametag.

She settled back in her seat, trying to adopt the appropriate level of grief. It wasn't hard. All she had to do was think of the woman by her side.

"Did you say you knew Teddy before Zach?"

Allison's question was softly spoken. The meaning behind it less so — was Claudia in the same situation as she or had her problem existed prior to Zach?

She curled her fingers over the other woman's arm and smiled. "A long time before Zach."

"Then you were able to leave and find happiness, like Linda Hanson."

Hanson? Claudia fought to maintain some level of composure. Was this the motive Vic needed? She forced herself to smile. "Yes, just like her, Allison."

Four women in front of them turned.

"Are you Teddy's weekend trip?" one asked.

Momentarily flustered, Allison clearly didn't know how to answer. Claudia squeezed her arm.

"Who wants to know?" she asked.

"Helen Moore. Are you Teddy's weekend trip?" she asked Allison again.

Allison nodded.

Helen nodded back. "You're to come with us. We'll take care of you now. Janie's got a room all ready for you. You and your baby will be safe with us."

Allison shot Claudia a nervous glance. All her secrets had just been revealed. "I-I can't. He's watching."

"Honey, they're always watching. Look around this church. You know how many women there are? Trust me. He ain't gonna dare screw with you here. Don't let Teddy's last act of kindness be in vain."

"But my clothes…my things."

"All that matters is your life and your baby's."

Strains of organ music died as the military chaplain stepped up to the altar to begin the service. Allison quivered while tears of grief and fear streamed down her face. She never uttered a sound, yet clutched Claudia's hand as if by letting go she would lose her last lifeline.

Claudia watched the women around her. Teddy's family sat in the front pew. The niece and nephew, now young adults, perched between his parents and Teddy's other sister and brother. Claudia felt like a fraud. She'd tarnished the memory of this man by pretending to be something she was not.

His last act of compassion mustn't be in vain. Claudia owed him that much. With his dying breath, he'd pulled her in as accomplice. She wouldn't deny him a final victory.

The mourners filed past pew by pew. One woman after another placed a pink rose for Julieanne on Teddy's coffin. *Who wouldn't be moved by such an act?* By the time Claudia and Allison stepped forward, she had tears in her eyes.

They turned to leave. Allison froze. Sinclair stood at the exit. By unspoken command, the women surrounded Allison, protecting her by their sheer numbers.

"All right. Let's go," Helen said.

"I...can't," Allison squeaked out.

"Yes, you can. Straight out the door."

To anyone else, nothing would seem out of order. They were friends filing as one from the church, supporting each other in this trying time. With each heart-pounding step, Claudia prayed they would make it.

She watched Zach ease in behind Sinclair. Montoya took the other side. Behind them all, Vic. The mass of women shoved by, out the door, down the steps. For a few glorious minutes, Claudia believed they were going to pull this off. She underestimated Sinclair's determination and control over his wife.

He called to her over the crowd. Not a shout, just her name. Then he walked their way. Allison froze.

Helen positioned herself between Sinclair and his target. "We were on our way to escort Teddy's coffin to the airport. After that, we were going to have a private condolence gathering."

"You can do it without my wife. Allison and I have our own condolences to make to the family."

He curled his hand over Allison's wrist and tried to pull her free. The women closed ranks, shoving him back.

Sinclair's lips thinned to a harsh white line. Through a tight smile he addressed Allison. "Darling, you've been sick, not to mention the strain of saying good-bye to a fine Marine. Come home where you can rest and I can take care of you."

There was enough of a hesitation to give him an edge. Only Helen stood firm. Claudia pushed to the forefront.

"Colonel, they mean no harm. We're friends of Teddy's who want to mourn him in private."

He smiled down at her but his eyes blazed with rage. His voice was low, for her ears only. "Frankly, Mrs. Taylor, I'm surprised to find a woman of your caliber associating with this cult. I can assure you, my wife will *not* be a part of it."

He tightened his hold and tugged again. Helen barred his attempt. Claudia gently pulled her away.

"I can certainly understand your concern." She forced a smile. "I'm grateful for the warning. Allison, I'm going away for the weekend and could use a little company. Would you like to go to San Francisco with me?"

Sinclair's smile turned to a grimace. "My wife goes *nowhere* with you. She's ill and needs her rest."

One final tug and Allison was his. In a last-ditch effort, Helen leaped for him. Sinclair clipped her ankle with his foot. She stumbled back. Claudia caught her before she fell. It was over in the blink of a moment.

In Sinclair's wake, Zach's shadow fell across them. "Let's go."

"But—"

"*Now*, Claudia."

His face was taut with anger. More mourners filed from the church. The last thing they needed was another scene.

Zach didn't say a word during the short drive home. He didn't have to. His clenched jaw said it all. He waited as long as it took to get inside the door, even had the presence of mind to shut it quietly. But as it clicked closed, Zach slammed his keys against the wall, denting the plasterboard. "What the hell were you thinking?"

Claudia splayed her hands across her chest. "It wasn't my idea."

"But you sure as hell went along with it. And when that didn't work, you invited her to San Francisco with you, for God's sake. Why the hell don't you just tattoo it across your forehead?" He drew a line in the furrows of her forehead. "'Come kill me, too!' Now pack your stuff and let's go."

"That's not fair, Zach. You're panicking for no reason. I'm perfectly capable of taking care of myself. I'm trained in self-defense."

He parked his hands on his hips. "I'd like to see you go one-on-one against a car or a bullet or God knows what else. And what about last night?"

She couldn't argue that point. "Granted, Vic and I were caught by surprise. We'll be more diligent—"

"But it could have been Sinclair!" Zach smacked his head. "This is insane."

"What is?"

"This. Debating this with you. This stupid investigation. Everything."

Now they were at the crux of the problem. "Everything, Zach?"

He paused as if considering his next words. "Yes...everything. I want you gone. I want you out of here *now*."

She curled her hand to the cleft between her breasts. "Are you telling me we're finished?"

Shoving himself upright, he stared down at her. "We didn't have anything *to* finish. It was sex, pure and simple, nothing more. Now, shall I help you pack?"

Claudia bit her lip and forced her chin up. This wasn't about him fearing for her safety or caring for her. He *really* wanted her gone.

"No, thank you. I believe I can manage on my own." Her broken heart was another matter.

Chapter Twelve

"I've listened to as much as I can take."

Claudia looked at Phillip from the corner of her eye while she blotted annoying tears away with the edge of a tissue. She'd thought she'd been discreet enough. It wasn't as if she was bawling her eyes out. In fact, the realization that she was crying at all made her angrier than she could say.

It wasn't supposed to have mattered. She had steeled herself to deal with whatever came her way and move on. Claudia wasn't counting on the pain of Zach's words to bring her down.

"You've been sniffling over there for four hours. Don't you even want to talk to me about it?"

"There really isn't anything to say. Even if there were, I don't want to talk about it."

The tremor in her voice told a different story. She longed to pour out her heart but hadn't the faintest idea where to begin.

"So you're back to keeping things bottled inside." Phillip snorted. "It's a wonder you don't have a stomach full of ulcers."

Claudia jerked her head around. "I'm not bottling things inside. It's just that it's none of your business."

"Fair enough."

To her disappointment, Phillip let the subject drop. The least he could have done was wheedle the information out of her. *What kind of brother is he?*

She drummed her nails on the armrest. At least his comment gave her the impetus to stop crying. Now all she had to focus on was her anger. She had been foolish to believe she'd seen something in Zach's eyes that obviously didn't exist and an idiot to let him have what he'd been after all these years. Although, why should she have done without? It had been very fine sex. So what if she was another notch on his bedpost. He was another notch on hers.

"How many women has Zach slept with?"

Phillip shrugged a shoulder and kept his gaze focused on the road. "At least a million."

Sarcasm. She needed comfort and he threw out sarcasm. *See if I talk to you again.*

On the north side of Bakersfield, Phillip pulled into a coffee shop. "I could use a cup of coffee and some dinner. How about you?"

"It doesn't matter to me. You're driving."

Her stomach was too tied in knots to eat. All she wanted was the comfort of her apartment.

While Phillip carved into a steak, it was all Claudia could do to pick at the small salad she'd ordered.

"I take it your part in the investigation is over?"

The question caught her off-guard. In the aftermath of Zach's rejection, she'd forgotten about the case. "Of course not. I promised the station a story and I'm determined to help Allison. When you go back to Twentynine Palms, I'm going with you. Why would you think otherwise?"

"Well, I know what a strain it is to have to live with someone you don't care for. You and Zach have never gotten along. I imagine the constant bickering has taken a toll—"

"Cut the crap, Phillip. I'm sure Rowan has already told you."

He chewed for a while before replying. "Rowan's told me a lot of things. To which specific thing are you referring?"

"I'm not in the mood to play games with you," she sneered.

He set aside his fork. "Good. Neither am I. Let's cut right to it. Why did you have sex with him in the first place…honestly?"

The intensity of his gaze was too much to bear. Claudia pushed her lettuce around. "Lust, I guess."

"So much for honesty."

Heads turned as her fork clattered to her plate. "All right. The more time I spent with him, the more I wanted to be with him—to see what I'd been missing all these years. I wanted him. I liked him. I went for him."

"Do you care for him?"

She looked away again. "I thought I did. I was wrong."

"Wrong—or too angry to focus on anything else?"

Claudia sagged under the weight of the question.

"Don't you think it's a bit odd that Zach would go from actively pursuing you to shoving you out of the house?"

She propped her chin in her hand. "I briefly considered that his actions were to keep me safe, but he made it quite clear this afternoon that it was about sex and nothing more."

"Read between the lines. What did he really make clear?"

A headache beat behind her eyes. She didn't feel like discussing this anymore. It'd been her choice to have sex with Zach. The consequences were hard enough to bear. Why did Phillip insist on dissecting her folly?

He smacked the table with his open palm. "I'm not playing this game anymore. Here's the bottom line."

When she looked up, he continued.

"My instructions from Zach are to take you to San Francisco and leave you there, even if I have to sneak out of your apartment to do so. Now, I'm not stupid enough to think that will be enough to make you stay. I argued with Zach until I didn't have a breath left in my body. He still won't listen to reason."

A new rash of tears blinded her. "Does he really hate me that much?"

Phillip reached across the worn table and cupped her hand in his. "No, Claudia. He *loves you* that much. Zach loves you."

Her jaw dropped and she could only blink uncomprehendingly at her brother.

He squeezed her fingers. "He is insane with worry, frantic that you're going to be killed. That's why he wants you gone."

"Why didn't he just tell me himself?"

"You're angry as hell with him right now and that's still not enough to keep you away. If Zach had told you how he feels, would it have made a difference?"

Claudia jerked away. "I don't know, but it would have been a hell of a lot nicer than being told I was nothing more than a sexual outlet."

"No one ever said a man in love made any sense — or so Rowan tells me. The questions now are... How do you feel about Zach, and are you going to stay in San Francisco like he wants?"

"That all depends. Are you on the man side or my side?"

He laughed. "I'm on whatever side Rowan tells me to be on and right now that seems to be yours."

"Why? Why tell me? Why help me? Why not let us screw this relationship up all by ourselves?"

The light faded from his silvery-gray eyes. "Rowan and I spent too many years apart because of a stupid misunderstanding caused by someone else. We aren't willing to let you and Zach go through that if being together is what you want."

Put in those terms, Claudia understood how they felt. "This is easily solved. When I get back to Twentynine Palms, Zach and I will have a calm and rational discussion about it."

Phillip's belly-shaking laughter brought the restaurant's attention their way once more. "There's nothing calm and rational about love. If you try to corner Zach on this, he'll deny everything just for the sake of protecting you."

"Then what would you suggest?" she snapped.

"Well, obviously nothing will keep you in San Francisco. If you're going back, you're going to have to get in under Zach's defenses. Make him say what he feels. That way, neither of you can deny it."

Claudia lifted an eyebrow. "That's very fine, but all I've heard is what Zach feels. I'm not going to trap him when I can't be certain how I feel."

A wide grin cut Phillip's features. "My dear, sweet, adorable little sister... If you didn't love Zach, you wouldn't be this upset. So, are you going to dig in and fight for what you want?"

"I don't seem to be very good at that, now do I?" She stared at the salt and pepper shakers. "I let Todd go without a fight."

"Todd Willoughby wasn't worth fighting for. Zach is. If our father had tried to buy off Zach to keep him from marrying you, Zach would have told you immediately then found a way to marry you, keep the money and humiliate Donald in front of a church full of people."

The image made her smile. Phillip was right. "I haven't the faintest idea how to go about this. I'm used to being more direct. What you're proposing is entrapment."

He laughed. "Zach was entrapped the minute he first laid eyes on you. He's been like a little boy these last five years, yanking on your pigtails to get your attention."

"And now that he has it?"

"Take it away from him. Ignore him. No more feuding. Just be yourself."

Myself — or the self I want to be?

* * * *

Zach checked the bedside clock for what must have been the thousandth time. Midnight. They should have gotten to San Francisco by now. *Why hasn't Phillip called? I did ask him to call when they arrived, didn't I?*

As much as he racked his brain, Zach couldn't recall. They'd discussed Claudia's safety, and his instructions for ensuring she remained in San Francisco were quite explicit. But calling? Had he forgotten to tell Phillip to call, no matter what hour they arrived? The question was driving him insane, almost as much as waiting to hear.

It was too much to bear. Zach snatched up his cell phone and got Phillip's voice mail when he called. *Should I call her apartment? Does she have a landline? What will I do when she answers?* He'd been pretty nasty in his attempt to keep her safe. It'd killed him to see the hurt on her face, but it would have killed him more to be staring into her coffin.

Zach flirted with the idea of calling Rowan. He tossed the phone to the nightstand and flopped down on the bed. It was much too late to call. She'd be asleep. He might wake the kids. Still, Rowan would know what was going on.

"No, she won't be asleep. Phillip definitely would have called her."

His actions justified, Zach reached for the phone once more. A muffled cry stopped him. He strained his ears but heard nothing. That alone bothered him.

With the tip of his index finger, Zach peeled back the edge of the drapes and glanced across the street. The only light came from the upstairs window. Sinclair's silhouette was outlined in sharp contrast. He reared back his arm and struck once...twice.

Zach's already-low spirits plunged into the sewer. Up to this very moment some part deep inside wanted to believe it wasn't true, that Sinclair was the model officer and leader he presented to the world. Here was irrefutable proof that he was not.

"Damned bastard," Zach said through clenched teeth and dialed the military police.

The desk sergeant wasted little time on preliminaries. If it was an emergency call, it would be handled immediately, even if he had to do so himself.

"My next-door neighbor is beating his wife."

Zach heard the sergeant's chair slide back.

"What's the address and the names of the parties?"

Once given, all urgency faded. Zach could hear it in the strained silence on the other end of the line.

"What's the problem, Sergeant?"

"Well, sir, I'm a little embarrassed to say. This isn't the first time a neighbor has called. I went out there a few times myself. We don't go anymore."

"But he's *beating* her."

"To be blunt, sir, that's how they…uhm…make love. Sorry, sir. I need to answer another call."

Zach stared at the phone. Sinclair had managed to foil Allison's only hope of protection. No wonder she'd given up so easily at the funeral.

He paced the length of the darkened bedroom and back. Frustration and anger boiled up in him. Someone had to do something. He imagined breaking into Sinclair's house. The image was followed in quick succession by another of him being hauled away in handcuffs.

Montoya. He'll know what to do.

Zach couldn't punch in the number fast enough. He expected to have awakened the man. Instead, there was soft music in the background, the sound of a woman's voice and irritation at the interruption.

"This better be good," Cruz snapped.

"Sinclair's beating Allison. The MPs refuse to come over. They've been told it's sex play. I thought —"

"I'll take care of it."

Again, he was left staring at the phone. He glanced out of the windows. Lights flicked on in the other house. Minutes later, Sinclair pulled out of the driveway in his car. Whatever Cruz had told him had worked.

Now Zach faced another dilemma. Should he go over and comfort Allison? Whisk her away to safety? Or just mind his own business and not risk embarrassing her? He wandered through the house, helpless for a solution.

Claudia would know what to do.

Zach traced the numbers on the phone. He could call her. Then what? What had happened with Allison would slip out, and she'd be back down here, putting herself in danger once more.

With a world-weary sigh, he set the phone aside.

* * * *

Claudia watched dawn lighten the San Francisco fog. She couldn't recall when she had welcomed morning more. Sleep had been elusive. Not even two glasses of merlot had helped. Normally, she would have occupied her mind with work or catching up on house chores. Phillip's presence made that impossible. The same thought that had been taunting her all night danced around in her head. Zach loved her, and she'd realized days ago that she loved him, too.

Her actions had betrayed her before her heart could admit it but it was true. There was no way she could deny it, no way she wanted to. Claudia longed to shout it to every car that had passed them on their drive, to talk Phillip's ear off about it, to run back to Twentynine

Palms and tell Zach, to hear him say it for herself. Instead, she'd reveled quietly in the knowledge.

It had been midnight by the time they had reached her apartment. The cheery rooms had seemed to greet her with a smile, but Claudia had missed Miss Kitty's greeting and the aura of Zach's presence, the way he'd swoop her into his arms and kiss her until she melted.

She must have reached for the phone a dozen times during the night to call him. Each time, she'd drawn back. *It's too late. He'll be asleep. I might let it slip that I'll be returning.* That would have sparked his defenses and possibly an argument.

So she'd paced, arms wrapped around her to ward off a sudden bout of the lonelies. Once in the night she'd heard Phillip talking to Rowan. The tender regard and humor in his voice had just made her feel worse. When would she and Zach have the freedom to behave that way? The answer had come too quickly for her liking — when they stopped playing these stupid games with each other.

Claudia hauled on her sweats and running shoes. With morning, her confinement was over. A peek into the spare bedroom showed Phillip was sound asleep. There was no one to stop her or insist on going with her. She took off toward the Embarcadero, one foot pounding after another.

Homeless people on the other side of the street ignored her and stayed huddled under threadbare blankets and cardboard shelters. Other joggers stared beyond her, absorbed in their own routine, their own thoughts, as she was.

She finished her five-mile route then circled back toward her favorite bakery for blueberry scones and Devonshire cream. They'd make a nice breakfast for her and Phillip. But when she returned to her apartment, she discovered Phillip was still asleep. He slept soundly while she ate, showered and packed the things she intended to take back with her.

By ten o'clock she decided to check in on him. The door barely made a sound when Claudia opened it but Phillip shifted to one side and muttered.

"Come on in, Ian, but be quiet. Mom's tired. The baby kept us up last night."

Smiling, Claudia shut the door. *I'll let him sleep.* She could occupy her time shopping.

She hailed a taxi outside her apartment building and directed the driver to the downtown area and the Neiman Marcus department store. Exiting the cab, she was assailed by the distinctive city aroma of automobile fumes mixed with the smells of the local grills preparing for the lunchtime crowds. *The city.* She was home. Yet, the sweet remembrance of desert air with its hint of mesquite and sage teased her memory. She missed Zach.

Pushing past a cluster of camera-toting tourists determined to stand and goggle at everything around them, she entered the store.

Clouds of expensive scents drifted around her, combined with the rich odor of leather handbags. The glitter of display stands, mirrors and to-die-for jewelry drew her gaze. Claudia wandered through the handbag section, pausing to examine the season's newest offerings. She caught herself admiring a buttery soft man's wallet and, on impulse, bought it for Zach. His was tattered beyond hope.

Humming, she continued on through cosmetics and wandered to ladies' apparel. Beyond the everyday wear and half-priced swimsuits lay her goal. The formal dresses were arranged and displayed as only an exclusive department store could. She began a slow circuit of the lushly carpeted alcove, her footsteps muffled by the soft pile. Shimmers of silk, the perfection of lace and the crisp lines of satin beckoned her. Every turn displayed a new marvel.

"Hello, hello."

The voice was loud, strident. Claudia jumped, startled out of her reveries by a sweaty palm on her shoulder. Instinct made her flinch and whirl around, heart pounding. A young salesman preened before her, adjusting his too-big suit and displaying himself under her gaze. He flicked a hand through his perfectly styled blond hair, worn a little too long in Claudia's opinion. *He might as well enjoy it while he can.* If the receding hairline was any indication, he'd be bald in five years.

"Excuse me, miss," he began again. "Could I help you find something?" He ran his gaze up and down her body in more than professional appraisal. "Something beautiful to fit a gorgeous woman like yourself?" The salesman smiled again. This time a touch of wolf gleamed in his gaze.

"No." Claudia's denial was flat, cold. She turned away and focused her attention toward the nearest rack.

"Haven't we met some place before?"

He moved closer. She could feel hot puffs of his breath on the back of her neck.

"I think not," she replied, willing him away.

"But I know we've met." He reached out to touch her hand. "You can tell me. Was it at a club? You've got a dancer's body. Did we dance?"

Claudia turned a lethal stare his way. "I'm a reporter for a local television station. I often appear on the evening news. I would never, ever associate myself with any entertainment establishment that would allow a boor like you inside. The closest we've ever come to meeting prior to this day was through a television screen. Now go away."

Shocked and embarrassed, the salesman gathered his tattered bits of composure and slinked off.

Claudia continued shifting through the rack of formal gowns, wishing she could get assistance of a more professional sort. Almost the instant she thought that, the department supervisor rushed forward.

"You'll have to forgive him. He's unseasoned and overly enthusiastic. I may have him moved down to men's footwear for a while to cool him off." She beamed a smile and clapped her hands together. "Now, how can I help you today?"

Claudia's irritability dissolved. "I need to attend a formal affair next weekend and was hoping to find something new to wear."

The woman stepped back, cocked her head to one side and appraised Claudia's figure. "I think I have just what you need."

Drawing Claudia away from the rack, she led her to an alcove where a solitary dress hung. With reverence, she took it down and shook it out.

Claudia's jaw dropped. The floor-length gown shimmered in a silver-blue dance. She had never seen a more beautiful color.

"It just arrived. Try it on."

A demand, not a request. Like an obedient child, Claudia followed the woman to the lush dressing room. Minutes later, she stared at herself in the mirror, still in slack-jawed wonder.

It was daring. That much was certain. Two strips of material crisscrossed over each breast then over her shoulders where they drifted to her lumbar, leaving most of her back bare. The bottom of the dress hugged her buttocks while the hem flared out.

The saleswoman tapped at the door. "How does it look?"

It's the most beautiful dress I've ever seen. "Very nice."

"Let me see."

With hesitancy, Claudia unlatched the door and stepped out. The woman gasped and clasped her hands under her chin.

"I was right. Absolutely gorgeous. Very few women have the body for a dress like this. You *must* buy it."

Claudia studied her reflection in the tri-fold mirror. Laughter bubbled to her throat. "Oh, I couldn't. It's too...too—"

"Stunning?"

She laughed. "It's stunning all right. I'm not sure it's me."

"Why not?"

Good question. She glanced at herself once more. It was unlike anything she had ever owned—completely seductive. Her smile announced her decision.

The woman clapped her hands once more. "Excellent. Shall I have it delivered to you?"

Claudia mentally ticked off the things she had to do then gave a short nod. "Thank you."

Her list was still foremost in her mind when Claudia left the store to continue her errands. Added to that were her plans to accessorize her new dress. Between the two, she failed to notice Franklin Delacourte coming her way until it was too late.

Claudia ducked into a fruit and vegetable stand, hoping to avoid him but he refused to be ignored. Focusing her attention on the produce displayed, she weaved her way through row after row. Each time, he followed. Finally, she saw no choice but to face him down.

"What do you want?"

He flashed his best anchorman smile and leaned over a bin of apples to reach her. "Still frosty over that nasty little scene at your brother's? I don't blame you. It was foolish of me. Forgive me?"

"Fine. Now leave me alone."

Franklin grabbed her wrist and held her in place. "Not so fast. I really don't blame you for being mad at me. I deserve it. If I'd taken the time to think, I would have realized there was nothing to your marriage."

Claudia slowly extricated herself from his grasp. "What *are* you talking about?"

He chuckled. "Don't play games. It's me."

She half-expected him to say, 'Franklin Delacourte, news anchor.'

"Ed told me everything about the fake marriage, that you're working something really big down there." He pressed closer. "So tell me, what is it?"

"As usual, you have your facts wrong, which probably explains why I am the investigative reporter and you are the news reader."

His face flushed a mottled shade of red. Claudia left him sputtering for a response. At least he had the sense not to follow her this time.

The encounter put a damper on her day. She'd expected her boss to be discreet, yet he'd given away her intent to the one person she would have never trusted. He'd probably done so to stir Franklin up and maybe squeeze a story from him.

A blast of cold wind cut into her. She tugged the edges of her jacket together, bent her head into the chill and pushed across the street to her next destination.

At the squeal of tires, she yanked up her head. A woman's warning shout pierced her confusion as a dark blue sedan barreled toward her. The idiot was going to run a red light.

Claudia raced for the curb yet couldn't keep her gaze from the approaching vehicle. In the back of her mind, she knew this was no coincidence, no red light run. The driver was aiming for her.

She needed a face... A glimpse of a license plate... Something, anything to identify who it was. Suddenly someone grabbed her from behind in a grip as tight as steel. She was lifted off her feet and hurled to the safety of a doorway. The man pressed her against the stone, using his body to shield hers. There was a hard bump as the car hit the curb, then another squeal, followed by the stench of burned rubber.

Reality slammed into her. She quivered from the shock. Slowly the man eased away, his hands softly caressing her upper arms, comforting her. Claudia dared to look up.

"Vic?"

He gave a shaky nod. "Let's get you back to your apartment."

"But who... How —"

"Hanson. I saw him follow you from Twentynine Palms, so I followed him. Been following him ever since. He was at the vegetable stand when that guy stopped you."

"And he overheard."

"Hard not to. The guy didn't exactly whisper."

She drew in a shaky breath to calm her nerves. "Hanson did have a motive, Vic. His wife. Apparently, Teddy helped her leave him."

He nodded, eyes puffy and tired. "That *does* tie it up. I'll check it out. Come on. Let's get you home."

Claudia let him lead her away. There was little more she could do. This was no mistake. This time there had been nothing discreet about the attempt. If Vic hadn't been there, she'd be dead.

There was no easy way to break the news to Phillip. Telling Zach would be even worse. They would insist she back off from the investigation, and Claudia couldn't say she blamed them. She'd faced tough situations before, but never once had she come this close to death.

Still, the choice was hers. She could fight to the end or stop and let the bastards get away with one murder after another. Then where would her conscience be? Claudia chose to fight, even if that meant beginning with Zach and Phillip.

Chapter Thirteen

Rowan opened the door before Zach could come to a full stop in the Stuart driveway. She watched him exit then tilted her head when he stepped from the vehicle.

"This is a surprise."

Not nearly as much as it was to him. He'd paced his house for the better part of the day, lost in the silence of Claudia's absence. Miss Kitty had ignored him. For the first time in his life, he felt lonely. The idea of going to Phoenix to visit his family was appealing until he realized his mother would bore through his defenses with nothing more than a look. In less time than it took to think about it, he'd be confessing all, so he'd come here.

"Got a minute?" he asked.

"For you, I've got five." Smiling, she shoved the door open wide. "Ian's at a birthday party. The baby's asleep. I'm all yours. Why the long face?"

Zach shrugged and stepped into the comfort of his best friends' home. "It's been a difficult night. I saw — let me rephrase that—I'm fairly certain I saw Sinclair beating his wife last night."

"Did you call—"

"Yeah," he snorted, "I called them, for all the good it did. I finally got hold of Cruz Montoya and he got Sinclair out of the house on some kind of ruse. I'll tell you, Princess. I've never felt more helpless in my life."

"Rowan."

Zach gave her a puzzled frown. "What?"

"My name is Rowan, not Princess."

Nothing like having your subconscious give you up. He didn't bother to try to cover his tracks.

"I presume they reached San Francisco all right."

"They did. Phillip called last night."

Rowan wandered through the house, picking up children's items scattered throughout. Zach followed.

"I kept expecting one of them to call me."

She tossed a handful of toys into the laundry basket nearby. "I don't know why. You made it quite clear to Claudia that you wanted her gone, and I would bet you weren't nice about it, either."

He was ashamed to admit she was right. "What else could I do? She wouldn't have left otherwise."

Rowan gave him a glare so filled with skepticism that Zach had to look away.

"Honesty might have been nice. You could have told her how you felt—that you love her so much and all you could think about was her safety. Instead, you got scared then you got nasty, which puts you right back where you were in the first place, because I doubt Claudia will ever trust you again. You'd better sit back and think about what your stupidity has cost you."

No solace here. He could have gotten the same lecture from his mother, not that he didn't deserve it. He just didn't like hearing it.

Zach sank to the nearest chair and buried his head in his hands. "I have thought about it. I haven't thought about anything else. The house is so empty without Claudia there."

Rowan nudged his leg with her bare toe. "So, what are you going to do about it?"

The answer was simple and hard at the same time. "The damage is already done, but she's safe. When this is over with, I'll try to explain."

"Hmph. Typical male response. But" —she tugged him to his feet—"you're not going to spend the weekend feeling sorry for yourself at my house. If you're going to be here, I've got painting for you to do."

"You've always got painting to do."

"Lucky you. Come on. The back fence has your name written all over it."

* * * *

Phillip shot a glance from Claudia to Vic then back again. Vic's presence would tell him something was wrong.

She was still quivering from the ordeal. She sought a corner of her sofa and tucked herself into it.

"What happened?"

A demand for information. She expected nothing less from her brother. She massaged the ache in her temple while Vic hesitated, sensing Phillip's anger. Already he'd be making decisions regarding her welfare and Claudia doubted he would give a damn what she thought of those decisions. Battle lines were being drawn, and although she had determined to fight for what she thought was best, she wasn't sure if she had the energy to do so at this point.

"Are you sure it was Hanson?"

Vic nodded. "Granted, I couldn't see well through the car's tinted windows, but he'd been following Claudia since the two of you left. The car was the one he'd been driving."

Phillip rubbed his chin. "And thanks to Franklin Delacourte, he now knows everything."

"No, he doesn't," Claudia told them. "That's one of the problems. Now that he knows I'm involved in an investigation, Franklin won't rest until he gets the scoop on the story. He wouldn't hesitate to break the news about our sham marriage and Sunline's death, just to leave me in the dust."

"Is Delacourte determined enough to follow you back to Twentynine Palms?"

Claudia stared at her brother. "Franklin has never been known to expend too much effort, but I've learned over the years not to second-guess him."

Vic cracked his knuckles. "I'll take care of Franklin. In fact, I've got a fish story he'll buy hook, line and sinker. When I get back here, we'll try to think of a way to get Claudia out of San Francisco without Hanson realizing she's gone."

An awkward silence grew once Vic left the apartment. Claudia nurtured it, afraid any conversation might change Phillip's mind and she'd be forced to argue with him.

"A package arrived for you today. Any chance it's a bomb?"

The sarcasm stung worse than any other words could. "Oh, Phillip, please don't be that way. It's a dress I bought for the Marine Corps Ball next weekend."

Sighing, he squeezed the bridge of his nose. "Sorry." Another sigh lifted his head. "Let's see it. Put it on."

"Phillip, I don't think either of us is in the mood — "

"It's the perfect time. We need something to take our minds off this crap."

Claudia gave in. Perhaps he was right. In fact, once she slipped the fabric over her skin, her mood lightened. To add to the effect, she slipped into a pair of silver heels. Without fanfare, flourish or any other type of announcement, she drifted into her living room.

It took a second or two for Phillip to notice her standing there. The wait was worth it. His jaw dropped and stayed there.

"Well, what do you think?" she asked with a smile.

"I think Zach's a dead man." Then he began to laugh.

* * * *

Once Zach got beyond cursing the day he'd ever met Rowan Stuart, he realized what she was up to. It was somewhere between him watching the baby while she picked up Ian and her having him grill hamburgers that he figured out she was trying to exhaust him. It had worked.

He dragged himself home, ready for a hot shower and bed. No thoughts of Claudia would keep him awake tonight. As he stepped over the threshold, the crunch of paper greeted him. He flicked on the light, expecting to see Miss Kitty's latest toy. Instead, he found photographs.

His mother would have called it a premonition that made him afraid to look. He squatted and spread the pictures out with the edge of his key. All were of Claudia going about her daily routine in San Francisco—jogging, at a bakery, walking along the street, in a department store, at a vegetable stand. And scrawled across the top of the last picture, one horrible threat.

I can get to her anytime, anywhere... Back off.

Zach left the pictures where they lay and fumbled for the phone. Maybe Vic could get some fingerprints off them. Twelve tries later and only getting voice mail, he tossed the phone to the coffee table.

"He picked a fine time to go out. I've got to warn Claudia."

Warn her? Hell, he still didn't have her landline number and knew she wouldn't answer his call to her cell.

Back to Rowan.

Zach drummed his fingers against the sofa arm while he waited for her to pick up. When she did, he didn't give her a chance to speak.

"I want Claudia's landline number."

"Why?"

Why the hell do you think? One minute, she was encouraging him to call, the next she was questioning his motives.

"Because I just received a threat against her life. She's being watched up there."

"Yes, I know. Zach, Phillip called a few minutes ago. Claudia was almost killed today. If it hadn't been for Vic, she might not be here."

Rage roared in Zach's ears. He'd sent her away to protect her and had thrown her right into the path of danger. And Vic... *He* should have been the one to rescue her, not Vic. Jealousy elbowed gratitude out of the way. Fear and panic nudged their way to the forefront.

Zach ground his teeth together. "Give me the number," he pushed out.

Rowan didn't hesitate.

His hand shook as he punched in the number. Claudia could have been killed and it was his fault. And on top of it all — she would have died without knowing how he felt. He had to talk to her, to know she was all right, to hear her voice, even if she was pissed as hell at him.

Hope plummeted when Phillip answered the phone.

"I want to talk to Claudia."

"Well, Zach, what a surprise to hear from you."

"Cut the crap. I want Claudia."

"She can't come to the phone. She's in the shower. Today was a little stressful for her."

"Yeah, I heard. Take the phone to her."

Phillip's intake of breath echoed on the line. "You wanted her gone. She's gone. Leave her be."

"I wanted her safe, not gone! Let me talk to her."

"Sorry, not possible." A click ended further discussion.

It was all Zach could do to keep from slamming the phone against the wall. The last thing he had patience for was games. He had one goal tonight and nothing, *nothing*, was going to stand in his way.

"Did I hear the phone?"

Claudia stood in the hall between the bathroom and the living room, towel-drying her hair. Neither Phillip nor Vic bothered to look up.

"Yep, it was Zach," Phillip answered.

Her heart skipped a beat.

"I told him you were unavailable."

She snapped the back of his head with the towel.

He whirled around, gray eyes flashing sparks.

"You had no right," she said.

"Fine. Call him yourself." Massaging the offended spot, Phillip eased back in front of the television.

"Will you two shut up?" Vic turned the volume up on the television. "The news is starting. I want to see if Delacourte bought my story."

"I'm sure he did. One fool always believes the other." Each word was scathingly sarcastic. Claudia didn't care and didn't wait around for his indignant response. She had enough reasons of her own to be upset.

How could Phillip do such a thing? He knew how upset she was. He knew she wanted to talk with...

Claudia drew up short of her bed. He didn't know anything. She'd kept it to herself.

Curling up in the center of her queen-size bed, she dialed his cell. All she got was voice mail.

"It's me, Zach. Call me...please."

She tried their house phone next and got the answering machine, leaving another message. His silence brought tears to her eyes. She set the phone aside. There was nothing more she could do except wait for him to call back. She'd get the call this time, even if she had to carry the damn phone all over the house with her.

After all she'd been through, Claudia wasn't up to playing games with someone else's emotions. She needed Zach, angry or not. With the phone clutched in her hand, she stretched out on her bed to wait. He'd call. She just knew it.

Hours later, a ring blasted through her dreams. Claudia yanked upright and pressed the phone to her ear.

"Zach?"

A dial tone was the response. There was a second ring. Through the fog of sleep, she realized it was the doorbell.

Struggling to her feet, she stumbled to the doorway. Phillip shoved her back.

"We don't know who it is. It might not be safe."

Claudia peeked around him. With gun drawn, Vic looked through the peephole.

"I don't know if we're safe or not." He holstered his weapon, unlocked the door and swung it open.

Zach charged in, shoving the door out of his path. "Where is she?"

Claudia tugged the belt on her robe tight and brushed around Phillip.

"How did you get here?" Phillip asked.

Zach jerked his arm Phillip's way, pointing his finger. "The red eye out of Palm Springs. I don't know what fucking games you and Rowan are playing, but don't *ever* keep me from talking to her again."

"Oh, Zach," she somehow managed to choke out, "I tried to call you back." The last word was strangled with tears. She'd meant to be discreet and calm, to force Zach to make the first move but at the sight of his disheveled appearance she crumbled.

Arms outstretched, she reached for him. "Oh, Zach, I…" She was wrapped in his embrace before she could say another word.

He cradled her on his lap, whispering soothing words of comfort while she cried against his neck. There was the clink of bottle to glass. Seconds later, Phillip handed them each a glass of wine.

He pulled back quickly, face screwed into a mask of disgust. "Phew, you smell ripe."

Zach flashed him an ugly glare. "No thanks to your wife. She worked me like a dog today."

"Painting the damn fence, I hope."

"Miles of it."

A broad smile cut across Phillip's face. "Excellent."

"I'm glad I could do you the favor. What the hell happened here?"

Claudia let Vic tell him. She had no energy left. With each word, she felt Zach's tension grow.

"What did you tell Delacourte to get rid of him?"

Vic smirked. "I told him that Claudia had heard a rumor that battalions of troops were being deployed for a Middle Eastern offensive and that she was trying to get verification for the station."

"Franklin broke the story on the evening news," Phillip added.

"He broke a story like that without confirmation?"

"He isn't the brightest star in the sky."

Zach traced circles on Claudia's shoulder with his thumb. "What about getting Claudia out of here safely?"

Vic laced his hands behind his head and leaned back. "She can fly out with you in the morning. Hanson won't want to tip his hand by getting on the same flight as you, and he won't leave his rental car here. You can get her back to the house before he's halfway to Twentynine Palms."

"Then what?"

He shrugged. "We cross that bridge later."

Zach set his glass down so hard the stem threatened to crack. "No. We cross it *now*. This is her life we're talking about."

Vic jumped forward, all semblance of friendliness gone. "Then take her away on an extended honeymoon and let the professionals finish this."

"Finish?" Claudia set her glass beside Zach's. "You'll have to start from scratch. We agreed the key was Allison. She'll never talk to you. You have to let me do this."

"Wrong, Princess." Zach snatched up his drink again and took a gulp. "I'd be willing to bet Allison won't be talking to anyone. He beat her last night. I called the MPs. There wasn't any—"

She pressed her fingers to his lips. "Shh, it's all right. You did all you could."

He clutched her wrist, kissed her fingers then curled her hand into his. "We finish this, Vic. It's become more than a matter of finding a murderer."

"You can't save the world, Zach."

"Not the world, Vic. Just one woman."

He polished off the remainder of his wine, set Claudia on her feet then stood. Twining his fingers through hers, she led the way to her bedroom and shut the door.

"We need to talk," he said.

Boy, do we ever. Claudia propped the pillow against the headboard and sat.

"Join me." She gave the mattress a pat.

"I can't." He motioned to his clothing. "Phillip's right. I'm filthy."

He squatted next to the bed and caressed her fingertips. "I used to laugh when my mom said men are stupid. Now I know exactly what she meant. The stupidest thing I ever did was convince myself that lying to you was a good idea. I tried to tell myself I was doing it to protect you."

She was glad he held her hand. It helped keep her from shaking. "What *exactly* have you lied about?"

"I lied when I said it was just sex. It wasn't. I love you, Claudia. I always have."

Her heart was beating so hard that she wasn't sure she heard him.

"It wasn't sex for me." Zach turned her palm over and traced the underside of her wrist. "It was love from day one, no doubt about it."

"It was for me, too." Her voice was barely above a whisper. "I love you, Zach."

He kept his gaze on her wrist, tracing the delicate blue veins with careful precision. "I want to believe that. God knows, I want to believe that. I can't stand thinking you might not. But, sweetheart, sex is a powerful emotion. How do you know it's love and not sex? Especially when the sex is so very, very good."

Claudia tried to keep her mouth shut, tried to keep the laughter from bubbling up. It was no use.

"Oh, my, but we *do* have an inflated opinion of ourself, don't we?" Clutching her sides, she doubled over while tears of laughter filled her eyes.

Zach stretched to his feet and stared down at her. It made her laugh all the more.

"Nothing like having your masculinity insulted by the woman you love." He snatched up his duffel bag. "Show me where the bathroom is so I can shower."

Still holding her midriff, Claudia pointed. "It's right down the hall. You can't miss it. We passed it on our way to the bedroom."

"Oh no…show me." He grabbed her hand and pulled her to her feet.

With her free hand, she wiped the tears from her eyes. "Now why do I suspect an ulterior motive?"

He waited as long as it took to reach the bathroom then pulled her into the room with him. "Because you're generally a suspicious woman?"

Before she could answer, Zach pressed her against the wall. As he devoured her mouth, the door clicked shut.

Claudia tugged the shirt from his trousers and dusted her nails across his belly. His muscles contracted with his sharp intake of breath. Emboldened, she flicked open his jeans' button then wiggled his zipper down.

Zach caught her wrist in a gentle hold. "Not yet. If you touch me now…"

The words died as she wrapped her hand around her target. He bit back a groan and nuzzled his face into the folds of her robe. Shoving aside material, he closed his mouth over her nipple.

Claudia tossed back her head in wonder and shrugged free of the garment. He was tenderness personified, caressing her to a fever pitch until all she wanted was to be possessed. Inch by inch, she stripped him.

Zach pulled back. "The apartment is small. They'll hear."

"Who gives a damn? Let's make their balls ready to explode."

"That's a little cruel. I love it." He grinned.

She watched with breathless anticipation as he twisted on the water then stepped into the tub. He extended his hand to her, making her feel like a princess. *His* princess.

Claudia stepped into the warmth of the spray. He eased her against the tile and wedged his cock between them. She writhed against it. He grunted and rubbed harder as he took her lips. His erection grew hotter with every sweep of his tongue. She tried to hook her leg over his hip and join them. Zach pushed her attempt aside and deepened the kiss, probing until her breath was ragged and shaky.

He tensed and dragged his mouth to her jawline. His cock thrummed against her stomach and she knew he was close to coming. Her slightest move would have him shooting over her stomach and breasts. *Be a lady and let him have the moment? Or be the vixen and take command?*

Before she could decide, he slid his tongue to the well of her throat, across to her collarbone then farther on. Her hard nipples were next. He flicked them mercilessly beneath his tongue until she was oblivious to everything else. He traveled onward, teasing her navel then the flat of her stomach and wiggled his way between her open legs. He dotted angel kisses on her inner thighs—up and down, up and down. Claudia quivered in response. Then she felt his hot breath against her pussy. She clutched the towel bar as he closed his lips over her clit. He lashed his tongue over his prize, kneaded her ass with one hand and delved the other down her crack and to her hole. Her tension rose with each circle he made around the tight muscle. He slid his thumb into her pussy then eased his finger up her ass. Orgasm washed over her seconds later, rattling her inside and out until she was spent and gasping.

Zach kissed his way back up her body as he stood. He held her upright with one strong arm around her waist. She lifted her leg over his hip. He tugged the other up and grinned.

"Hold on tight, baby."

"Don't worry. I'm never letting you go." She locked her ankles at his waist.

He groaned and pivoted into her body. His frenzy brought her to a fever pitch once more. She writhed against him, clutching the towel bar with one hand and his shoulders with the other. He cupped her ass, helping her keep the position. He fingered her hole again. Her clit hardened all the more.

"I wish I could reach your ass," she whispered against his ear.

He smothered his groan against her neck then kneaded his lips along the extra-sensitive tendon. Shudders of pleasure washed through her.

"I'm coming," she whispered.

"Good," he said through clenched teeth and stabbed deep.

They wriggled against each other, dragging the intensity out a little longer, mouths welded together to keep their sounds muffled as they came. Their kiss gentled in the afterward. Spent, they sagged to the bottom of the tub under the onslaught of the shower spray.

Chapter Fourteen

Zach stood on what little patio Claudia had, letting the night chill and the wine in his hand ease his worries. They loved each other—with a passion they couldn't deny. It was all he'd ever wanted and now it was his. *She* was his. Hell, they were married. Reality wasted little time intruding on his bliss. *How in the hell are we going to make this work?* She had a career and a home in San Francisco. He lived in Twentynine Palms, for now. Who knew where the Marine Corps would send him next? Overseas? Across the country? He wasn't ready to put his career aside any more than Claudia would be.

By rights, they should talk about this. Zach didn't want to, though—not now, not when their love was fresh and crazy and finally acknowledged. *Don't we have enough to worry about with this investigation?* A time would come soon enough once the dust settled for them to realize there were obstacles on their road to happiness. Until then, he'd treasure the minutes with her, commit them to memory and pray to God that their eventual breakup didn't kill him, because he couldn't see any way they'd survive a long-distance relationship. He couldn't breathe without her by his side.

The sliding glass door opened, bringing a touch of warmth to his back. He hoped it was Claudia and was disappointed to discover Phillip.

"You want to share that?" Phillip shoved a glass his way and, when Zach poured, braced his arms on the iron railing to stare into the play of streetlights on the light fog.

"Can't sleep?"

"No," Zach muttered in response. *I don't feel like talking either, so shut the fuck up or go away.*

"So, now what happens?"

"I'll wake her in a little bit and we'll head to the airport."

"That's not what I mean."

Zach covered his eyes. There was no getting around this. "I know how I feel. I've let her know. This isn't your normal relationship we're talking about. Most romances evolve. You date, have sex, live together *then* get married. We've gotten it all backward. I don't know what to do here and I'm sure Claudia doesn't, either. Just…just give us some breathing room and back off…please."

Phillip slugged down the wine like a shot of whiskey then moved toward the door. "All right. This is me…backing off."

Left alone again with his thoughts, Zach wasn't any happier than before Phillip had intruded. He pulled his phone from his pocket. It wouldn't be the first time a Taylor son had called home in the middle of the night.

His mom answered on the first ring. She brushed aside his apology. Without prompting, he unburdened his heart, confessing all.

"I wasn't aware you had psychic abilities, Zach," Mom said when he'd finished.

"I don't understand."

"How can you assign feelings and emotions to Claudia that she has not expressed? How can you know what's truly in her heart? Don't put words or thoughts in her head that don't exist. Good night, sweetheart."

He could almost see his mom's smile as she hung up. She was right, but it didn't quell the fear in his heart. It only made him more cautious about expressing it aloud.

Zach raised the bottle to pour the last drink. It shattered in his hand. Glass exploded behind him.

Vic bolted upright from where he slept on the sofa. "Get in here now! Everyone stay down!"

A stupidly obvious remark. Zach called nine-one-one while he hunkered down behind a large decorative planter. With one foot, he shoved open the remains of the door and eased over the pile of glass. He spied Claudia belly-crawling along the hallway. Once he spat instructions to the operator, he waved her back.

"Start packing. We're leaving now. Once the police get here, we'll have them give us an escort to the airport."

"No." She crawled forward. "Come into the bathroom. There are no windows there. We'll be safe."

"Damn it, Claudia, I said — "

"You're hurt. You're bleeding."

Zach glanced down. A gash along the underside of his arm oozed blood.

The police arrived while she bandaged him. Both he and Claudia strained to pick up pieces of their conversation with Vic. The officers were noncommittal in their responses, and after careful evaluations, they came up with one conclusion—a random act of street violence. They'd even managed to find the weapon but no shooter.

It was too much of a coincidence. Zach let Vic argue with them. His goal—his only concern—was to get Claudia out of there. Since the police refused to ensure their safety to the airport, Zach decided to take advantage of the distraction their presence created to leave.

Two hours later, when the plane was airborne, they were able to relax. He waited until Claudia was asleep then allowed himself to do the same. He jerked awake when the tires bounced onto the tarmac in Palm Springs.

"If you'd like, I'll drive us home," Claudia told him.

Zach nodded. Two nights without sleep had caught up with him. He was out again before she could leave the parking lot. The next thing he felt was her shaking his shoulder.

"Hold your temper. This shouldn't take long."

He squinted into bright daylight then gave her a look that screamed of treachery.

Claudia arched her eyebrow. "Yes, the Naval Hospital. You need stitches and you're going to have them."

Hard to argue when she'd already alerted the medical staff.

Claudia slid into the molded plastic chair while Zach was hustled into the examining room. The attempt on her life with the car had been scary enough, but to come so close to losing Zach was frightening beyond belief. It seemed too pat to be gang related, especially since there had never been any activity of that nature in her neighborhood.

This went way beyond a warning or an accident. Even if they were to turn back now and let Vic take full control of the investigation, the murderer — Hanson or Sinclair — would never allow them to be free. They were in this for the duration. Now all they had to do was survive it.

"Mrs. Taylor?"

Claudia glanced up at the Navy corpsman and got a clipboard shoved under her nose.

"Your husband is being most disagreeable. If you would fill out these forms, we would appreciate it. How did he cut himself?"

It's quite simple. You see, a killer is after us. He decided to use my husband for target practice.

"A glass bottle shattered while he was holding it. I cleaned the wound immediately, but it took me this long to convince him stitches were required."

"Very good. It shouldn't be long. It's not as bad as it looks."

At least the man didn't hover over her while she wrote. There was a ton of information she didn't know — height, weight, date of birth, Social Security Number, unit. As far as she was concerned, they could yank the information out of Zach later.

She slid the clipboard across the counter to the corpsman, daring him to say something. Her glare kept him quiet. Claudia returned to her seat undisturbed.

By the time Zach was finished, she was ready to get back to the comfort of bed and a long sleep. By his droopy eyes and sour disposition, she could tell Zach was as well. A large bandage covered his arm.

Without a word, he walked to the Jeep and crawled into the passenger seat. "I hope you're happy," he grumbled.

Claudia smiled. "Ecstatic. I'm sure if the situations were reversed, you would have done the same. Deny it and I'll call you a liar. How many stitches?"

"Six paper butterfly ones." He tucked his arms over his chest, shutting out further discussion.

She resisted the urge to laugh at him. *Had* their situations been reversed, her behavior would have been no better. The least she could do was humor him and see he got some well-deserved rest before they moved in the few belongings Phillip was bringing from her apartment.

He drifted off once more before they could get home. Claudia hated to wake him. She didn't have to. His eyes flashed opened the second she turned into the driveway. A muttered curse set her heart to leaping. Sinclair cut across the street toward them. He hailed them with a wave and a fixed smile.

Zach jerked open the Jeep door and jumped down, intercepting Sinclair's path. "What can I do for you this morning, sir?"

"I came over to invite the two of you to a barbecue this afternoon at my house."

"Who's cooking and who will be there?" Zach shot back.

Sinclair's humor faded, but his smile remained fixed. "Friends, neighbors, office personnel... I do the grill work. Allison takes care of the kitchen. It's the only proper way to do it. Shall I count on the two of you?"

Zach was a breath away from refusing until he felt Claudia's fingers against his back.

"That's very kind of you but we've had a long, exhausting weekend and want to spend the day resting. We'll see you tomorrow night for the football gathering."

"Suit yourself. If you change your mind, come on over. There's plenty for everyone."

"Yeah, we'd love to have you poison us," Zach muttered under his breath once Sinclair was out of hearing range. "The guy has balls, asking us over after that performance at Sunline's funeral."

"Yeah, and I'd like to cut them off and shove them down his throat."

Chuckling, Zach pulled her arm through his. "Now that's something I'd really like to see. Come on, Princess. Last one to sleep is a rotten egg."

Miss Kitty opened one eye as they walked through the door, offered a half-hearted meow then rolled her back to them and returned to her nap. The answering machine greeted them. Its red light flashed, indicating twenty-five messages.

"God, how many times did you call me?" he asked.

"Once."

He sucked his teeth. "This can't be good."

There was a message from Zach's mother, wondering if he was all right, and one from Rowan to call when they arrived and that Phillip was on his way. Vic called as he and Phillip passed Bakersfield, reporting no sign of trouble. Four were hang-ups. And lastly, a series of calls from what had to be everyone in Zach's family welcoming Claudia to their ranks. Each ended with, *"See you at Thanksgiving."*

Zach buried his head in his hands and braced his elbows on his knees.

She lifted a brow. "This Thanksgiving thing seems to be really big deal. I presume it is a family gathering."

"Everyone will be there."

"I see. May I also presume from some of the comments that my procreation potential will be evaluated?"

Zach tossed back a laugh. "Must you be so precise and formal?"

"Reply to the question."

"Yes, yes, yes. They are going to size you up. They are going to inundate you with warmth and love and smother you until you can't stand it. The kids will want you to play catch and chase and tie shoes. And above all, they will all look at you as the hope and salvation of the Taylor clan."

Wrinkling her brow in confusion, Claudia cocked her head to one side. "Why so?"

Zach caught her waist and drew her astride his lap. "Because, Princess, there hasn't been a girl born to the Taylor clan in four generations."

She tensed. "A heavy responsibility."

"Very." He drew circles along her ribcage with his thumbs. "I'm not going to lie to you. There have been enough barriers between us since we met. No more. Here it is." Pulling in a deep breath, he went on, "I love you. Honest to God love you. I always have, from the second our lips touched under that mistletoe. I want nothing more than to see our child growing in you, to feel it move beneath my hand, to pamper you throughout the whole ordeal. Hell, right now I'd lay the world at your feet if that's what it would take to make sure you stay with me always. My brothers would call me a crazy fool in love. Well, I might be crazy, but I'm no fool."

"Zach, I'm not ready for children."

"That's fine with me. I don't think I am, either. You tell me when you are and we'll take it from there. What I'm trying to say is that I don't want anything to make you feel compelled to stay here. We have a backward relationship. Once this other business is taken care of, if you want to start from scratch and build—"

She covered his mouth with her hand. "Shut up and stop thinking, Zach. You married me. You're not going to get rid of me that easy. Now call Rowan, call your mom and I'll whip up a breakfast that will knock your socks off."

* * * *

"Paella!" Cruz Montoya scooped a healthy portion onto his tortilla then took an equally healthy bite and rolled his eyes heavenward. "Delicious. What else is there to eat?"

Claudia lifted the lid on another pot. She liked this man—his sense of humor, the way his eyes laughed. "Seafood gumbo and sourdough bread."

Closing his eyes, Cruz inhaled the aroma. "A woman after my own heart. Wouldn't you say, Kurt?"

Kurt smiled and cocked his head to one side. "Definitely one to be admired."

Cruz's eyes sparkled as he smiled down at Claudia. "If you ever decide to give Zach the boot, let me know."

Zach raised his hands. "All right, gentlemen, that'll be enough. Kurt, don't you have a self-defense class to teach?"

"I do. I have quite a crowd of women waiting for me in the backyard, including the wives who came tonight for football. Obviously, they're more intrigued with developing a strong right arm than watching a bunch of sweaty guys in tight pants throw a ball and pat each other on the butt. Come on, Claudia." He motioned to her to follow him.

"Coming, Allison?" Claudia asked.

"I...couldn't. My clothes —"

"Easy. Run home and put on some sweats. We'll wait."

Sinclair pushed his way to the stove and snatched the lid from the gumbo. "Allison doesn't own sweats and she doesn't want to roughhouse."

Tension crackled in the atmosphere. No matter how nonchalantly Sinclair may have presented the words, menacing control seeped through.

"Well then, she can chow down with the rest of us." Always the peacemaker, Cruz's smile seemed forced.

Claudia blessed him for trying to cover the awkward moment. Sinclair ruined the attempt.

"Allison won't be eating tonight. She's on a diet. Getting a little thick in the belly." He seated the lid and turned around. "Where's the meat?"

"There's chicken in the paella and shrimp in the gumbo," Claudia managed to say, despite her clenched jaw. "If you're referring to red meat, there is none."

"No meat? Little lady, a man's got to have red meat. If you'd come to our house yesterday, you would've seen that."

Claudia curled her fingers over the doorknob to keep from making a fist. "Strange that you're the only one with that opinion. Everyone else seems to be enjoying the food. And you will not refer to me as *little lady*."

His false smile faded. "Taylor, what the hell kind of home are you running here? Haven't you taught her respect for rank?"

Zach leaned against the counter. "Sir, with all due *respect*, while you are in *my* house, there is *no* rank. You're free to enjoy the food, the company and the game. If you don't want to do any of those things, you're free to leave."

Sinclair's pulse throbbed at his temple. "If I go, so will your guests. Unlike your wife, who seems to enjoy sticking her nose in other people's business, they know what side their bread is buttered on."

"That almost sounds like a threat, Colonel."

"Take it as you wish, Captain."

Zach pointed to the front door. "There's the exit. If anyone chooses to leave, that's their business. This whole football thing was your idea, not ours."

Claudia's heart beat against her ribs while the two stood there, gazes fixed in an unspoken standoff. Minutes passed before Sinclair gave a nod.

"Allison, run home and fix me two steak sandwiches. I think the game's started."

Zach barred his way. "You don't understand. You are no longer welcome in my home. Allison can stay however long she wishes, but I want you out of here...*sir*."

"Unlike your wife, Captain, mine knows her place."

"Unfortunately, I'm sure that's true."

Sinclair's eyes blazed with fury. He caught Allison's upper arm and steered her to the door. Half-dragging, half-pushing, he took her home. The slamming of their door reverberated through the neighborhood like a gunshot. Seconds later, there was a crash then another from across the street.

"Get off your ass and fix me some fucking dinner!" Sinclair bellowed.

Tears welled up in Claudia's eyes. She refused to let this happen. She looked at Zach, then at Cruz, and shook her head. "No, not if I can help it."

Whipping open the door, she sprinted for the Sinclairs'.

"Claudia, no!"

The words came from Zach, Kurt and Cruz. Claudia disregarded the caution, ran across the street and yanked open the Sinclairs' door. Allison lay sprawled among the toppled over kitchen chairs, her husband hovering over her with fist raised. He whirled around at the intrusion while two of Allison's friends zipped by Claudia to help Allison to her feet.

"What the hell is this?" Sinclair yelled.

Claudia ignored him. "Bring her to my house."

One of the women nodded. Sinclair shoved his hand into Claudia's chest. Claudia drew back a fist and plowed it against his nose. He fell back, clearly startled that someone—a *woman*—dared oppose him. She pulled back another, ready to let him have it again.

Zach caught her wrist and pulled it down. "Enough."

Sinclair used pressure to stem the blood dripping from his nose. "Lady, you've made a big mistake and a very powerful enemy. I don't know who the hell you think you are—"

"You're one to talk. Who do you think *you* are, beating a helpless woman?"

He snorted. "You're crazy. Allison fell." He glared down at his wife. "Tell them."

She was shaking, frightened beyond words. This was an escape for her. All she had to do was take it.

"I...fell. I slipped and fell."

"You see?" Sinclair pulled her away from the other women. "Now get out."

The women did so with hesitance, but Claudia held firm.

Sinclair pushed his wife toward the living room then faced down Claudia. "You try a stunt like that again, Mrs. Taylor, and I'll personally see you're permanently kicked off this base and any other."

She raised her chin, meeting his challenge. "That goes for you, too, Colonel."

Zach draped his arm around her shoulders and led her back to their house. She was conscious of Cruz walking alongside them, of Kurt behind her, of the other wives in a semicircle, whispering in her backyard. All she could think about was the terror in Allison's eyes.

The women surrounded her as they neared, words of support ready.

"You tried. We all have."

"You can't help someone who isn't willing to be helped."

"Come on, ladies. Let's get back to our class." Kurt herded them into position.

Claudia couldn't force herself to move. She was too angry, too shocked.

Kurt chucked her under the chin and edged closer. "Come on, girlfriend." He was Kiki again, for her ears only. "Remember this... Never wrestle with a pig. You get all dirty and the pig likes it."

She gave a half-hearted smile and he stepped back.

"Okay, ladies. First rule of defense. You're women. You've got to fight like women, not like men. Kick, gouge and pull hair. Claudia, you first. You need a target."

He hauled on his protective clothes and helmet. All padded to avoid injury, he looked more like a kid ready for a day in the snow. Without warning, he lunged for her.

Claudia dug in. Falling with him, she kicked out.

"That's one hell of a woman you've got there, Zach. I don't suppose she has a sister."

Zach forced himself to smile. Cruz was right. She was something. 'Crazy' came to mind. "Nope, no sister. Sorry."

"Then you're one lucky man."

They watched her pummel Kurt with kicks and punches, yelling at his direction. "No! No! No! Go away!"

Cruz smiled and shook his head. "I'm actually beginning to think she could have taken Sinclair."

Zach sighed. "I'm learning to not put anything past her. Tell me. How often does he beat her?"

The smile disappeared. "Whenever the mood strikes him. Whenever she does something that displeases him or when he's in a bad mood, had a rough day at work, angry."

"Sounds like constantly."

"She's always walking on eggshells. She's a nervous wreck, trying to keep him happy."

"Is she in danger tonight?"

Cruz thought for a moment then shook his head. "He'll be extra careful if he thinks the neighbors are watching. He knows he's on the sky-line right now and can't afford adverse publicity, especially since he's up for promotion."

"What about at the Marine Corps Ball? They'll be at a hotel. Would he take a week's worth of anger out on her then?"

Again, Cruz gave it careful consideration. "I doubt he'd find the Palm Springs police as easily fooled as the military police."

"That would depend on the people in the neighboring rooms reporting him. A lot of people don't want to be involved."

Cruz smiled. "Oh, I can think of one or two who wouldn't hesitate, and I think I might just have come up with a plan."

Chapter Fifteen

Claudia beat her feet on the pavement with a force she knew she'd feel later. She didn't care. This was now and she was mad.

The jerk had actually had the nerve to issue a restraining order against *her*. The official hearing wasn't for a week, but already the temporary order had instructed her to stay away from the Sinclairs.

Zach didn't know. She was too angry to tell him. Her first instinct served her best—to run it off. It was all about control, something at which she was an expert.

She heard footsteps pounding behind her. Fear made her pick up the pace. She should have stayed in the house. Anger had made her reckless.

Even though she was still on base property, she was between the housing area and the business side of the installation. Open desert bordered the road on both sides. If someone wanted to, Claudia would be easily disposed of before the next car drove by. In her mind, she rehearsed what she would do if the person following her attacked.

The runner closed the gap. Claudia darted across the street.

"For cryin' out loud," Vic called out through pants for air. "Give me a break."

Claudia jerked to a stop and turned around. Vic stood behind her, drenched in sweat, doubled over in an effort to catch his breath.

Smiling, she trotted back to him. "Stand up. Walk. You'll be okay in a few minutes."

Grudgingly, he fell in step with her. "What are you trying to do? Kill me?"

"You scared me. I was doing my best to protect myself."

"You've got no business being out alone." He doubled over once more, blowing hard, hands braced on his knees.

Claudia tugged him upright. "Yes, I know. But if Sinclair or Hanson is coming after me, they can do so just as easily in the house. Besides, you've obviously been guarding me, so my safety is ensured."

"Why do I detect a note of sarcasm in your voice?"

Claudia smiled and pulled him in the opposite direction. "Come on. You need to get out of the sun. I can't believe how out of shape you are."

"Forgive me. I'm not used to chasing marathon runners. You know, I used to think you were a nice woman. Now, I'd swear you have a sadistic streak." He pulled in a deep breath and let it out slowly. "Who was the guy at the door?"

Outrage rushed back in. "Sinclair issued a temporary restraining order against me. The hearing is next Monday."

"The bastard will try anything."

"He's going to have to do better than that if he thinks a little piece of paper will scare me away from protecting Allison."

* * * *

A summons before the royalty of base. At least that was what it felt like. But if the Commanding General and Chief of Staff also intended intimidation, Zach wasn't buying into it. He was right. The facts were there. Now all he had to do was convince these superior officers.

Colonel Scott was by his side, ready to defend whatever actions Zach, Vic and Claudia had taken. He didn't know what had swayed the man, and he frankly didn't care. Sinclair was going down and Zach was making sure Hanson went with him, even if that meant fighting the good-ole-boy system all the way back to Headquarters Marine Corps.

General Drummond folded his hands on the big oak desk before him, focusing all his attention on Zach. "As I'm sure you are aware, Captain Taylor, the chief and I had a very long talk with Colonel Sinclair this morning."

His Virginia accent was as sweet and rolling as the Charlottesville hills. Zach didn't allow that to lull him into a feeling of complacency. The hidden message was clear — *explain yourself*.

"Yes, sir. I believe most of it centered around my wife."

The general gave a slow nod. "That it did."

"Sir, I'll be blunt. Martin Sinclair is a wife beater."

General Drummond's knuckles whitened, the only indication of his distress. "That's a very serious accusation, Captain."

"My wife and I suspected from the moment we moved in across the street. Major Cruz Montoya can verify the abuse. I personally witnessed it myself on Friday evening."

"Yet you allowed it to go unchecked?"

Zach burned with anger but kept his gaze locked on the general's. "No, sir, I did not. The military police refused to act on my call. The desk sergeant indicated they'd received calls in the past regarding the Sinclairs. Each time they checked into the matter, the Sinclairs dismissed the action as sexual play. Colonel Sinclair apparently talked the Provost Marshal into keeping the report off the blotter."

The general eased back into his leather chair, fingers steepled beneath his chin. Before he could comment, Colonel Scott jumped in.

"I've spoken to several of the people who were there last night, sir. All of them verify what Captain Taylor is saying."

Zach leaned forward. "The problem is Allison. She's too frightened to go against her husband. The one time she did confide in someone, that person was killed."

"Gunnery Sergeant Sunline?"

The general's voice was incredulous. Zach didn't blame him. It was a hard story to hear.

"Yes, sir. We don't know how, but we have a suspect."

"And that would be?"

"Sir, I'd rather not say until we have proof." When the general nodded, Zach continued. "We believe Sinclair was an accomplice and the instigator. We also believe

Allison may have witnessed the entire thing, and that's why she's so frightened now."

The general tapped his chin. "These are serious charges, Captain Taylor, but you seem to have sufficient witnesses to Sinclair's actions. I don't care what rank he is, I want him and his cohort arrested. I will not have wife beaters and murderers in my Marine Corps."

"I understand your feelings, sir, but with all due respect, we must have solid proof and evidence. Major Montoya and NCIS Agent Brownell have a plan they're working on for the Marine Corps Ball this Saturday." At least that was what Cruz and Vic kept promising him, although he didn't have a clue what the plan was.

General Drummond frowned. "I don't like the idea of putting this woman in further jeopardy. Are you sure this will work?"

"I've been told it will, sir."

"Very well. Trust that I'll be paying very close attention to all parties at the ball. Until then, Colonel Sinclair has issued a temporary restraining order against your wife. I trust Mrs. Taylor will adhere to it."

Zach's skin bristled. He could imagine Claudia's reaction and it wouldn't be pleasant. "The only thing I can guarantee is that Claudia will not sit back and allow someone — *anyone* — to be abused."

"And damn the consequences?" General Drummond resumed his initial position. "I'm surprised you have so little control over your wife, Captain Taylor."

Zach had to laugh. "Sir, my parents have been married a long time and one thing I do know is that no man has *control* over his wife."

The general smiled. "True. I look forward to meeting this extraordinary woman of yours on Saturday. Until then, I shall pray the rest of the week is peaceful in the Sinclair house, as well as the neighborhood."

His meaning was clear. "I'll do my best, sir."

* * * *

"Wake up, sleepy-head."

Claudia ignored Zach and tugged the blanket over her head. He peeled back a corner and when the scent of coffee wafted to her, she opened one eye.

"That's better." He pulled her upright and shoved the cup in her hands. "I have a surprise for you. Grab your running shoes and be ready to leave in twenty minutes."

"Where are we going?" she managed to mumble but Zach had already left the room.

Bleary-eyed, she swallowed the coffee and wiggled into shorts and a fleece sweatshirt. Every muscle in her body ached—retribution for the punishing workout she'd given it the day before. The temptation to crawl back into bed was great but curiosity wouldn't let her. Cursing herself for answering his challenge, she stumbled downstairs.

Zach was already outside, door opened on the Jeep like it was a coach ready to spirit her away. And like a diligent footman, he helped her inside then trotted around to slip behind the wheel. Before she quite knew what was happening, they were breezing down the desert highway, one of the few vehicles in the darkness.

Claudia hunched into her sweatshirt, trying to avoid the chilly bite of dawn air. Though scorching hot during the daytime, the nighttime temperatures dipped low. Zach had even mentioned seeing several inches of snow dusting the area the previous Christmas. She'd have liked to have seen that.

Slowing the vehicle, he made a quick turn off the highway onto a narrow road and they drove deeper into the desert backcountry. Now they were on land bordering Joshua Tree National Park—a solitary area that appeared devoid of all human habitation.

The just-emerging light of dawn created huge purple shadows upon the mammoth boulders piled throughout the desert. A faint electric glow shimmered along the eastern sky, darkening above to a deep, velvety blue. The last remnants of night were vanishing with the dawn. It was one of the most beautiful sights she'd ever seen.

A glimpse of a small sign flashed by. She caught the word 'oasis.' Intrigued and now fully awake, she craned her neck for some view of it.

"Where are we going?"

"Hiking."

"Why now?"

"Why not now?" Zach glided into a parking slot and killed the engine.

The silence was complete.

Claudia strained to hear a sound, any sound in the wilderness. Not a bird or animal noise intruded, only the slight rustle of the wind as it moved the scattered brush to and fro.

The rocks rose around them like enormous blocks piled by a careless child. As the morning light grew brighter, she could make out the wooden marker indicating the beginning of the hiking trail.

She turned and caught Zach watching her as if he were trying to memorize each facet of her face. There was no mockery, no barriers of any kind. To think they'd achieved this level of their relationship in so short a time...

But it hadn't been so short after all. It had taken them five years to get here. The wasted time made her want to cry.

She glanced away from the intensity of his gaze. The landscape was pink and golden with the sunrise. A bird fluttered to the trail marker. The world was waking up.

"It's beautiful."

"Wait till you see the end," he said.

"How far is it?"

"A mile and a half."

Claudia's muscles groaned.

"Are you ready?"

She nodded and stepped out of the vehicle.

They stretched, warming up in preparation for exercise. Zach pulled a bulging backpack from the rear of the Jeep and put it on. Then he handed her two insulated carriers, each containing liter bottles of water. Claudia crisscrossed the straps over her shoulders as Zach did with the other two.

He shut the hatch. The slamming, though slight, tore the blanket of silence around them. A covey of quail burst into the air.

"Let's go."

A simple proclamation Claudia had no trouble following, now that she was awake. Once they got moving, the rest of her body would catch up.

Zach led the way. The trail weaved in and out of boulders, twisting back and forth at steep angles and sharp drops. The ridges of reddish-brown hills jutted upward like gigantic backbones pushing their way through the skin of the earth. At times, Claudia wasn't sure if they were climbing or descending. A glance behind her provided the answer. The Jeep was toy-like in the distance below.

"How are you doing back there?" he asked over his shoulder.

"Fine," Claudia said through pants of breath. *And I thought yesterday's workout was a killer.* Now a simple climb kicked her butt. She slugged down some water.

Zach wore hiking boots, which gave him a superior grip on the rocky trail. Her trainers were fine for jogging but didn't provide much ankle support for the uneven surface. If they were going to do this in the future, she was going to have to get something sturdier. The second the thought left her head, she stumbled.

Zach caught her before she could fall. "Are you okay?"

"I'm fine." Claudia pulled upright and sucked in a breath. "Can we stop for a minute?"

"Sure."

She made her way to a smooth rock and slumped into the shade beside it.

"Drink." He nudged her bottle of water. "You're a little flushed. Hiking really gets your heart pounding."

"You're not kidding." Claudia took a few desperate gulps.

"We're almost to the end of the trail. How are you feeling?"

She grimaced. "I thought I was in good shape, but I think I'm using muscles I've never used before."

"You'll be sore tomorrow. Think of it as nature's stair-climber." He chuckled and held out his hand to help her up. "Come on. I have a surprise for you."

"If it's anything like your earlier one, forget it. I don't think I can take it."

Laughing, he tugged her to her feet. "I think you'll like this one. It's breakfast."

That diverted her attention. Suddenly, she was ravenous. "All depends. What did you bring?"

"You'll find out at the end, Princess," he taunted and continued on.

Claudia took a swig of water and followed.

The hike took another thirty minutes. Just when Claudia thought she couldn't take another step, they scrambled over one last boulder onto a level ridge overlooking the desert valley on one side and the oasis on the other.

The view was spectacular. Below them spread an undulating ribbon of tan and gold flecked with dark browns, reds and purples. Here and there the spiked red globe of a barrel cactus dotted the landscape.

The morning sun was starting to warm the rocks, drawing the small whiptailed lizards out from their holes to bask in the heat. Larger chuckwallas, their cousins, joined them. But nothing could compare to the oasis. Dozens of towering palm trees were clumped together in the damp earth, creating a shady haven. Riotous birdcalls drifted out from the fronds. Farther on in the rocks above were more palms.

Zach pointed in that direction. "That's where the water is. We'll go up in a bit. Aren't you glad I got you up for this?"

She nodded. "It's lovely."

Zach slid off the backpack, unzipped it and withdrew a tightly folded blanket, which he shook open and spread upon the ground. Claudia dropped the water containers on it, followed by her sweatshirt. The next items to appear from his magician's pack were some beautifully shaped croissants and a container of fresh, hulled strawberries. The ripe smell of the fruit made Claudia's mouth water. Next, he pulled out a thermos and two collapsible camping cups, followed by a tiny plastic container.

Claudia's eyebrow rose with curiosity.

"Honey," Zach said. "I really love honey on bread." He opened the lid of the container then muttered a curse as a drop slid over the edge. Catching it carefully with one finger, he licked the golden bead off with one quick flick of his tongue.

Claudia's body tightened. Memories of his tongue dancing through her pussy overwhelmed her. He waved her to the blanket and they sat together to eat breakfast.

The croissants were flaky and filled with butter, the strawberries juicy and sweet and the coffee strong. Everything was just the way she liked it.

Zach ate beside her, gazing out over the panorama that spread before them.

She fiddled with her empty cup. That old awkwardness between them built. Claudia refused to let it take hold.

"Why are we here, Zach?"

"*Here* in the big scheme of things?"

"You know what I mean." She bit her last strawberry in two for emphasis.

Zach flashed her his most beguiling smile. "Consider it our first official date."

The urge to say 'aww' was too great. This simple picnic meant more than all the fancy dinners in the world.

"Plus, I thought it would do us some good to get away from everything—to just be together."

He cupped her chin, leaned forward and kissed her. It was soft. Sweet. Perfect. He leaned into her, moving his lips against hers — not demanding, only giving.

Zach nibbled at her lower lip, teasing her mouth open, his warm breath scented with honey and strawberries, a heady mixture. Claudia's breath shortened. If she lived to be a hundred, she doubted she would ever tire of his kisses. Her answering moan and response drew a deep growl from within his chest. She caught his lower lip between her teeth, at the same time reaching around him to run her hand beneath his shirt along his tight back muscles.

He worked his hands under her thin T-shirt and slid up the jogging bra beneath. Unfettered, her breasts surged into his hands.

She gasped into his mouth.

Gathering her into his arms, Zach rolled onto his back, scattering their remaining dishes and pulling Claudia on top of him so that she straddled one leg.

A high trill of laughter made them freeze.

Startled, she jerked up her head, searching for the source.

"There are hikers coming up the trail." She rolled off Zach and yanked down her bra and T-shirt.

He sat up, adjusted his shorts and took several measured breaths of air.

Claudia gathered up the containers and tried not to laugh. Zach's snickering didn't help. She stole a kiss then another. He cupped her between the legs and rubbed. The voices grew closer. She smacked his hand away playfully. He winked and returned everything to his backpack. By the time the hikers arrived, Claudia was folding the picnic blanket while Zach searched the area. The group paid little attention to them as they followed the trail on over the edge of the ridge to the palm trees above.

Claudia chuckled and peeked at Zach from the corner of her eye. "I don't believe I've ever felt so naughty in my life."

Zach wasn't laughing. She realized he was scanning the area now as a military man, probably seeing places for a potential ambush wherever he looked. What had been a great place to relax could have well been a death trap. The hikers had proved that by how easily they had come upon them.

Claudia stepped closer and planted a kiss on his lips. "There's always later. How about showing me the rest of this place?"

A war waged in his expression. Clearly fearing danger, he wanted to leave.

"This wasn't smart," he said. "I'll be damned if I'm going to take chances with your life again."

Laughter filtered down from the tree grove above. She cupped his face. "There's safety in numbers."

Sighing, he relaxed visibly. "There is." He grabbed her hands and pulled them both to their feet. "Come on. And later..." He left the suggestion open.

Claudia smiled. Nothing was going to ruin this hike for them. They deserved at least that much.

Chapter Sixteen

Zach tossed their suitcase on the hotel luggage rack while Claudia parked the hanging bag in the closet. In a week of quiet surveillance, neither had made any progress. Sinclair was being the model Marine officer, Allison the loyal and dutiful wife.

It was the weekend of the annual Marine Corps Ball, celebrating the anniversary of the founding of the Corps. She and Zach had driven down to Palm Springs and booked into the luxury hotel where the gala would be held, where Cruz's plan to save Allison would be set in motion.

On the investigation front, there were no new leads and nothing to tie Hanson to any crime. In fact, he seemed to make it his mission to avoid them at all costs, where the week before they had run into him constantly. Even when they'd picked up her car from the body shop, they'd discovered Hanson's vehicle long gone. There had been nothing Vic could do to keep it there.

Claudia had bided her time working on her news report. She'd lost the stomach for it. It wasn't her desire to protect the Marine Corps but the thought of exposing Allison's humiliation to the rest of the world that bothered her. If they could manage to wrest Allison from Sinclair, she deserved as much privacy as possible to heal, psychologically as well as physically.

"What exactly is this plan of Cruz's?" Claudia stretched out Miss Kitty-like on the king-size bed. She missed her but was certain Kitty had Phillip's family wrapped around her paw and their dog terrified. "It's got to involve more than us being in the room next to the Sinclairs."

Zach sat in the chair and propped his feet on the end of the bed. "If it is, he hasn't shared it with me. Each time I've asked, he says he and Vic are still working out the details. We're supposed to play nine holes of golf this afternoon. I'm hoping he'll fill me in then."

"It's too bad Vic hasn't been able to find Linda Hanson."

"I can't see what good that would do, anyway. We know there was motive. What we need is a witness." He nudged her foot with his. "What are you going to do until it's time to get ready?"

"Indulge myself in a little princess treatment with some of the other women." Sitting up, she hugged her knees to her chest. "We're going to the spa to get pampered and massaged."

Zach grinned. "A little rubdown by some Nordic guy named Sven?"

Claudia laughed. "Actually, I understand her name is Bonnie. But I rather like the idea of a muscular blond god running his hands over my body."

"I swear you've turned bawdy on me."

"I always have been. I've just let you have the full experience." She crawled over to him. "If you think I'm bawdy now, wait until you see me tonight."

He closed the gap between them and kissed her. "I can hardly wait. And if I don't leave now, I won't wait."

Claudia bounced from the bed. "Don't let me keep you then." She gave him a wink at the door. "See you later."

It was hard to let him leave. Danger lurked in all corners and not only for her. She shoved worry aside and focused on the evening to come.

She couldn't wait to see the look on Zach's face when he saw her in *the dress*. It made the anticipation all the sweeter and the preparations for the evening that much more luxurious.

* * * *

Zach's game was off and it had little to do with his stitches. Everyone played poorly. It was no wonder. They were setting Allison up. There was no other way to trap Sinclair. All they needed was to have Sinclair take the bait and act.

There wouldn't be a problem as far as Zach was concerned. Once Sinclair saw Helen Moore with Vic and Janie Brighton with Cruz, his paranoia would take over.

Zach was working on a little bit of paranoia of his own. If Claudia found out about this, she'd have a fit. Nothing would keep her away from Allison. She couldn't be allowed to learn the truth. Everything must appear as natural as possible. *He* had to be as natural as possible. It wasn't easy when it seemed Claudia's ability to read his every emotion increased with each day that passed.

He returned to their room, hot and sweaty from an afternoon on the golf course, ready to put one of those hateful walls between them. It wasn't necessary. One glance at Claudia took all other thought away.

Zach's jaw dropped. He hardly knew where to look first. She was the perfect incarnation of his Ice Princess, shimmering in a dress of blue ice. Her hair was swept back in a French twist, one tiny curl left to dangle enticingly around the curve of her neck.

Platinum and pearls danced from her earlobes and her slender throat. The dress skimmed her curves. He forced his gaze down the column of iridescent material to her feet. Her toes peeked out from the silver strapped heels she wore. Each one was painted with a translucent sparkle to match the dress, as were her fingernails. She did a slow turn, displaying the bare back.

Damn!

Zach drew in a shaky breath. It didn't help. He was hard as a rock and suspected he was going to stay that way until the evening was over unless he took matters into his own hand while he showered. *And she watches?*

"My God, you're beautiful, Princess," he said in a rush of breath.

Claudia glided forward. "I'm glad you're pleased."

The gown moved with her like a second skin, begging the question, "What are you wearing under that?"

She traced her finger over his erection. "Almost nothing at the moment." Smiling, she pressed his hand over her breast. Her hard nipple kissed his palm.

He glanced at the clock on the nightstand, weighing his options. As much as he wanted to fuck her, there wasn't much time. Sex would mess up her makeup and hair. He was on the edge of disgusting after nine holes of golf in the sun, but she kept running her hand up and down his cock, sending a signal any idiot could understand.

"I better get ready to go. I don't have much time." Zach ran his hand down her bare back. "I suppose a kiss is out?"

She grinned. "I'd hate to mess up my makeup."

He slipped his hand beneath the material and cupped her bare ass. Claudia gasped and arched her neck. He licked his tongue up her throat.

"You'd better be able to get out of that dress fast when we get back to the room. Once I start loving you, I don't intend to stop."

She slipped away and grabbed his hand, tugging him toward the bed. "I don't think I can wait that long. I have the perfect solution. You don't have to do a thing."

In one firm shove, she had him on the bed. When he reached for her, Claudia batted his hands away.

"I think I'm scared."

She laughed. "Put your hands beneath the pillow and keep them there."

"Okay, maybe I'm a little turned on." He tucked his hands behind his head.

"Only a little?"

She flicked open the fly button on his shorts and slithered the zipper down until his cock sprang free. "I said *beneath* the pillow."

"Yes, ma'am." He did as ordered and discovered a rectangular piece of plastic there.

Hiking her dress to her waist, Claudia straddled his hips and gave him a good view of the strap-on vibrator nestled against her clit. "Connected the dots yet?"

"Oh yeah." He danced his thumb over the buttons. "Eeny, meeny—ahh."

She plunged his cock deep inside her. Pressing her hands on his chest, she tightened her pussy muscles around him. He punched one of the buttons wondering for a half second why he heard nothing. Then the vibrations shuddered through him. He reared up on a hard growl. Claudia writhed on him, unleashing a contented moan as she flexed her fingers on his chest.

She leaned closer until her red lips hovered over his. "Be very still. Let the toy do all the work."

"You're asking the impossible."

"Trust me. It will be extremely rewarding." She flashed her tongue over his chin and righted herself.

Zach fisted the pillow. Being still was impossible, especially when Claudia couldn't follow her own decree. With every pivot of her hips, he ground into her. Her eyes were closed, lost in the sensations building between them. She came on a sharp gasp, head tossed back, throat exposed, fingers digging into his chest. He gripped the pillow harder, fighting the urge to roll her beneath him and pound into her.

"Come with me, love," she whispered.

On a strangled cry, he thrust deep and let go.

Claudia leaned forward, shoved her hand under the pillow and turned the device off.

"Is that what they give you as swag when you get a massage?" he asked.

She grinned. "I brought this from my apartment."

"Any other toys in your bag of tricks?"

Laughing, she pulled her dress to her waist and unlinked them. "Oh yes. Come on." She patted his thigh. "Time to get ready."

"Gonna watch me shower?" he asked.

"And let the steam mess up my hair?"

"What was I thinking?" He vaulted from the bed. "I'll let you clean up first."

"Thanks." She dropped the barest of kisses on his lips then headed for the bathroom.

He plucked the remote from under the pillow. "So, can I take this with me tonight?" He flicked it off and on, off and on.

She flashed that curved-eyebrow look over her shoulder. Holding her dress with one hand, she wiggled the vibrator off with the other.

"I think I've created a monster," she mumbled.

"Yeah, but I'm all yours, baby."

"Remember that when you see what my bag of tricks contains." She snickered and ducked into the bathroom.

And he was hard once more.

* * * *

Passion still shimmered beneath Claudia's skin when they walked into the ballroom an hour later. Protocol demanded they be on time, otherwise they never would have bothered to make it.

They made the round of introductions — the Commanding General, the Chief of Staff, Zach's Staff Judge Advocate. Then they found their table with the other attorneys from Zach's office.

Every military member was dressed the same — in the crisp dress blue uniform. Claudia didn't see how the men could breathe with the jacket as tight around the collar as it was. She'd spent five minutes listening to Zach curse the thing before she'd finally helped him fasten it.

Despite the discomfort, Zach was devastatingly handsome. He fit the uniform well. The blue trousers with the blood-red stripe down the side emphasized his height. The midnight blue jacket spread across his broad chest, medals winking in the light from the ballroom chandeliers. It was no wonder women's heads turned their way.

"I feel like the luckiest man here tonight," he said against her ear.

Claudia smiled. "Then I suppose it's a good thing you're with me, because I feel like I'm the lucky one. See how all the women look at you?"

Zach chuckled. "They're looking at you. They're jealous."

She drew back with a disbelieving laugh. "Impossible."

He shrugged a shoulder and leaned away.

She'd been to one other Marine Corps Ball—as Phillip's date when he'd first entered the Corps. The ceremony and pageantry had impressed her then. That hadn't changed. Who wouldn't be moved by the history, the symbolism, the patriotism? A glimpse across the room spoiled it all.

She waited until a break in the festivities before tugging on Zach's arm. "Why didn't you tell me Vic and Cruz were bringing Teddy's women to the ball?"

He curled his hand over hers. "Shh... Now's not the time. Besides, I didn't know."

"If Sinclair sees... My God, he's at the same table as Cruz."

There was a firmer squeeze on her hand, a warning to keep quiet, calm. "It'll be all right."

"It won't be. He'll blame Allison and beat the hell out of her."

"This will be one time he won't get away with it."

"I thought human sacrifice went out with the pagans."

He looked at her then, his gaze shutting out further discussion. But he also couldn't hide his discomfort. She could tell that he didn't like this any more than she did.

Dinner was wasted on her. Claudia could only pick at the pasta primavera. Zach didn't do much better with his prime rib. When the band cued up, she was grateful for the excuse that put them as part of the crowd and away from forced socializing. Dancing in Zach's arms, she found comfort from the turmoil in her soul. They also had a close view of the Sinclair table.

Allison wore a sequined royal blue gown that was much too tight for her current condition. Her cheeks were pale, her smile forced, her hand firmly clenched by her husband's. She spoke to no one, but every so often she allowed her gaze to wander to Janie Brighton, sitting close to Cruz and Helen Moore at the table next to them with Vic. Sinclair's lapdog, Hanson, spent his time wandering from table to table, sucking up to the higher-ranking officers. He didn't seem to have an escort.

"I don't know how much more of this I can stand," she told Zach.

"We'll leave as soon as protocol allows. I want to be back in the room before the Sinclairs. He mustn't know we're in the room beside them."

"Who's on the opposite side?"

"Cruz and Vic. Helen and Janie are across the hall. The general and Colonel Scott flank them."

"Surrounded on all sides."

He peered over her shoulder to the Sinclair table. "I sure hope so. We won't get another chance like this."

It was another two hours before Zach and Claudia could slip away. Once in their room, they changed into jeans and shirts and waited.

We should be tearing up the sheets, not waiting for disaster. The tension was enough to make her cry.

At some point, she drifted off. A crash from the neighboring room jerked her upright. There was a muffled cry. Sinclair screaming. There was a dull thud against the adjoining wall.

"My God, did he throw her against the wall?" She leaped from the bed.

Zach grabbed the phone to call it in. Claudia raced from the room. Vic and Cruz were already at the Sinclairs' door. Helen and Janie hovered in the doorway of their room while the general and Colonel Scott hurried forward, hotel manager in tow.

The manager gave a warning knock. Silence descended. Seconds later, Sinclair cracked open the door.

"Is there a problem?"

Cruz muscled his way forward. "I believe you know the answer to that, sir."

"I don't have a clue."

"Open the door, Colonel," General Drummond said.

Sinclair stared at each man, ignoring the women. Then, realizing he had no choice and wouldn't be able to talk his way out of it, he let them in.

Claudia ran forward. Allison was doubled over on the floor between the two beds, her gown ripped down the front. A pool of blood stained the carpet beneath her.

"Someone get a towel!" she shouted.

Sinclair grabbed Claudia by the hair and yanked her to her feet. "Get this woman out of here. I have a restraining order against her."

Balling up a fist, Claudia threw her weight behind the blow and punched him in the solar plexus. Sinclair fell back, gasping for breath and damning her with his eyes.

She knelt beside Allison and drew her into her arms. Helen and Janie darted in, forming a circle of protection around them.

"Go ahead, Colonel," Zach snapped. "Want to feed us that line again about her falling?"

"I don't have to listen to this."

When Sinclair tried to stagger past them into the bathroom, General Drummond hauled him into the hallway. "I believe you do. You may have gotten away with this in the past, but I'm not a subordinate to be browbeaten into turning a blind eye. You've disgraced my Marine Corps, and I'll see you finished."

Allison raised her bruised and bloodied face to Claudia. "A doctor. Please get me a doctor. I think I'm losing my baby."

Claudia squeezed back her tears. The baby was already gone.

Chapter Seventeen

Zach paced the length of the hospital corridor. It looked like a war zone in the waiting room. Claudia had managed to curl herself into a chair, using the arm of it as a pillow. Vic's broad shoulders served as a cushion for Helen and Janie's heads. General Drummond and his wife merely propped their heads against each other. And Cruz? He paced, too, passing Zach on a parallel course.

No one had spoken since Allison had been brought in. They just waited. Even Vic's news that Colonel Scott had made sure Sinclair was arrested had been greeted with silence.

Zach saw movement from the corner of his eye and looked up to find the doctor coming their way. He appeared weary, sad. Zach tapped Cruz on the arm to get his attention. The two of them met the doctor halfway. He stopped and motioned them to a lounge nearby.

"Coffee, gentlemen?"

"No, thanks," they replied together.

"How's Allison?" Cruz asked.

The doctor took his time pouring himself a cup before giving them his attention. "I'm afraid there was nothing I could do to save the baby. She was hemorrhaging too badly. It was a girl. She was sixteen plus weeks into her term."

"Allison will want to know," Cruz said.

The doctor glanced away. "She already knows. It was the first thing she asked about when the anesthetic started to wear off."

"Can I see her?" Cruz asked.

Dark eyes glared up at him. "Are you the husband?"

Cruz's jaw tightened. "No. The bastard is in jail. I'm her friend."

Zach positioned himself between the two men. "We're all friends and very concerned."

Sighing, the doctor rubbed his eyes. "You should be. He messed her up pretty badly. Poor little thing has bruises all over her body. She has a hairline fracture on one of her ribs and a broken wrist. There is evidence of old fractures, old scar tissue. She's been suffering for a long time."

Zach heard Cruz's sharp intake of breath seconds before he darted from the room. His instincts screamed at him to follow. The need for more information kept him in place.

Still staring at the door, he asked, "Is there anything else? When can she have visitors?"

"Those are the immediate problems. X-rays will probably reveal other damage, but her emotional scars are what will be the hardest to heal. As for visitors... She said she'll only see Claudia."

Zach nodded. "That's my wife."

"Ask her to wait until Mrs. Sinclair's less groggy. She needs the rest."

He left the doctor to his rounds and went in search of Cruz. He didn't have to look far. Cruz sat in the garden courtyard, tucked away on one of the wrought-iron benches. His shoulders were bent, shaking. Zach faltered. This was too much emotion to deal with. He was intruding on another man's pain, his secret, his heart. Where were the words to understand?

Quashing his feeling of ineptitude, Zach stepped forward, sat and curled his fingers over Cruz's shoulder.

"How could he do that?" Cruz demanded to know. "She's so tiny, so delicate, so beautiful. How could he hurt her like that? How could he crush her? How?"

He buried his face in his hands. Zach wanted to do the same. There were no answers, only questions.

"Does Allison know you're in love with her?"

Cruz jerked up. "Of course not. Do you think I'm crazy? I'm supposed to go to the wife of another man — my commanding officer — and tell her I love her? Where's the honor in that?"

"How long?"

He sagged into his former position. "From the moment I first met her. I told myself I was insane and tried to be her friend. So many times I wanted to hold her. Once I even got to dance with her." He held up one finger. "Once. You can imagine how helpless I felt when Sunline told me his suspicions. All that mattered was to make her safe. I can't tell you how many times I longed to put a bullet in that cruel bastard's head. Right now, I wish I had."

Zach squeezed his shoulder. "It's over. Time for a new beginning. Maybe one day soon, you can tell her how you really feel and the two of you can—"

"*That* will take a small miracle, my friend. I could never make up for the hurt she's been through."

"No, you can't, but you can show her life doesn't have to be like that. Patience and time. Trust me."

"I'd like to believe that, but I keep asking myself one question. What would a woman like Allison want with a man like me? I'm just a reminder of her years of torture."

Zach was at a loss to answer.

* * * *

A gentle shake pulled Claudia from a fitful sleep. She forced her tired eyes to focus on the culprit—Zach.

"Sorry, honey. Allison is awake and asking to see you."

She unfolded herself from the chair, stretching out the kinks in her muscles to avoid cramping. It was a wonder she had managed to ball herself into the position in the first place.

A strand of hair fell in front of her eyes. Finger combing put it in place but there was nothing she could do about the cotton taste in her mouth.

She ran her tongue over her teeth, hoping to alleviate some of the morning breath. To her relief, Zach gave her a stick of gum. After popping it in her mouth, she kissed his cheek. His smile, his thoughtfulness fortified her for the ordeal ahead.

She pushed open the door to Allison's private room, expecting to find her waiting for visitors. Instead, Allison lay there like a broken doll, staring out of the window at the palm trees rustling in the dawn breeze. The hospital gown hid little. Bruises dotted her arms, ringed her throat, a splint weighed down her left wrist.

"My baby's dead. My little girl. She was just starting to move. The sensation was..."

Allison broke down into sobs so full of anguish and despair that all Claudia could do was hold her and cry with her. Allison held on until she was spent. Hands shaking, Claudia poured them each a glass of water.

"He's in jail now, Allison. He can't hurt you anymore."

"I guarantee he won't stay there for long." There was no emotion in her voice, only resignation.

"What will you do?" When she didn't answer, Claudia pressed on, "Allison, how much longer? The next time he could kill you."

She glanced to the window where birds wiggled among the palm fronds. "I can't stay with him. I *won't* stay with him. I've been holding on, hoping I could find happiness like Linda Hanson...like you. But I'm so afraid. I don't know what to do."

"We'll help you. We'll all help you."

"The last person who tried to help me is dead."

"Did you see what happened?" Again, silence. Had she not been so battered, Claudia might have grabbed her shoulders and given her a little shake. "Allison, *did* you see what happened?"

"Yes."

The response was barely audible.

"Are you willing to make a statement?"

"Yes."

Firmer, surer. At least she was showing some willingness to fight. She squared her petite shoulders and focused determined eyes on Claudia.

"I want this over with. I want Eric Hanson behind bars. I want Martin Sinclair out of my life by the fastest means possible. Still, I've never been more frightened."

Claudia laced her fingers through Allison's. "Zach will help you file for divorce and get a restraining order against Martin. The Marine Corps will prosecute him for abuse...murder, too, if we can prove his involvement. You'll probably have to testify. In the meantime, there's a women's shelter up in the mountains near Big Bear. I believe that's where Teddy was going to take you. You'll be safe and can take the time you need to strengthen yourself."

She clutched Claudia's hand as if it were a lifeline. "He's very clever. He mustn't suspect I've gone there. He'll try to find me."

"We'll find a way. I'll get Vic so you can make that statement."

Allison refused to let go. "Not without you. Don't leave me, Claudia. I'm so afraid."

* * * *

Vic pressed the button on his recorder and placed it on the food tray before Allison. "This statement is made by Allison Sinclair." He added the date, location and who was present. "The case is the investigation into the death of Gunnery Sergeant Theodore Sunline. Mrs. Sinclair, you may begin. Tell us everything you can."

Her hand in Claudia's, Allison started. The words came slowly at first. She detailed her first meeting with Teddy, their friendship, how he suspected her abuse based on his own history with his deceased sister and, finally, the plan to get her away.

"He told me how Julieanne was killed by her husband while their children slept in the next room. I was scared to death to leave but even more frightened to stay. I couldn't put my child through that. I didn't care if it was taking Marty's child away from him. I had to go.

"We made plans to meet out in the desert. Cruz was to keep Marty occupied that night so I could slip away. I met Teddy and we'd driven a short distance when a car cut across our path. Teddy told me to get in the back seat on the floor then he got out.

"I heard Eric Hanson ask Teddy what the hell he thought he was doing. Eric said, 'You don't actually think the colonel is going to let you get away with fu...with screwing his wife?' Teddy tried to tell him the truth. Eric didn't want to listen. He said it was all lies and he'd be damned if he let someone like Teddy ruin Marty's life like he had ruined his. Teddy said, '*You* ruined your life, Captain.' He told him that he was going to make sure I was safe and that Marty could never hurt me again.

"I heard a car door slam, tires spit gravel, Teddy cry out then a horrible thud. When I heard the door slam again, I peeked over the seat and saw him sprawled in the desert fifty feet away with Eric standing over him. I crawled out of the car and hid in the desert. I watched from behind a bush. Eric pulled a sleeping bag from the trunk of his car, put him in it then dragged him onto the back seat and drove away.

"Once they were gone, I walked the two miles back to my car and went home. I didn't know what to do. I knew Marty was responsible. I just couldn't prove it and I was so afraid I would be killed next. When he came home that night, he...he hinted as much, told me to clean the car spotless or he would see that I was the one in jail for Teddy's murder."

Vic clicked off the recorder and tucked it in his pocket. "I'll have the statement typed up for you to sign by the end of the day."

Claudia showed him to the door. "You can bring them up when Zach brings up the other legal papers for her to sign. She'll be released tomorrow and we'll be going to court from there. Make sure Hanson is locked up before then."

He gave her a mock salute. "Yes, ma'am. By the way, your friend Kiki is in the waiting room."

"Good. Send her in."

Panic shadowed Allison's face. She had been very specific. No one must come in without her approval. Claudia just smiled.

"It'll be all right. Trust me."

Kiki breezed in a few minutes later in a subdued fifties retro-dress. Somehow, she made it look contemporary.

"You called and here I am."

Allison eyed her suspiciously.

"Kiki, I have a task for you." Claudia pushed her to the vacant chair.

"Anything for you, darling."

"Thank you." She pointed to Allison. "Can you make her look like a man?"

She gave the other woman the once-over. "A boy, yes, but a man? No, sweets. She's much too small."

"Then a boy will have to do." Claudia strode to the door and called to Helen and Janie. Their entrance earned her another glare of betrayal from Allison. Claudia just smiled.

"What about these two, Kiki? Boys or men?"

"Older boys, I think. Girlfriend, what are you up to?"

"Take whatever measurements you need, Kiki. I want you to make Boy Scouts out of these women by tomorrow afternoon."

She pulled her phone from her purse and called Phillip. "How would you like to take a bunch of Boy Scouts camping to Big Bear tomorrow afternoon?"

She glanced down at Allison. Gratitude brought tears to the battered woman's eyes.

* * * *

It was inevitable that something would go wrong. However, Zach hadn't been expecting all his plans to go awry at the same time.

Sinclair had used his one phone call to contact Hanson. Hanson had hired a civilian attorney then had taken off for parts unknown. Sinclair would be released on his own recognizance before the day was out. Fortunately, it would be after the Monday morning hearing to issue a restraining order against him.

They'd all agreed that Allison mustn't know when he was released. She was still frightened but her inner strength had allowed her to rise above it and push on. Once the hearing was complete, they could whisk her off to the mountain town of Big Bear.

Allison stayed close to Claudia, but her need to constantly clutch her hand had disappeared. Even Allison knew that help only went so far, that she had to help herself at some point. This hearing was one of those situations. Zach had filed all the necessary paperwork, but it was Allison who would have to speak with the judge. Although, had it been up to Cruz, she wouldn't have to do so.

When it was time for the hearing, he sat in the back of the courtroom with Claudia and Zach, ready to leap to Allison's aid if necessary. It wasn't. She stated her case in a strong, yet quivering, voice. In the end, the judge awarded a permanent restraining order against Martin Sinclair.

She withheld her joy until they stepped into the corridor then hugged Claudia. "Thank you."

"Any time. Now, let's get you out of here."

Another elaborate scheme that he thought spelled disaster. Zach kept his mouth shut. At this time, he couldn't come up with anything better.

Back at Phillip's house, he watched the transformation. Under Kiki's direction, three attractive women became Boy Scouts of varying ages. Using young Ian as a model, she even managed to give them that not-quite-clean appearance of an active boy.

Kiki stood back to admire her handiwork. "Well, what do you think?"

"Helen's breasts still stick out too much," Vic said.

"Oh, you would notice that," Helen shot back, laughing.

Vic winked at her. "Just fix it, Kiki."

A few minutes later, adjustment made, they returned to the living room.

"Perfect," Claudia declared. "Let's move out."

Phillip gave each a backpack and motioned them to the door. "Last one to the minivan is a rotten egg."

Vic waited until they pulled from the driveway. "Guess it's our turn now. Check your radios to make sure they work. Space yourselves in fifteen-minute intervals. If Hanson or anyone else is going to follow, one of us should catch him. Keep in constant contact."

Zach took up the rear. Claudia stopped him at the door. "Call when you get there."

"I will." He kissed her, lingering, deepening with every sweep of their tongues, then finally pulled away and left.

* * * *

Claudia hugged herself long after they'd departed. *Almost over.*

"How long to get to Big Bear?" she asked Rowan.

"Depends on the traffic. Give them at least two hours." She tugged Claudia's arms away from her chest. "Come on. I've got something to keep you occupied while we wait."

"You're not going to have me paint the fence, are you?"

Rowan laughed. "Actually, I thought we might try that quilting project we keep putting off."

"Neither of us is very good at it."

"Yeah, I know, but it passes the time."

"How about you, Kiki? Up for a little quilting?"

"Kiki has other plans. Ta for now, girlfriend." She blew Claudia a kiss and left.

Time didn't pass quickly enough. Claudia checked off the minutes as they went by, counting down thirty, an hour, then two. Still, the blast from the phone was so sudden that she jumped.

Rowan picked it up before it could ring a second time. It was Phillip. They'd arrived safely, Allison was at the shelter and they were heading home.

A single tear slipped down Claudia's cheek. It was over. She tied off her thread and stood.

"I'm going home to wait for Zach."

"Sure you don't want to stay for dinner?"

"Frankly, I'm too exhausted."

And elated and sad and everything. By the time Claudia reached her own front door, she'd run the gamut of every emotion there was. One thing was certain. There would be no story for her news station. Let them think the base was gearing up for a major deployment. She would not violate Allison's privacy.

She pushed into the kitchen, waiting for Miss Kitty's traditional greeting. A low, rumbling growl greeted her instead.

Claudia had never heard a cat growl before and didn't take time to question it. A warning was a warning. She fumbled for the doorknob to ease back out. A man's shadow fell across the kitchen floor. The door behind her moved.

In the back of her mind, Claudia knew she was surrounded and knew who her captors were. Crouching low against the refrigerator, she prepared to defend herself. She never got the chance. A police baton snapped out, clipping her leg and knocking her to the floor.

Claudia scrambled for a weapon—a knife, a pot, anything. Sinclair shoved her against the cabinets. She reared back to kick. He was too fast. He slammed her to the floor facedown, his body pressing against hers.

"I saw you outside that night. Don't you think I watched your moves? You're great on your back, but once you're flipped over, you're nothing."

Want to bet?

Gritting her teeth, Claudia banged her head backward against his face.

Sinclair cried out and jerked back, but the bulk of his weight still covered her.

"Bitch." He grabbed a handful of hair and yanked her head. "You're good, little lady, but I'm better." He was excited, aroused, enjoying himself and his power. "Now, you're going to tell me where my wife is or I'll see you regret it for the rest of your life."

"Go to hell."

"Have it your way. It doesn't bother me to put a woman in her place."

With Hanson's help, Sinclair bound and gagged her then hauled her through the house, into the garage and dumped her in the backseat of his car.

"Keep her still and quiet," he told Hanson. "If it weren't for you, we wouldn't be in this predicament. Push me any further and I won't hesitate to turn you in."

Hanson shoved her to the floor. For extra measure, he added his own weight. "Nice and cozy. Move and I'll strangle you." He tossed a blanket over them and signaled for Sinclair to leave.

Chapter Eighteen

Zach's radio crackled to life on the seat beside him. Puzzled, he brought it to his ear.

"Yeah?"

"Pull into the next shopping center," Vic said.

"Is something wrong? We're almost home." *Thirty minutes tops.*

"Just pull in."

He tossed the radio aside and made a sharp right into the parking lot. Vic was already there. Cruz was right behind him. Phillip drove on with Helen and Janie.

"What's up?" he asked.

Vic didn't waste time on preliminaries. "Sinclair and Hanson broke into your house. They have Claudia."

The world exploded before Zach in shades of red. Vic kept talking. Zach couldn't understand a word. Only one thing stayed in his head. Claudia was in danger.

Vic shook his arm. "Did you hear me? You and Cruz go back to your house and wait until you hear from me."

"The hell I will. I'm going after her."

"You don't even know where she is."

"But you do."

Braced on the car door, Vic hung his head. "Yes, I do. I didn't want to take a chance. I've had one of my fellow agents watching her from the start. He knows exactly where she is and will do his best to protect her."

"Not good enough. I'm going with you."

Vic shook his head. "No. It's too risky."

A snarl ripped from Zach's throat. He grabbed Vic's shirt in his fist and yanked him close. "Goddamn it, that's my *wife*! Take me to where she is *now*."

Cruz peeled his hands from Vic's throat. "Take it easy. We'll all go."

Released from the stranglehold, Vic adjusted his clothing. "We're wasting time."

* * * *

Claudia wanted to vomit in Hanson's face. The man took take great delight in her discomfort, using each jolt of the car to grind himself against her. She prayed whatever they planned for her wouldn't come to *that*.

Courage. That was what she needed — and strength. And to hold on to the belief that somehow, some way, Zach would find her.

"We're here," Sinclair said. "Get her in the cabin before some damn hiker sees us."

Hanson yanked her up by the arms. Pain knifed between her shoulder blades. Claudia refused to cry out, refused to give them the pleasure of knowing they had hurt her. They grabbed her from either side, dragged her to a dilapidated mining shack miles from civilization and shoved her inside.

"Now what?" Hanson pulled off her gag and rubbed his thin hands together. "Going to rough her up a bit?"

"Shut up and sit down. You've already caused me enough problems by not disposing of Sunline's body like I told you." Sinclair pushed away the cardboard covering one of the windows and peeked outside. "I'm sure our intrepid young captain will want his wife returned to him undamaged. We'll give him the chance to respond to our ultimatum first. If that fails…" He shrugged and faced them once more. "I'll get what I want one way or the other, little lady."

Hanson snickered. "Colonel Sinclair always wins."

Claudia struggled to sit on the worn cot. "You would do well to remember that, Hanson, or are you really foolish enough to believe that Sinclair's going to take the fall with you? By the time he's through with you, he'll make sure you get life in prison and that he gets away scot-free."

Hanson's cocky smile faltered. "You don't know what you're talking about."

She jerked her head toward Sinclair. "Ask him. This is a man who managed to convince the military police the beatings he gave his wife were a sexual game. What scenario do you think he'll use to discredit you? We already know you killed Teddy and we know why. Sinclair won't go down with you. He'll blame it all on you. He'll even say you set him and Allison up just to get to Teddy. That would be first-degree murder. Who knows? Before this is over, the authorities might even find you dead — a victim of your own 'suicide'."

In one stride, Sinclair hovered over her. "Shut up."

She glared up at him. "It's the truth. Ask him. He can't stand for you to hear it."

Sinclair cracked his hand across her face with enough force to split her lip. Claudia's head snapped back. A muffled cry tore from her throat. Tears stung her eyes. She blinked them away then flashed him another hate-filled glare.

"Don't tempt me, bitch." He pivoted on his heel and marched to the door. "Watch her. I won't be long."

Claudia waited until she heard the car drive away then shoved herself into the corner of the cot. Blood trickled from the corner of her mouth onto her neck.

"See? I told you. He's going to let you take the fall for kidnapping me. You're already wanted for murder. He's probably on his way to call the police right now. He can't afford loose ends and that's all you are to him."

Hanson wiped the sweat from his brow with the back on his arm. "Get on your feet. We're getting out of here."

"I'd love to oblige you, but you've tied my feet together."

"Keep your mouth shut, bitch, or I'll slap you myself." He cut the cords free and pulled her upright. "Move."

"It will be faster if my arms are free, too. Plus, it might help your case if the police find you trying to help me."

Mumbling curses, he cut her arms loose. "You keep ahead of me at all times. No funny stuff."

Claudia rubbed the circulation into her arms. "I wouldn't dream of it."

He led her down a dirt road. Claudia had no idea if he knew what direction to take or where they were. It didn't matter. As long as they were in the open, there was a better chance they would be found.

There was a rustling behind them. Hanson froze. Claudia kept walking.

"Stop," he growled. "Stay where you are."

Hands on hips, she turned to face him. Ten feet beyond, Kurt hid behind a cluster of creosote bushes. Relief flooded through her. Hanson started to turn.

"It's a coyote, you coward," she said. "It's just curious and shouldn't bother us if we keep on and ignore it."

He turned around, scanning the bushes suspiciously. "Yeah, well, you're going first in case it decides to attack."

She'd given Kurt the break he needed. When Hanson walked on, he made his move. Claudia had barely had time to put one foot in front of the other before Kurt dashed forward. In less time than it took for her to realize what was happening, he had Hanson facedown in the sand.

Plucking a pair of handcuffs from the back of his jeans, he gave her a wink. "You know I'd never let you down."

Two quick gunshots swallowed her reply. Blood exploded from Kurt's shoulder. He fell back, clutching the wound.

Claudia skidded to her knees beside him. Hanson lay nearby, his blood staining the sand. She couldn't tell if he was alive or dead — and she didn't care.

"Get down," Kurt snarled.

"Your shoulder." She feathered her hands over the wound, trying to ignore his wince.

"I'm all right," he ground out through clenched teeth.

"But the bleeding."

He shook his head. "There's a kubaton on my key ring."

"A...what?"

"A small, steel baton. Get it. Defend yourself." He chucked her under the chin. "You can do it, girlfriend."

She slipped it from his pocket and nestled the cold metal in her palm.

"Good. Now into the bushes before he realizes I don't have backup and comes out of hiding."

"Kurt, he has a gun."

"He needs us to get his wife. She's his possession, his property, and he wants her back."

"He's absolutely right about that." Sinclair's shadow fell over them. "On your feet, both of you."

"He can't. You've shot him."

"An accident. I was aiming for the man who murdered my Marine. I was defending your friend. I can't be all bad if I was doing that."

"Very clever, but it won't hold up in court," Kurt sneered.

A demonic grin spread over Martin Sinclair's face. He kissed the barrel of the pistol, levered it at Kurt and fired into his leg. "It doesn't have to. I'm not the one accused of murder." He dug his fingers into Claudia's upper arm and yanked her to him. "I want my wife."

"Too bad."

Sinclair seized her throat in one hand and squeezed. "I'm not playing games with you anymore, little girl. Give me my wife."

"Claudia, fight!" Kurt shouted.

Gasping for air, she flicked the weapon like a whip, slicing the keys against Sinclair's cheek. He reared back with a howl.

"Now, Claudia, get him! Fight like I showed you!"

Fury unfurled, she attacked. In her hand, the keys became razors gouging into every area of exposed skin. He lunged for her and Claudia jabbed the kubaton under his chin, trying to stab into his jugular. Overbalancing, she staggered back.

Sinclair lunged, triumph on his face. Exposed and vulnerable, Claudia kicked out. He caught her ankle and yanked her down.

She lashed out with her feet, digging into his ribs, his face, his stomach, his groin. He rolled away and leaped up. She jumped with him, nails curled for battle, teeth bared.

"Come on, you bastard," she snarled. "Come at me. Give me the excuse to beat the shit out of you."

Too late, she saw him reach for his gun. Her heart was suspended in time. Glee spread over his face as he pointed the weapon at her.

Claudia crouched low, digging her hands into the sand. She had one chance. With a shout, she stood and tossed a fistful of sand into his eyes.

Sinclair screamed and stumbled, hands raking at his face. There was a dart of movement to the side. She jerked around in time to see Zach tackle Sinclair to the ground. Still blinded, Sinclair lashed out with the pistol, clipping Zach on the cheek. Zach rolled away, taking Sinclair with him.

She flinched with each blow Zach took. He gave as good, or better, than he got. He ducked each flailing swipe of the pistol until he seized Sinclair's wrist in a viselike grip.

Sinclair cried out. The weapon fell from his fingers and skidded across the sand. He refused to admit defeat. With one heave, he toppled Zach backward.

The men rolled down the incline, each refusing to release the other. Claudia grabbed the gun and ran behind, hoping for something that would give her an advantage to help Zach.

Suddenly the ground beneath the men gave way. Claudia's scream pierced the air as the vertical mine shaft opened. Dust hurled into the sky, obscuring her vision. She dropped the gun and crawled forward, fearful of the silence. A dark hole opened inches before her. She eased closer.

"Zach?"

There was the sound of someone spitting, a sharp intake of breath then...

"Here," he gasped.

Claudia fanned the dust away. Ten feet below, Zach dangled from a worn rope. "Hang on. I'll try to pull you up."

"Just stand away. I can do it."

Breath held and hands clutched under her chin, Claudia watched his slow ascent. Sinclair was right behind him and gaining. He grabbed for Zach's ankle. Zach kicked him away, but it seemed like he still had miles to go.

The rope groaned from the weight. A cord snapped. Claudia grabbed hold with both hands, digging in with her heels.

Sand skidded beside her. She couldn't spare the time to look. Whoever it was had to be help. There was no one else left.

Vic pulled her gently to one side and grabbed the rope. Cruz took up the slack behind him.

"Hang on. We'll have you out in a minute."

"He doesn't have a minute," Claudia cried out. "Sinclair's trying to knock him off."

The rope groaned again. Another thread snapped. Vic flopped forward, hanging over the edge while Cruz continued to pull. Claudia saw a hand clasp Vic's arm.

Seconds later, Zach scrambled for safety and into her embrace.

She wrapped him in a tight hug, not bothering to hide the tears drifting down her cheeks. With shaking hands, she touched his wounds.

"I'm okay, honey. I'm okay."

His gaze fell to the cut on her lip, the bruise on her cheek. He touched both then tucked her head under his chin. From the corner of her eye, Claudia saw Sinclair crawl from the mine shaft. His breathing was labored but hate still glared from his eyes. Sirens echoed across the landscape.

"It's over, Sinclair," Vic said, trying to catch his breath.

"That's what you think." In a lightning-fast move, he dived for the fallen pistol and swung around on them. Claudia was his first target.

Zach pulled her behind him. "You just don't get it, do you? It's over. You're history. Your career is over. You're going to jail. Shooting us isn't going to change anything."

The sirens drew closer. Sinclair glanced over his shoulder then at the four of them. He pulled the pistol up then turned it toward himself.

"No!" Vic leaped for him. It was too late.

Claudia buried her head against Zach's shoulder as a final shot rang out and Sinclair's body crumpled to the desert sand.

Zach turned and wrapped his arm around her. "Come on, honey. You don't need to see this."

Her knees threatened to give way. She forced them to hold her up. "I knew you'd come."

He held her close. "I would have been here sooner but I couldn't run any faster. We split up to surround him. I hate to think what would have happened —"

She pressed her fingers to his lips. "I'm fine but Kurt's been shot. We have to get him to the hospital."

Vic hurried over to where Kurt lay. "He's lost a lot of blood but should be fine. Problem is, it will take a while for an ambulance to get here. It would be best if you took him to the hospital."

"Not a problem," Zach replied.

A few yards farther up the hill, Hanson groaned and struggled to sit up. Blood saturated his side. Still, Vic took the precaution of handcuffing him, reading him his rights as he did so.

"You do-gooders are always interfering," Hanson sneered.

Vic propped him upright. "Someone has to protect the world from people like you."

He glared up at him. "You're a fool just like Sinclair. A puppet just like him."

When Vic ignored him, Hanson snickered. "Doesn't matter. I got what I wanted — Sunline's death. Hell, I was even gonna bury him. I should have done it as soon as I crushed the bastard."

"I'd advise you to keep quiet," he said and put a little distance between them. Claudia touched Vic's arm. "How did you know I'd been taken?"

"I didn't, but I don't take chances with the lives of civilians, even the extra special ones. I've had you watched from the start. I knew from talking to Phillip that you'd be suspicious of a man, so…"

Kurt struggled to speak. "Yeah, and the next time *you* can shave your legs and be the woman."

Vic smiled. "You're the one who minored in Theater Arts."

"I mean it, Vic."

Cruz knelt beside him to prop him up.

Zach helped haul him up from the other side. "I believe there's a hospital bed waiting for you. Claudia, if you'll drive?"

Her head was still reeling from the news that Kurt aka Kiki was an undercover NCIS plant assigned to protect her. She felt as if she'd lost a dear friend. By the time they reached the emergency room on base, she was crying.

"I'm not dead yet," Kurt managed to say.

She dabbed at the corners of her eyes. "I'm going to miss Kiki."

He forced a smile. "Aw, she's not gone, girlfriend, just tucked away. Have the doc take a look at those cuts on your face then go home and get some rest. You deserve it. Your husband is one lucky guy."

Zach tucked her under his arm. "Don't I know it."

But once Kurt and Cruz left them, Zach's arm tensed.

Tracing his cheek, she forced him to look at her. "What's wrong?"

He cupped her chin, gently tracing the livid bruise. "What happens now? What happens to us?"

Smiling, she cuddled closer. "Well, first you take me home and pamper me a little. Then this weekend we rent a truck to finish moving me out of my apartment and — "

"You don't want to leave? You don't want to start from scratch?"

She brought her lips to his. "I told you. You can't get rid of me that easy."

A smirk lifted one corner of his mouth. "We'll see how you feel after a Taylor Thanksgiving."

* * * *

The next few weeks had been gloriously mundane as Claudia and Zach had settled into married life back in Zach's house in town. Kurt had done his recuperating at the Taylor home while Miss Kitty lavished all her attention on her captive audience. Claudia had packed up her San Francisco apartment and merged all her possessions with Zach's. She'd even managed to find a job with a television station in Palm Springs. They had passed the parenting test by babysitting for Phillip and Rowan one weekend. Everything was as close to perfect as possible.

So Claudia couldn't understand why Zach had suddenly become so morose. She chalked it up to a case of nerves over her meeting the Taylor clan. That had to explain why he hadn't uttered more than a few terse words during their five-hour drive to Phoenix.

When he pulled into the overcrowded driveway of his parents' home, Claudia was certain of it. Before they could step out of the car, they were inundated with family.

Zach's mother swept her into a smothering embrace, ignoring her son as she drew Claudia toward the sisters-in-law. A tribe of boys, large and small, stared at her from different angles.

"Would you people give her a break?" Zach snapped. "She's not a brood mare."

His father laughed. "You can't blame us for trying."

Zach's mother hugged her tight. "He's one to talk. Zach is the middle boy. He was *supposed* to be the last child."

Claudia's eyes sparkled. "Hence the name Zach?"

She laughed. "Exactly. You can see how far that got us. Maybe you'll have better luck pulling that extra X chromosome from him."

"I'll do my best."

"As long as the child is healthy, dear." She pulled Claudia toward the house then called over her shoulder. "Zach, bring in those pies Claudia made. I have a feeling a few of them might not last until Thanksgiving dinner tomorrow."

A big family. It was wonderful, but as Claudia settled in, Zach's sour disposition worsened. Finally, she'd had enough. Snagging his arm, she drew him into the room they were assigned.

"What's wrong?"

He shrugged. "Nothing."

"Hmm, why do I doubt that? Come on, Zach. This is me you're talking to. No barriers, no walls, nothing between us anymore. Remember?"

He studied his toes and scuffed at the carpet. "I have orders to Okinawa, Japan. I leave in March."

"That's it? That's what has you in such a nasty mood?"

"You don't understand."

"Then explain it to me."

"It's for a year. It's unaccompanied. The Marine Corps won't pay for you to go there and live."

"And?" She tucked her arms under her bosom.

"I'm going to miss you. That's all."

"You don't think I'll wait for you, right?" The fact that he refused to meet her gaze answered the question.

Claudia wanted to cry. Who would have thought that big, tough Zach Taylor would think he was unworthy of her?

"Will you?" he asked. "A year is a long time."

"It is. Too long. I won't wait."

He closed his eyes. Claudia caught his face in her hands. "You dope. I'm going with you. I'll pay my own way if I have to. Remember, we still have the Vegas money we haven't touched. Nothing's going to come between us ever again—not an ocean, not even the United States Marine Corps."

"But you just got a job."

"Screw the job. I'll find another or maybe even start on this granddaughter your family is craving. You're all that matters. I *love* you."

Zach smiled, his dark brown eyes filled with relief and adoration, then laughed, yanked her close and kissed her. "I *am* the luckiest person in the world."

Claudia hugged him close. "No...I am."

Want to see more from this author? Here's a taster for you to enjoy!

Rules of Engagement: Beneath the Layers
Caitlyn Willows

Excerpt

Midge Ellis stared in shocked disbelief at her reflection in the bedroom mirror. 'Hooker' was the only way to describe her. It wasn't even remotely what she'd had in mind when she'd grudgingly agreed to celebrate her birthday at the Lost Oasis, and she was beyond pissed to learn Susan Bolotnik had discovered it *was* her birthday by snooping in her medical records. Susan's *'but you're my friend and I wanted to help you celebrate'* dowsed some of Midge's ire, yet irritation still hovered at the fringes of her mind.

How am I even friends with these two?

Susan and her boyfriend slash BFF Jeremy had descended on Midge one day while she'd been enjoying a good book and a sandwich during her lunch break. They'd overwhelmed her with friendship. She'd yet to shake them in those six weeks. She hated confrontation and had had enough to last a lifetime. Midge didn't want any more. It was easier to go with the flow and put up with crap than to deal with it. But for Susan to use her job at the base hospital to extract personal information had crossed a big line, despite her 'good' intentions. Midge was beyond tempted to file a formal complaint through Susan's chain of command. Being a Navy corpsman didn't give her the right to access Midge's medical records.

Then there was Jeremy. A Marine didn't go absent without leave and not expect some ramifications. From what Midge had heard, it hadn't been his first time being charged with unauthorized absence. He'd deserved being busted from staff sergeant down to private first class. By all rights, she shouldn't be associating with him. Even after all these years, she worried someone would try to pin something on her. Hanging out with a dirtbag like Jeremy would be a career killer. Plus, he was now a private first class and she was a staff sergeant. Fraternization was a big no-no, punishable by court-martial. It was the perfect excuse to send the two packing. But that involved the dreaded *confrontation*.

I am such a fucking wimp.

The thought made her want to cry. She used to be a hard-charger—the person who stood up for someone and did the right thing. Then she'd found herself caught in an impossible situation and her world had turned upside down. Few had remained her friends during and after the debacle. The ordeal followed Midge wherever she was stationed. In a world where everything was a mouse click away, her past was there, waiting to be rediscovered. She'd learned to lock herself away, keep her head down, do her job and not draw attention to herself. Once her current enlistment was up the next year, she was leaving the Marine Corps behind. *Far behind.*

Midge reached for the wig. She'd had enough.

Susan swatted her hand away. "Relax and get a grip."

She tugged the red wig into place. Midge blew the flaming red bangs off her eyebrows then flicked them aside when that didn't work. The get-up was outrageous and much too revealing.

"Please tell me there's more to this somewhere."

Susan's glower screamed exasperation. "You look fabulous." She tilted her bleached-blonde head to one side and smiled. "I should become a makeup artist."

"What *would* the Navy ever do without you?" Midge let the sarcasm speak for itself while she evaluated the results of Susan's over-the-top cosmetic work.

Where am I underneath all this makeup?

Heavy liner highlighted with a luminescent silver powder made her gray eyes enormous behind her black-rimmed glasses. Dark red lipstick gave her lips a lush, sultry pout.

She twisted away from the mirror and paced the confines of her bedroom. Walking to-and-fro always made her feel better. The problem with her circuit in the small room was the tell-all mirror giving her glimpses of the transformation from mild-mannered court-reporter to... *Hooker from hell? Vamp? Wicked city woman?*

The crimson wig was straight and heavy. The flipped-up ends brushed past her shoulders. Midge's dark curls were stuffed under a wig cap that threatened to suck out her brain.

Susan had delved into her vast wardrobe for Midge's transformation. The stylish, black silk tank top with a scoop neck felt like heaven against her skin. But the soft leather mini-skirt that looked cute when Susan wore it was much too short on Midge. All the tugging in the world wasn't going to lengthen it. Though she and her nemesis were about the same height, Midge's curves filled out the form-fitting clothes to the point of indecency. What was sophisticated on Susan oozed provocative on Midge. It was amazing the clothes fit at all. Susan's body was H-shaped while Midge's was hourglass.

The crowning touch to the evening's ensemble was a pair of thigh-high leather boots with three-inch heels. They hugged Midge's calves. With every step, their *shush-shush* told the world she was coming. A bell around her neck would have been less intrusive. The ensemble demanded male attention and forced a sway into Midge's walk that made her want to crawl into a hole and die.

"I'm not wearing this. I'll get arrested for indecent exposure." Midge stumbled to the bed, sat and tugged at her left boot.

"You're wearing more right now than you do when you're at the pool."

"I don't go to the pool." The boot refused to budge. "Can you see me swimming around in front of two billion twenty-year-old Marines? No way."

"Yes, God forbid any man should see what a great figure you have underneath that frumpy uniform."

Midge couldn't disagree. It was part of who she'd become. She didn't want anyone to notice her — at least no one in the Marine Corps community. It had been easy to be anonymous when stationed near a big city. Now she was in the fishbowl of a small town, living in Twentynine Palms. A person couldn't go anywhere without running into an acquaintance. It made hooking up impossible.

But you're anonymous now, her conscience whispered.

Standing, Midge studied her reflection through narrowed eyes. No one would recognize her. Hell, she didn't recognize herself. A hookup would be nice, though. She hadn't had sex since the incident. All the masturbation in the world hadn't cut the edge on her horniness, and she'd masturbated a lot since she'd arrived at this duty station, lusting after a man she couldn't have. Her rules forbade it.

Questions assaulted her... *Can I get away with it? Will the wig stay in place? How will I face the guy if we run into each other later? Isn't this lying?* With the disguise, her hookup would never know it was her.

"These boots have to go."

"No, no, no." Susan's bobbed hair bounced with every shake of her head. "Let's get Jeremy's opinion."

Midge frowned at her. "I don't care about his opinion. Why did you have to invite him anyway? You said girls' night out. At least it was before you turned it into sluts' night out. I'm not in the mood for Jeremy's running commentary."

The man never shut up, even when he was eating. Left to his own devices downstairs, he'd probably devoured half the contents of her refrigerator.

Susan laughed and leaned toward the mirror to blot her glossy lipstick with a tissue. "Cut him some slack. Being busted rattled him. I thought we could give him some company. Anyway, going out is a good stress reliever, right?"

She fiddled with the neck clasp on her halter-cut cranberry jumpsuit. Her adjustment deepened her cleavage.

Midge lowered her foot with an exasperated thump. "Jeremy needs to be rattled. If he keeps up his crap, he'll be dishonorably discharged. I'm not in the mood to play babysitter to him tonight." *Or ever.*

"He's harmless, and don't try to change the subject by starting an argument." Susan shook her finger. "You're trying to wiggle out of our big adventure."

Midge glared at her. "I'm not comfortable with this. When you mentioned having some fun for my birthday, I thought you meant going to a movie in Palm Springs, not all *this*. It's not me." It never had been.

Susan whirled around and parked her fists on slender hips. "You're impossible. You don't date, you don't socialize and you're either squirreled up in this wannabe home or that damn bookstore."

Anger flared to the forefront. Midge willed her temper to cool. "How dare—"

"Forget work, forget those stupid books, forget about being a mousy little court reporter…just for this one night."

She grabbed Midge's wrists, hauled her to her feet then let go. Midge flailed her arms for balance. Susan righted her before she fell.

"I want you to have some fun. Come out tonight and have the time of your life. Be someone else. Make this evening a birthday gift to yourself."

On firm feet once more, Midge stood there, stomach clenching, heart pounding with a raw combination of rage, indecision and anxiety. She studied her reflection again—at the wig, the over-the-top makeup, the skin-tight mini—and knew true fear. She'd wanted to go incognito, not shout her presence to the world. This getup would garner too much attention. She couldn't pull it off.

"I'd really rather stay home and read."

"Seriously?" Susan screeched. "It's your birthday. You need to go out and get laid."

Midge wouldn't argue that. But no matter how horny she was, relationships took too much energy. What she *needed* was a one-night stand. What she *wanted* was a forever kind of guy. She wanted a man who had her back, one for whom the past didn't matter, a man who understood and supported what she'd done, one who didn't condemn her for having done the right thing. Oh hell, she wanted that delicious-looking Kurt Davidson, but work relationships were off her list. It might be all right, since they worked for different agencies, but she still had to see him on an almost day-to-day basis. She wouldn't risk it. But he *was* a sweet fantasy with his light blue eyes, sandy blond hair and a smile that turned her insides to mush. When they'd first crossed paths, he'd been somewhat attentive, sharing gum and mints with her. She'd been too tongue-tied to speak and too fearful of having attention on her in the office to respond. He'd said little to her since but had occupied the prime spot in her nightly fantasies. That was too much information to share with her pushy, so-called friend.

"Fine," she snapped.

"Lovely." Susan sniffed. "With an attitude like that, you can forget about getting laid."

Midge looked her in the eye. She was crossing one line after the other. "You're starting to piss me off." They were well past that point.

"Because I want you to get out and have fun?"

"All I want is a normal life."

"Then start living that way," she replied.

Susan had a point. Normal was what made people happy. Midge couldn't honestly say she was happy anymore. She watched her coworkers with their families and longed for that kind of life — especially children. She knew what she wanted, and maybe now it was time to go out and get it. She wasn't going to find the man of her dreams by sitting at home every night with her cat and a good book...or by bringing herself off to images of a man she could never play with.

Midge tugged at the annoying boots once more. "Enough. I promise I'll try to be charming and exciting, not nerdy and boring."

Susan clasped her hands to her chest. "Thank you. One more thing... Let's lose these."

Before Midge could stop her, Susan snatched off her glasses and tossed them to the queen-size bed. Midge grabbed them and put them back on.

"Are you two done in there yet? It's getting late." Jeremy cracked open the door.

"Not yet." Susan dashed to the door and smacked it shut.

A muffled 'ouch' came from the other side. "You're the meanest corpsman I've ever met. What happened to being kind and gentle?"

"I'm off-duty," Susan replied. "Are you ready to see the new Midge?"

"If I say yes, can we get going? I want to hit the bar. Plus, this fucking cat keeps giving me the evil eye. He's already scratched my hand, and I think he's going to bite me or something."

"Hades doesn't bite," Midge replied. But he was a pro at letting his displeasure be known. Susan and Jeremy had been on his hate list from the second he'd met them.

Midge wiggled her foot, trying in vain to get some breathing room between it and the leather boot.

Susan performed a drum roll on the dresser. "And now, for the first time in public…" She threw open the door and Jeremy fell in. He rolled to his back, laughing.

God, is he already drunk?

"Are you all right?" Midge wobbled toward him and was forced to grab the dresser to keep from crumpling on top of him. She still managed to slide down the wall and land on her backside with a thump.

Susan had always referred to Jeremy as her pretty surfer boy. His wavy white-blond hair was cut in the longest style Marine Corps regulations allowed. His eyes were blue-violet fringed with thick, dark gold lashes. Jeremy matched Midge's five-foot-five inches, but what he lacked in height he more than made up for in muscle. If he spent half as much time working on his education as he did lifting weights, he might attain reasonable intelligence. While funny and good-natured, he wasn't the brightest bulb in the pack. Instead, he excelled at being a testosterone-laden jerk.

Take a stand. Dump these two.

As she clambered to her feet, Jeremy's laughter faded and his eyes widened in lecherous appreciation.

"Wow. If I didn't know it was you—"

"Stand up, you idiot, and quit trying to look under her skirt." Susan yanked on his arm, hauling him to his feet. "What do you think of her outfit?"

He ran a slow gaze down her body, making her feel dirty and shamed and damned uncomfortable. *Just say no. These aren't real friends.*

"If I were drunk in a bar, I'd hit on you," he declared. "Love the wig. Hot, hot, hot."

"High compliments, indeed," Midge muttered.

"Are we going or not?" Susan demanded. "If we hurry, we can get to the club before the DJ sets up." She snatched her purse from the bed. "Once he starts spinning tunes, it'll be impossible to find a table."

Jeremy draped an arm around each of them. "If any guys from my unit are there tonight, I may have to tell them I'm dating you both."

"Cut the crap. It's irritating." Midge shrugged off his arm and sank to the edge of her bed to remove the torturous boots.

"What're you doing?" Susan screeched. "You *have* to wear those. They're part of the outfit."

Midge glared up at her. "I'll wear your wig and this hideous outfit, but I am *not* wearing these boots. Give me your heels or I'm staying home."

Faced with that ultimatum, Susan grudgingly complied. Wearing four-inch heels didn't help Midge's equilibrium, but at least her legs could breathe. She took a fortifying lungful of air and picked up her small black leather purse — a birthday gift from her father and stepmom.

"Let's go before I lose my nerve and run for the shower to get this gunk off my face."

"I'll join you in the shower anytime, hot stuff." Jeremy waggled his eyebrows at her.

The thought curdled her stomach. She curled her fingers into a fist, ready to plow it into his solar plexus if he dared come near her. A sibilant hiss from the doorway drew everyone's attention and saved Midge from a response. Hades stood there, back arched, black fur puffed out and yellow eyes huge. He hissed again before leaping to his accustomed perch on the windowsill. Tail curled around his legs, he continued to watch her, emitting little angry chuffing noises.

"There's a critic in every bunch," Susan said. "And get these rid of these damn glasses."

She had them off before Midge could stop her.

"Are you crazy? I can't see without those." She also couldn't see what Susan had done with them. Everything was a fuzzy blob—like a picture in desperate need of focus.

"Put in your contacts."

Jeremy edged toward the door, rubbing his right hand. He must have done something to deserve that scratch. Hades didn't lash out unless someone he didn't like invaded his space.

"I don't have contacts," she answered.

It was a lie, but she was careful about when and where she wore them—and certainly wouldn't in this town. She kept her guard up for a reason. It was one of the things she'd sacrificed to keep attention off her—and one of her biggest regrets. In reality, it was a small price to pay for her peace of mind.

"You look like a nerd. No way." Susan caught her arm and dragged her from the room.

"I can't see." Midge squinted. Her surroundings were a blur at best.

Susan gave her a little shove. "Go."

"Don't worry, cutie-pie." Jeremy followed. "We're your friends. We'll take good care of you during your birthday bash."

Midge winced. "That's what I'm afraid of."

The Lost Oasis was within walking distance of her place, but maybe they could get a cab. Navigating the two miles without glasses and in four-inch heels wasn't the smartest thing to consider, but if this night went further downhill, she was out of there. As a Marine, she'd handled worse on forced marches.

With 'friends' like them...

Home of Erotic Romance

Sign up for our newsletter and find out about all our romance book releases, eBook sales and promotions, sneak peeks and FREE romance books!

About the Author

Blessed (or cursed) with a vivid imagination, Caitlyn Willows eventually learned to turn that talent inward. Readers will find deep emotions and sizzling sensuality seamlessly woven into her action-filled stories. Believing life is to be lived and felt, not merely watched, Caitlyn delivers real-to-life characters in unforgettable tales of love, adventure, and always steamy passion. No one is more surprised than she at the direction life has taken her. She is also a mosaic artist and an avid crafter with a passion for cross-stitch. Caitlyn lives in the beautiful desert of Southern California with her husband (a genealogist). She is always on the lookout for the next interesting tidbit that will help fill her writing well.

Caitlyn loves to hear from readers. You can find her contact information, website and author biography at http://www.totallybound.com.